BURN

STARSHIP FOR SALE, BOOK 5

M.R FORBES

Quirky
Algorithms

Published by Quirky Algorithms
Seattle, Washington

Cover illustration by Tom Edwards
Edited by Merrylee Lanehart

CHAPTER 1

"Dropping out of hyperspace in one minute," Alter announced through *Head Case's* shipwide comms.

"Everybody buckle up," I added, making sure the rest of the crew would be prepared for our loss of FTL travel.

The announcement was mostly for the sake of Quasar and Druck. Keep, Matt and Gia were already locked in on the sofa behind the pilot station, keeping an eye on space through the forward viewport and the sensor grid that would fill in once space flattened out around us. I didn't know where the former Royal Marine and the soldier of fortune were on the ship at the moment. Hopefully, if they were still in bed, the announcement would get them up and moving to the lounge or joining us on the flight deck where they could strap into the extra jump seats near the back.

Not that I wanted re-entry to be that frantic. In fact, Alter had set coordinates for nearly six hours away from the planet Atlas' typical drop zone to avoid the potential for immediate confrontation. Nobody on board had forgotten that we were still fugitives wanted by the Royal Guard, our ship an easily identifiable target at close range. Unlike on Furion, we wouldn't be able to bribe Atlas Orbital Control to mix up identifiers and make it easier to avoid detection. There was a reason we had a new addition to the family. A smaller space hopper just big enough to carry our crew and make hyperspace jumps to adjacent systems and just small enough to fit inside the hangar. Of course, Druck had been upset when we'd chosen to make that purchase instead of picking up the Avenger on our way to the Hegemony homeworld, but he didn't have much of a leg to stand on after I told him he was free to go when we landed on Jafar to pick up the space hopper. He chose to stick around. He had said escaped convicts needed to stick together.

I agreed.

Other than that, the trip had been mostly uneventful. The highlight for me at least was that I had managed to go three days between bouts of nausea and dizziness, though I'd also developed a light cough I knew was going to continue to get worse. The symptoms were an internal timer, counting down to the moment I wouldn't be part of this fight anymore. With Atlas nearly in sight, I was hopeful we could find a way to pass the responsibility for Sedaya's sigiltech-focused scheming to the Empress. Maybe she would even pardon us for giving her the heads-up. Either way, our part in the story would be finished and I could turn my concentration to finding a cure for my cancer, whether that came from rediscovering the sigil carved on the inside of Keep's skull, locating another skilled surgeon who might be able to clean it out, or finding some other means to save my own life.

Barring that, I wanted to see as much of the Spiral as possible, especially the most exotic planets. I wanted to swim in unbelievable oceans, take in more alien landscapes, meet more exotic intelligent races. For all I had been through, the violence, trouble, and fear since Keep had sent me that first text message, was equally met with excitement, awe, and friendship that I wouldn't trade for anything. I was grateful for the opportunity to be exactly where I was, no matter what happened in the end.

That didn't mean I wanted the end to come soon, but I had made peace with the idea that it might. Once we met with the Empress, I could at least rest easy knowing Matt and the others would be safe.

"Here we go," Alter said, flipping the toggle on the co-pilot console to bring us out of hyperspace. The darkness surrounding us faded as starlight was able to catch up to us once more, becoming brighter as the hyperspace field dissipated. From six hours away, Atlas was about the size of a pea. Even from this distance, I could make out the shades of blue, green, white, and silver that announced it as a highly-populated Earthlike world.

"So far so good," Matt said. "It's always nice not to be attacked the moment we come out of hyperspace."

"When have we ever been attacked the moment we come out of hyperspace?" Keep asked. "That's not a thing that happens."

"So far," Matt added. "Which is still nice. And if it couldn't happen, then why do we need to be buckled up?"

"You never know when you'll drop into an asteroid field or something," Keep said. "Or wind up in a crowded drop zone and need to make emergency maneuvers."

"That's not a thing that happens either," Matt countered.

"It's a lot more likely to happen than being attacked right away. It's not like a ship can target the exact position where you're going to appear."

"I'd be a lot more worried about being attacked."

"Then you'd be worrying about the wrong thing, Sherlock."

"Can you guys, I don't know, give it a rest?" I asked, glancing back at them over my shoulder. "It's better to be prepared for any situation than to be caught with our pants down."

"Speaking of which," Alter said, motioning to the sensor grid as it started populating.

"What the hell?" I said, staring at it.

I expected the grid to be active. As the seat of the Hegemony government and the Empress, Atlas was the most trafficked planet in the Spiral. There were always hundreds of ships orbiting the planet or in transit to and from the atmosphere.

I didn't expect a handful of them to be headed right for us, including a Royal Sentry.

"You were just saying?" Matt quipped, no doubt looking at Keep.

"That's impossible," Keep replied. "They couldn't know we would come out of hyperspace right here, right now."

"Yet here we are."

We were six hours out from Atlas. The ships coming toward us were only thirty minutes away, which meant they would have had to leave the planet's orbit some time ago to be where they were now.

"Keep's right," I said. "This doesn't make sense. But sense or not, that flotilla is coming our way."

The glow of the ships' main thrusters became visible through the forward viewport, with dark centers that would form into the starships themselves once the range between us closed a bit more.

"Maybe we should get out of here," Matt suggested. "Come back later."

"Yeah, maybe you're right," I agreed. "Alter, can you enter coordinates? Not too far, but far enough we can slip away without a trace."

"On it," she replied.

"They're firing," Keep said, thrusting a finger at the

sensor grid as the system picked up a handful of torpedoes, outlining them in red.

"Shit!" I snapped. "Get ready for—"

"Ben, wait," Alter said. "They aren't targeting us."

Looking at the sensor grid again, I didn't see another target. Eight large ships were headed in our direction, their distances staggered but all within an AU of one another. The Royal Sentry near the center of the group had fired the torpedoes, which shot past the lead ship, continuing forward into the space between us and them. If the torpedoes were locked onto us, the PSC would be blasting my ears with frenzied warnings. So she wasn't wrong. We weren't the targets.

But if not us…?

"Who are they firing at?" I asked, confused.

"Unclear," she replied.

"Ben, I think I've got something," Gia said. "I'm passing the connection."

The center console slab display changed, offering a connection to a wideband audio feed as her top-of-the-line neural link continued to outpace our seventy-year-old comms array. I reached down to the slab and tapped the button to tune in to the broadcast.

"...all armed vessels. Attention all armed vessels. This is a Blue Burn. This is a Blue Burn. Unidentified starship identifier 74K3NP21NC3 has been designated as an L6VOI. A twenty million credit bounty has been issued for the disablement or capture of the ship. Again, unidentified starship identifier 74K3NP21NC3 has been designated as an L6VOI. A twenty million electro bounty has been issued for the disablement or capture of the ship."

The feed went silent for a few seconds before repeating.

"Blue Burn? L6VOI?" Matt asked. If he hadn't, I would have.

"Level Six Vessel of Interest," Alter replied. "A fugitive,

like us. Blue Burn is a special status given to a vessel the Royal Guard wants to get a hold of very, very badly. It suspends certain rules and regulations with relation to private ships engaging targets within range of an inhabited planet and/or a Royal Sentry. Even your escape from Persiphon didn't rate a Blue Burn."

"What do they want it for?" I questioned.

"There's no way to know. In most cases, the Royal Guard will never say. It's enough to know that the ship is wanted, and for twenty million electro. That's a tremendous bounty."

"It sure is," Keep said. "Maybe we should try to nab it ourselves."

"Do you think that's where the torpedoes are going?"

"Without a doubt."

"But there isn't a ship with that identifier on our grid."

"If it's small and fast enough, it won't show up on the grid until it's within a few thousand kilometers. But we can estimate its position once those torpedoes detonate."

"The message just said disablement or capture. Won't a torpedo blow the VOI to smithereens?"

"They were fired from the Royal Sentry. They're likely disruptor warheads, not explosive."

The thruster glow of the torpedoes came into distant view, all of them moving along the same course. They shifted vectors, spreading apart as they turned to follow the unseen ship, which was obviously fleeing.

"Where's the blueburn's thruster flare?" I asked. If I could see the glow from the torpedoes, there was no reason not to see the light from the fugitive vessel.

"It may be shrouded," Keep replied. "The ship may have sensor blocking surfaces as well."

"You mean it's stealth?"

"Bingo. Very illegal, but I imagine whoever's flying it doesn't care. Ballsy to operate a ship like that. Steel ballsy to bring it to Atlas, whatever they used it for. Badabing badaboom."

The torpedoes began twisting and corkscrewing through space, spreading further apart as they tried to follow the blueburn. I thought I caught a glimpse of something as it crossed ahead of one of the more distant vessels. Nearly twice as long as *Head Case,* slender like a needle, it barely had a side profile save for the rear protrusion that shrouded the thrusters. I had a feeling they just couldn't make engines as skinny as the rest of the ship.

"What should we do?" I asked.

"It's twenty million electro, kid," Koop replied. "And we're closer to them than anyone else."

"But we're fugitives too."

"They're on a Blue Burn. We stop that ship, and the Empress will probably pardon you."

"I was hoping she would pardon us for warning her about Sedaya."

"Maybe. If that's the case, you still get twenty million."

"Aren't the ion cannons lethal?"

"That's the good thing about ion cannons," Alter said. "We can dial them back. A clean hit to the shroud will block the thruster exhaust and disable the ship."

I glanced at her, a smile spreading across my face. "In that case, let's go bag us a criminal."

CHAPTER 2

"Zar, Druck, I hope you two are locked in, wherever you are," I said over the comm device Miklos had implanted behind my ear. "It's about to get a little tight in here."

"We're good, Captain," Quasar replied. "Strapped into the couch in the lounge."

"Are we gonna die?" Druck asked.

"Not likely," I replied, opening the throttle and turning the stick to send *Head Case* rocketing along a new course. One that would hopefully cut the blueburn ship off at the pass. The combination was too much for the inertial negators to absorb, leaving me tightening my gut against the sudden G-force. "But you never know," I added through gritted teeth.

The G-force subsided quickly as I straightened the ship out, still accelerating rapidly. At the same time, Alter activated our newly renovated shields. In addition to the space hopper, we had picked up more robust nodes during the stop, which she and Druck had been installing over the last week. The forward shields were still using the original configuration, but we had managed to improve the robustness of our rear protection by over fifty percent. A pricey upgrade, but I was certain it would pay for itself before all was said and done.

I still couldn't see the escaping ship. Neither could the sensors. Instead, I had chosen our course based on the path of the torpedoes. While somewhat confused by the stealth systems of the blueburn, they managed to at least provide a general vector. Meanwhile, the larger ships further back, including the Royal Sentry, continued to give chase but seemed to be falling further and further behind. It seemed the captain in charge of the Sentry had the same thought, because a second barrage of torpedoes launched from the huge ship, nearly a dozen zipping off toward the first group on a more direct course. My guess was that the second grouping of torpedoes was able to use the positioning of the first as part of its targeting solution.

We streaked across space from the opposite side of the torpedoes, gaining ground on the assumed position of the target. I finally got a look at the needle-shaped vessel as one of the torpedoes got close enough to it to detonate. A flash of blue energy expanded out from the warhead, the blueburn skipping sideways and dropping below the explosion to narrowly avoid being hit by the resulting disruptor field. The ship slowed and slipped up and to starboard as a second torpedo exploded behind it. It became easily visible for a few seconds after that as bright tracers flowed out of both sides of the ship, spraying out in both directions and creating a small starfield behind it.

"Jamming chaff," Alter explained, knowing I hadn't seen the rounds before.

"Why don't we have that?" I asked as the rest of the first group of torpedoes rammed the chaff and exploded in rapid succession. While the blueburn's tactics had helped it to evade the first strike, the maneuvering and chaff seemed to give the second batch of torpedoes a better lock. They zipped toward the ship in a tightly grouped straight line.

"We don't need it," Keep replied. "We have better shields. Chaff runs out."

"And shield nodes overload," I countered.

"True, but most of the time we can repair shields. Chaff is an ongoing cost."

"*We* repair shields?" Alter asked.

"Fine. Alter can repair the shields," Keep corrected.

We had gained nearly five hundred kilometers on the blueburn, still accelerating, the gap shrinking faster and faster. The warships fell further behind, quickly making it clear the second volley of torpedoes was probably the best shot they were going to get. It might possibly be the only shot they would need to take.

The torpedoes spread apart again, only this time they remained on a direct course. They had simply widened the net. The blueburn stayed on a straight vector too, inexplicably trying to outrun them.

"If those torpedoes hit the target, we're out twenty million electro," Matt said.

"What?" I replied. "Do you think we should shoot them down?"

"I don't know. Maybe."

I glanced at Alter, who shook her head. "There's no guarantee we'll be able to stop them. And if we help them get away..." She trailed off. The sentence didn't need finishing.

"Point made," I said. "If we lose the electro, that's one thing. If we lose the blueburn, we'll never get a chance to talk to the Empress no matter what kind of intel we have to share."

The flight deck fell silent again as the scene continued to unfold. The torpedoes moved to within one hundred kilometers of the fleeing ship. We closed to under a thousand. Close enough to start shooting and possibly hit the vessel. Too far to risk missing and hitting one of the torpedoes instead. I cut the burn, pausing our acceleration, staying on a course to lead the blueburn right into our line of fire, assuming it made it that far.

My heart pounded, nerves tensing as the chase reached its sudden crescendo. The blueburn blipped onto our sensors around the same time it became clearly visible ahead. I shifted my eyes to target it with the guns, getting a lock but holding fire. The torpedoes were only seconds away from either being chaffed out, maneuvered through, or taking out the target.

"Get ready," Alter said, seeing the same thing.

"I'm so ready," I replied, resting my finger lightly on the trigger.

Chaff spewed from the sides of the blueburn, trying to confuse the torpedoes. The jamming signals sent four of the warheads off course, enough that their control system decided it was safer to detonate them than let them drift into space with their warhead armed. They exploded one after another, close to the rear of the fleeing ship, too far away to harm it. The chaff continued shooting out, three more torpedoes blowing up before the defensive measures stopped.

"They're out of chaff," Alter said.

"That would be good for us if we had torpedoes."

"We don't need them, we're almost in range. The blueburn pilot's so busy with the torpedoes he hasn't even noticed us."

At least, that's what we both thought.

We were wrong.

The blueburn changed course suddenly, redirecting nearly one hundred thirty degrees in a blink. One second, we were coming up on the ship's rear from the port side, the next the needle-shaped starship pointed directly at us, like a dagger ready to slice us in half.

"Shit!" I cried, barely getting the first half of the word out before the blueburn shot past us.

"That's impossible," Matt exhaled behind me. "The G-forces—"

I didn't hear the rest of whatever he said. We had no chance of catching up to the blueburn now. We had lost it before we could take our shot. That was a secondary concern.

The seven remaining disruptor torpedoes were struggling to make the same crazy turn, their limits pulling them directly into our path.

I pushed the stick forward, twisting it at the same time, desperate to move away from the torpedoes. If our ship were needle or wedge shaped we would have made it. But we were riding around the universe in a giant robot head, its profile nearly identical on all sides.

We couldn't get out of the way.

Not completely. Three of the torpedoes swept past, still trying to chase their intended target. The other four hit us in the face, detonating against the shields and sending a spike of energy through the nodes. If only one or two had struck us in the front of the ship, we probably would have been okay. But four at one time?

The shields failed. The energy from the disruptor warheads dug into our patchwork aluminum shell, reaching into the electronics and overloading them. The PSC reacted by going offline and taking all of the other systems with it.

The bridge went dark. My helmet blanked out. Life support stopped functioning. Gravity failed. The thrusters shut down, leaving us adrift and unable to escape the Royal Sentry, who would no doubt come for us the moment its captain accepted the truth:

The blueburn had gotten away.

CHAPTER 3

"Shit!" Matt cried, shaking his head. "Shit, shit, shit, shit, shit!"

"Relax, Sherlock," Keep said, remaining calm in the darkness of the flight deck. "It isn't that bad."

"Are you kidding? Going after that ship was your idea, and now look at us." He kept shaking his head. "We should have dropped in a different system and jumped here in the hopper."

"Matt, freaking out isn't going to help," I said, ripping my flight helmet off and locking it to its post on the back of my seat. "We dropped out of hyperspace far enough away to avoid sensor detection from Atlas' orbit. There was no way to know we'd have company out here."

"Exactamundo," Keep agreed. "What he said."

"Fine, but we still should have left the blueburn alone." He thrust his finger toward Gia. "Aren't you like a super billionaire or something? Why did we need to chase after twenty million electro?"

"Whoa," Gia said. "Don't drag me into this. I already explained why I can't fund this expedition."

"Can't or won't?" Matt pushed.

"Aiding and abetting fugitives will ruin me. I'll lose the deed to my planet."

"But you are aiding and abetting us. You're part of the crew."

"Nobody knows that. I start sending funds to strange accounts, and that'll change in a hurry."

"Newsflash, G," Matt continued. "If they capture us, they'll know you were here."

"I can tell them you abducted me. That I'm a prisoner."

"You wouldn't do that."

Her face hardened. "You may have the chance for me to prove I would. I want to help you crush Sedaya, but you know I won't risk everything I've worked so hard for to do it."

"That's enough," I snapped. "We're wasting time. Alter, how long will it take us to get back up and running?"

"We've been through this before," Alter replied. "I can reset the PSC, but rebooting will take more time than we have before those ships arrive."

"How do you know?"

She pointed out of the forward transparency. My final maneuvers combined with the torpedoes had left us in a spin, bringing the trailing warships across into view for only a few seconds. "They're already coming about."

Their thruster trails told the tale. They knew they couldn't catch the blueburn, not with its new heading and current velocity. But why not go check out the ship that had tried to help them catch the escaping fugitive? Right now, they probably thought we were just some random mercenary or private starship owner who had been in the right place at the right time and wanted to earn twenty million electro. Which was almost true, save for the one minor detail that turned the whole occasion to hell.

We were fugitives too.

We could change our identifier to help our disguise, but

nothing we did would help once the Sentry drew close enough to get a solid visual. There just weren't many giant robot heads flying around the galaxy. In fact, I was pretty sure we were the only one.

"What do we do now?" Gia asked. "And how much time do we have to do it?"

"Five minutes, give or take," Alter replied. "We have the space hopper. We can evacuate in that."

"You want to abandon ship?" Matt asked.

"Of course not," Alter answered. "But I also don't want to go to prison."

"There's no guarantee we'll go to prison," I said. "We still have intel to share with the Empress. If we convince the captain of the Sentry to listen to reason, we might be able to wiggle our way out of trouble before we wind up incarcerated again."

"I wouldn't lean too heavily into those odds," Keep commented. "There's a reason we developed an actual plan to get an audience with her."

"A plan that's gone to hell now," I replied. "Which means we need to improvise."

"I'm not disagreeing with you there, kid. But letting them take us in is the wrong move. Believe me."

"Okay, grandpa," Matt said. "What do you suggest?"

"Bailing in the star hopper won't work. They'll pick us up on sensors the moment we light the thrusters and all we'll succeed in doing is starting a new chase. I highly doubt they'll waste more disruptor warheads on the likes of us, which means badabing badaBOOM!" He spread his hands apart, making the sound of an explosion.

"There's no sound in space," Matt pointed out.

Keep glared at him. "Seriously? It's for dramatic effect."

"So how do we get out of this?" I asked. "It seems like you already have a..." I trailed off. It was my turn to shake my head. "No. Nope. Nuh-uh."

"Bennie, it's the only way," Keep pressed.

"What's the only way?" Matt asked.

"Forget it," I said. "We'll use the star hopper. If we calculate jump coordinates ahead of time—"

"As soon as we make a move to jump, the Sentry will pick up the energy signature and blast us with torpedoes while our shields are down," Alter said. "We'd need to outrun them first, just like the blueburn did."

"You just said we could escape in the star hopper," I complained.

"That was thirty seconds ago. The Sentry is that much closer now."

"Crap."

"It doesn't matter," Keep said. "We weren't getting out that way."

"Uh, did somebody turn out the lights?" Druck asked over the embedded comms.

"You just noticed that now?" Quasar replied.

"I was taking a nap."

"During combat maneuvers? Have you even noticed there's no gravity?"

"I was tired. What did I miss?"

"You missed us getting hit with a disruptor torpedo," I said. "There's a Royal Sentry coming our way. We have four minutes to do something."

"Do what?"

"Something," I repeated.

"You know what we need to do, kid," Keep said. "Why are you so reluctant?"

"One, I don't want to leave the Star of Caprum behind."

"We don't need to. It's portable. Alter can go get it."

"Really?" I replied.

"Yeppers. No problemo there."

"Two, I don't want to lose my starship."

"Our starship," Matt said. "And that probably should have been mentioned first."

"The Sentry will confiscate *Head Case* and take it to the Royal Guard base on Atlas," Keep said. "Alter can recover the ship there."

"I can?" Alter said.

"Can't you? I would think it would be pretty easy compared to some of the other things you've done."

"You *did* recover *Head Case* on Kasper," I said before looking back at Keep. "Three, I don't want to upset Mom again."

He shrugged. "Well, I guess being sent back to Persephon is definitely better than seeing your mother again. What was I thinking?"

"Ben, what is he talking about?" Matt asked.

"He wants to use the Mustang to transit back to Earth," I explained, keeping my eyes on Keep. "And once we're there, how long before we come back? And do we have to traverse the galaxy again to get back here?"

"I'm not exhausted like I was the last time. A few days. And we can transit to Atlas' surface. I know the coordinates. Badabing bada—"

"Why the hell didn't we just do that in the first place?" I shouted, interrupting him. "We didn't need to come all the way back across the Spiral. And we didn't need to buy the space hopper."

"Believe it or not, transiting isn't the bees knees. I don't really like the idea either, but there's no other way."

I stared at him, hesitant to abandon *Head Case*. At least the Royal Guard wasn't an actual enemy. Both the ship and the Star would stay out of Sedaya's hands.

"Do you want to stand here and argue about it while that Sentry pulls us into its hangar or do you want to escape?" Keep pushed. "Tick-tock, kid."

I exhaled sharply. "Fine. Alter, can you go get the Star?"

"Of course," she replied, unbuckling herself from her seat and planting her magboots on the deck.

"And maybe make sure the Grimoire is tucked away somewhere safe too?" Keep added.

"Already on my emergency todo list," she replied, clomping her way across the flight deck to manually crank open the door.

"Matt, Druck, Zar, make a pit stop at the armory and grab as much gear as you can in the next two minutes. The rest of you head for the hangar. It's going to be a tight fit in the car, but we'll make it work. I'll meet you there."

"Where are you going?" Matt asked.

"I need to get something from my room," I replied, glancing out of the transparency. The warships again appeared to rotate through our line of sight, a lot closer than before. "Let's move it team, we don't have a lot of time."

We all headed for the door. Alter had already slipped through the space between the two panels and made it to the elevator, having already dumped her off on Deck Six. She'd sent the cab back down so it was waiting for us when we arrived.

"Here's to emergency power," Matt said as we all boarded.

"Tell me about it," I replied. "Otherwise I'd have to navigate Deck Three full-sized, and Druck, Zar, and Shaq would be pint-sized."

He laughed, releasing some of his nervous tension. "Darn. I wouldn't mind seeing that."

"You never know. You might still get the chance," I said as the elevator stopped at Deck Three.

The trio waited outside when the doors opened. Shaq hopped from Quasar's shoulder to mine as I passed them, headed in the opposite direction, as they floated into the elevator cab. I pulled myself hand over hand along the bulkhead to get to my room as fast as I could. When I arrived, I grabbed the gift George had given me. I still didn't know what was in the box, but I definitely didn't want the Royal Guard to have it.

"Let's hope emergency power lasts another minute," I said to Shaq as I hurried back to the elevator. "Or Matt's going to wet himself when we get to the hangar."

CHAPTER 4

The emergency power held out long enough for all of us to reach the hangar. Shaq and I arrived just ahead of Matt, Druck, and Quasar, who each carried a space pack laden with hastily gathered goodies from the armory. I flinched as a car horn blared, my head whipping toward the sudden appearance of headlights in the hangar's back corner.

Keep leaned out of the Mustang's front passenger side window. "Can we get a move on here?" he shouted at us. As if to emphasize the urgency in his statement, *Head Case* jolted. The sudden change in inertia would have knocked me off my feet if I hadn't been magnetically connected to the deck. "That was the Sentry locking on a drone to stop our spin."

"Is Alter with you?" I asked as we all raced for the car.

"I'm here," she said, waving out the rear window.

"There's no way we'll all fit," Matt said, racing ahead of me and heading for the driver's seat.

"Where are you going?" I asked.

"It's my car. I'm driving."

"You don't know how to transit."

He released the maglock on his boots to hurdle over the top of the car, grabbing the roof and landing cleanly on the other side. It was a far cry from his first intentional zero-g experience, which had ended when he vomited on the deck. Again.

"Matt!" I shouted, annoyed he had chosen this moment to break the chain of command.

"It's okay, kid," Keep said. "He can drive. I've got the catalyst." He pushed open his door. "Squeeze in."

I shoved him toward the middle of the forward row of seats with Shaq still on my shoulder. Quasar beat Druck to the back. If we had anyone else with us we probably could have fit four across. She took up too much space, leaving the soldier of fortune as the odd man out.

"What about me?" Druck whined.

"Trunk it is," Matt said as the deck started to vibrate. "Hurry."

Druck grumbled under his breath and circled to the rear to pop the trunk. He climbed in and ducked down, pulling the lid closed behind him. I could still hear him muttering his complaints through the rear seat.

"How do we drive with no gravity?" I asked.

"We don't need to move much to transit," Keep replied.

"Since when?"

"Since ever. I don't make the rules, kid."

"Wait, I don't actually get to drive?" Matt asked.

"Nope. That's why it didn't matter that you got behind the wheel."

Matt's face fell. "Damn. No shrunken Ben, no driving the Wickmobile. This escape stinks."

"Better to escape stinky than not escape at all," Keep replied. He reached into his pocket, producing one of the sigiltech rings and handing it to me. "Bennie, when the portal opens, give us a push."

"What about the anchors holding the car in place?" I asked, excitedly sliding the ring onto my finger. I hadn't used a single sigil in weeks. I had missed it.

"They're magnetic. Push hard enough to break the grip, but not too hard."

"You do know pushing not too hard isn't my strong suit."

"Just do your best not to give us whiplash." Keep flipped open the transmission gear selector, revealing the needle beneath.

"What's that for?" Matt questioned.

"This," Keep answered, slamming his hand down on it. Matt winced and turned green as blood ran down the sides of the selector. Keep's jaw tightened in pain but he didn't cry out. Instead, he whispered his focus word under his breath, activating the catalyst in the car. The dark transit portal opened ahead of us. "Now, kid," he said, voice strained from effort.

"Distra," I whispered, *pushing* the car forward similarly to how I had *pushed* the hovercart on Sedaya's space dock, only with a much, much lighter touch, at least for me. It was still enough to yank the Mustang forward, shoving us all back in our seats as it broke free of the magnetic anchors and launched toward the portal. The Royal Guard had done us a favor by stopping our spin, allowing the Mustang to go straight into the void.

My heart lurched as we entered. I didn't want to leave *Head Case* behind. I didn't want strangers combing through it, raiding the armory, confiscating everything including the space hopper. We had spent a week working on a plan to get a message to the Empress, and in five minutes a random encounter with an L6VOI had screwed everything up. At the same time, it was a reminder of how fast life could change, and that I shouldn't take a single second for granted.

Passing through the void always seemed to be like dropping a wet blanket on my mood, but that thought helped get me through without falling into a sudden, deep depression. Glancing around the car, I couldn't say the same for any of the others save for Keep. Unsurprisingly, Alter looked the most distraught, though maybe that was more because she was leaving her home behind than because of the void. Matt's head slumped forward, eyes tearing up. I didn't know what thoughts came into his head, but I had a feeling they involved his father.

"Mattie!" Keep shouted, getting his attention as we passed to the other side of the tear in spacetime.

His head snapped up, hands gripping the wheel as we emerged into the middle of a cornfield. The car dropped about six inches from the air, bouncing hard while smashing down stalks as the momentum of my push wore out. We came to a stop surrounded by the crop. Humid air and a hot sun immediately started baking us.

"Where are we?" I asked.

"Bill's farm," Keep replied. "We were supposed to come out in the barn. My aim was a little off, I guess."

I couldn't see the barn past the height of the stalks. "Yeah, just a little. What if we came out into a wall or something? Or off the side of a cliff or on top of a building?"

"That can't happen."

"Why not? Depending on where you're aiming, that could be a little off."

"It didn't happen," Keep said, updating his original response. "Tally ho, Sherlock."

Matt glanced at him before starting the engine, a smile spreading across his face in response to the resulting purr. "Does transiting always feel like someone tore your heart out and stomped on it?"

"Only when you're awake," Keep replied.

Matt eyed him for another second. I could sense the

light bulb going off in his mind. "You *calmed* us, didn't you?" he said. "The first time we met, when you brought us to see *Head Case*."

Keep shrugged. "You got me red-handed. I didn't exactly want you to know I moved you to another planet."

"At least it makes sense now," Matt replied. "I don't usually fall asleep on car rides. Can you put us in drive? I'm not touching that."

Keep smirked, using his impaled hand to use the shifter.

"Shaq," I said, rolling down my side window. "Can you get up on the roof of the car and point us in the right direction?"

"Mmm-hmmm," Shaq replied, climbing out of the window. I couldn't see him spring up, but I heard his clawed feet on the metal.

"He's going to scratch the paint," Matt complained.

Shaq leaned down over the top of the windshield, pointing a finger a little to our right. Matt accelerated slowly, knocking down more corn as he steered us toward the edge of the field.

It took about twenty seconds to clear the cornfield. Bill's barn came into view the moment we broke through the last of the stalks. There was no immediate sign of Bill, Marie, Mom, or anyone else, but I could hear the engines of farm machines elsewhere on the property.

"Are we really on Earth?" Gia asked. "This is totally cotton…so wicked," she corrected, using her favorite of the expressions Matt and I had run past her.

"It is really incredible," Quasar agreed. "Not this so much. There are other planets with corn. Just the idea of being here." She reached forward, putting her hand on my shoulder. "And meeting your Mom. I can't wait."

"Me neither," Alter seconded. "Not everything about this is bad."

"You never know," Keep said. "This could turn out to be the best decision we were ever forced to make."

"Don't jinx it," I replied. "Our decisions don't usually turn out the way we want. Matt, take us up to the house. We'll see if anyone's home."

CHAPTER 5

We stopped in front of the house, all of us piling out of the car like a bunch of clowns. Locked in the trunk, Druck pounded on the inside of the lid, eager to be let out.

"I've been in some small mech cockpits before," the jockey said as Matt opened the back and helped him out of the tight space. "But at least the pilot suits are temperature controlled." He wiped at his sweaty brow with his already sweat-soaked shirt.

"Summer in southern California," Matt replied. "I'm surprised they're able to grow anything."

"They have water rights," I said. "But plantings are still only about seventy percent of where Bill wants them to be." I looked over the hood of the car at Alter, who held the clear cylinder containing the Star of Caprum against her chest. Even though it was disconnected from the ship, the Star remained active—a bright, miniaturized sun leaking plasma into the container. "Are you sure that's safe?" I asked, turning my attention to Keep.

"For now," he replied. "The Star can't stop giving off energy. The insulation in the capsule can hold the power as heat for about twelve hours before we need to release it."

"Release it how?"

"We could spike the power grid, but that might draw attention. Alternatively we can use *absorb* and *disperse* to send it into the atmosphere. It's nothing to worry about, especially since we'll only be here for a day or two."

I nodded, accepting his explanation and climbing the steps to the front door of the farmhouse. I rang the bell, immediately hearing light footfalls inside as someone rushing down the stairs and quickly approached the door. Heavier footsteps trailed slowly behind.

The main door opened, leaving Sally looking up at me from the other side of the screen door. She immediately beamed up at me. "Ben!" Her head whipped over her shoulder. "Daddy, it's Ben!"

"What?" I heard Bill say.. His footsteps sped up as he hurried to the door, quickly appearing in the short hallway behind Sally. "Ben, what are you doing here?" His forehead wrinkled with concern, though I wasn't sure if it was for me or himself. "Is everything okay?"

"Yes and no," I replied, happy to see him. "Don't worry. I didn't come to enlist you again."

Bill put a big hand on Sally's shoulder and looked past me to the rest of my crew. "Yeah, you don't look like you need as much help as you did the last time." His eyes shifted, widening as he noticed Shaq. "You know you have a blue squirrel on your shoulder, right?"

"Squirrel?" Shaq buzzed in annoyance.

"Come on Bill, I told you about Shaq," I said with a smile.

Bill let out one of his deep belly laughs. "I'm just messing with you, Shaq. Ben told us all about you. It's great to meet you."

"You too," Shaq replied, chittering happily.

"Ben!" Sally laughed. "Can I pet him?"

"He's not a dog, Sally," Bill explained. "He's from another planet. And he's as smart as a human."

"Smarter," Shaq corrected.

Bill laughed again. "I don't doubt that."

"Okay," Sally said, looking up at Shaq. "Maybe we can be friends, then."

"Mmm-hmm," Shaq agreed.

Bill unlocked and pushed the screen door open. "Come on in."

I didn't move right away. "Is my mother around?"

"She went into town with Marie to do some shopping. They'll be back in an hour or two."

"She's doing well, though?"

"Oh, yeah. She's great. The hardest worker I have on the farm. We're real happy to have her here. Your sister too. She's out in the stables brushing the horses."

"I'll check in with her soon. Let me introduce you to my crew. You already know Keep."

"Always a pleasure, Bill," Keep said.

"And this is Matt," I continued, pointing him out.

"Your fellow Earthling," Bill said. "Any best friend of Ben's is a friend of mine."

"That's Emil, Quasar, Gia, and Alter," I added, pointing to each one in turn. "And FYI. Out there…" He pointed to the sky. "...everyone calls us Earthians."

"You don't say." Bill shifted his attention to the others. "Welcome to my farm." He gave them a long-suffering look. "Though my wife would say it's her farm. It isn't though."

"Yes it is," Sally corrected.

He laughed. "Smart kid. This is my daughter Sally. At least she knows who the boss is."

"Hi, Sally," Quasar said with a big smile.

"Hi," she replied, shifting closer to Bill, suddenly a little shy. "You're so big."

"Sally," Bill admonished.

Quasar chuckled. "No, it's fine. I am big. But I use my size to help people."

"Quasar used to be a Royal Marine," I explained. "She protected the most important person in the galaxy she's from."

"Wow," Sally said, impressed. "I like your name, too. It's different."

"Thank you. I like your name too."

"Ben!" I whirled around at the shout. Sheri was running up the path from the stables, and I went back down the steps to meet her next to the Mustang. "You're back!" She skidded to a halt in front of me, eying Shaq. "You're the Jagger."

"Mmm-hmm."

"I'm Ben's sister, Sheri."

Shaq buzzed something I assumed was a warm greeting before leaning forward to nuzzle her neck. She started to draw back until she felt the softness of his fur. "Oh, that's nice," she said, leaning into it. She kept coming forward until she had wrapped her arms around me, showing an affection we had never shared before she had been taken by Alonzo Dellacqua. She pulled away. "And you brought more friends." Her eyes widened. "Matt! You're here too!"

"Hey, Sher," Matt said with an easy grin. "Good to see you."

She beamed at him, barely disguising her forever crush on him as I introduced everyone to her.

"It's so cool to meet you all," she said. "But it's so hot out here. Why are you all standing outside?"

"I told them to come in," Bill replied. "I guess they want to stay out here and bake."

"I definitely have had enough baking for today," Druck said, slipping past Bill into the air conditioned house. "Ahh, that's so much better than being locked in the trunk."

"What?" Bill said.

"Long story," Druck added. "You don't have anything to drink, do you?"

"Kitchen's in the back. Help yourself to anything in the fridge." He looked out to the rest of us. "Same goes for any of you. My house is your house."

"Thank you, sir," Druck said, heading for the kitchen.

"He's military too, isn't he?" Bill asked.

"He is," I replied. "He's our mech pilot. And a damn good one."

"Mech pilot?" Sheri said. "Like in those video games you used to play?"

"Yeah, pretty much. Why don't we all go inside?"

We all filed into the house. Druck carried out a six-pack of beer from Bill's refrigerator, offering it out to whoever wanted one. Matt and Quasar took him up on it, as did Bill. The rest of us declined. We made our way to Bill's den, each of us finding seats. It was a surreal experience to go from chasing a fugitive starship to having beers in a farmhouse all within twenty minutes.

"So Ben, what brings you back here?" Bill asked. "You said things both are and aren't okay."

"Wow, what is *that*?" Sally asked, approaching Alter and looking at the Star of Caprum. "It's beautiful."

"It's called the Star of Caprum," Alter replied. "It's the energy source that powers Ben and Matt's starship."

"That's so cool," she said, staring at the mini-sun. "How does it work?"

"Honestly, I don't know."

"Really? It reminds me of Tinkerbell."

"Who?"

"Tinkerbell. From Peter Pan. She's a fairy, and she glows and flies around."

"Oh. The Star isn't a fairy. It isn't alive."

"If you don't know how it works, then how do you know it isn't alive?"

Alter opened her mouth to answer before realizing that she couldn't. "I'm pretty sure it isn't alive," she corrected.

"Sally, stop hassling our guests," Bill said.

"Okay." She sat on the floor next to Alter's legs, gazing longingly at Shaq, still on my shoulder.

"We were hit with a disruptor warhead," I said. "It knocked out the ship's computer and left us dark and adrift. It was either come back here or be captured. So, we're okay because we're safe. Not okay because we lost our ship."

"We'll get it back," Keep said. "I just need a couple of days to recharge and we'll be on our way."

"If you're going to stay a couple of days, I'll call George," Bill said. "I'm sure he'd be happy to see you too."

"Sure, why not?" I replied, settling back in my seat and sighing heavily. There was no point obsessing over whatever was happening to *Head Case* right now. There was nothing we could do about it. At least we were all alive. All healthy and present. We had a little time to rest. And we still had the Star. "Druck, can you pass me a beer?"

CHAPTER 6

We spent the next hour chatting with Bill and Sheri. I found out early on that she and Nick had gotten back together before breaking up a second time, which turned out to be mostly my fault. It seemed Nick's experience at the processing facility had changed his perspective on a lot of things, and he'd decided to enlist in the Marines. Not that they had to break up because of that, but Nick felt it was better for him to get a clean start on what he called his second life.

I was angry with him for leaving her, proud of him for following his heart. Sher wasn't really that broken up about it anyway. She had already questioned their relationship, and Nick coming to the same conclusion made it easier for everyone.

Quasar was telling Royal Marine stories when Mom and Marie returned from their shopping trip. I heard the car pull up, followed by her rush into the house. She knew what the presence of the Mustang meant.

"Ben?" she said as soon as she made it into the door. "Ben, please tell me you're here."

I stood up, a big smile on my face. "I'm here, Mom," I replied.

She came around the corner, her expression joyous. "Oh, thank goodness," she exclaimed, dropping the bag she had in her hand and throwing herself at me without paying Shaq any mind. He jumped off my shoulder before she could accidentally knock him off. I returned her embrace, an excited squeal nearby telling me Shaq had decided to humor Cally and get close enough for her to touch him.

"It's good to see you," I said, squeezing her tight. At that moment, my thoughts turned to the cancer that had moved into my lungs. She would want to know, but did I want to tell her? Not right now.

"I wasn't sure I should expect you back at all," she said, stepping away. "And I definitely didn't expect you back so soon."

"Yeah. I didn't plan to be here either," I admitted.

"What happened?"

"We were in the wrong place at the wrong time. Our ship was captured. We escaped in the Mustang by coming back here."

"Oh. So you'll be staying for a while?"

"No, only a day or two while Keep gets some of his mojo back. We're still trying to get an audience with the Empress. We have proof that she's in danger now."

"So you got it," she said excitedly. "How?"

"Ben!" Marie finally caught up to Mom. "I figured you had to be here. How are you?"

"I've been better, but I've also been a lot worse," I replied. "So we'll call it even."

"Take what you can get, eh?"

"Exactly."

"I hope Bill's been a good host while we were out?"

"Of course he has," I said.

"He gave us beer," Druck added, drawing Marie's attention.

I quickly introduced Mom and Marie to the crew. Of course, when Mom saw Matt she hurried over to him and wrapped him in another bear hug, happier to see him than his father would ever be. I knew he appreciated the gesture even though he played macho about it.

"Well, it's great to meet all of you," Mom said.

"You're all in luck," Marie added. "We just got back from grocery shopping. There's forty pounds of burgers and dogs in the trunk. I think this is a good time to barbecue it."

"Any time is a good time for a barbecue," Bill said, standing up and rubbing his hands together in anticipation. "I'll go set up the grill. Sally, help your mother with the groceries."

"Do I have to?" Sitting on the floor with her legs crossed, Shaq had settled into her lap, looking content while she stroked him between his ears. "I'm making a new friend."

"I'd be happy to help," Alter said, springing to her feet.

Bill smiled. "Okay, Sally. Thank Miss Alter for volunteering to take your place."

"Thank you Miss Alter," she said.

"You're welcome," Alter replied, turning to Marie. "Just tell me what to do."

"Follow me," Marie said.

"I'll come too, Quasar decided, catching up to them. "I've never been to a barbecue before."

"Then you're in for a treat," Marie said. "I think you can carry all of the bags yourself."

"If that's what you need," Quasar replied. She and Alter followed Marie out of the farmhouse.

"Ben, we should talk," Mom said, glancing at the others. "Privately."

The way she said it made me nervous. I nodded. "Sure, Mom."

"Let's take a walk outside. We can go out the back."

"Uh-oh," Druck teased. "Somebody's in trouble."

Shaq perked up, ready to follow. "It's okay, bud," I said. "I've got this." He dropped back into Sally's lap. I followed Mom through the house and outside. The direction didn't really matter, so we headed down the dirt road toward the barn. "What's up?"

"How are you feeling?" she asked.

"I'm fine, Mom," I replied. "Still taking my meds, getting treatment from the autodoc on the ship. And Keep is using sigiltech on me at night to slow the spread of the cancer cells."

"That's great. What aren't you telling me?"

"What?" I replied, surprised by the question.

"I saw it in your eyes the moment I first looked at your face. A sadness I didn't see when you talked about your crew or your ship. Which means it has to do with your health."

"I can't hide anything from you, can I?" I asked.

"You never could. Do you remember that time you stole twenty dollars out of my wallet and spent it on cookies? I didn't realize the money was gone."

"But I missed one crumb."

"And you looked guilty as anything."

"No, I didn't."

"Yes, you did." She laughed, taking my hand. "What's going on, Ben?"

I stopped walking, turning to face her. Biting my lower lip, I fought to hold back tears. I'd put on a brave face for my crew, and for myself. But I couldn't hold them back when I looked at her. "The cancer's in my lungs now," I gritted out as the tears rolled down my cheeks. "It's spreading."

She stared at me, tears bursting from her eyes as she reached out to pull me in. "Oh Ben." We cried on each other's shoulder. I hadn't realized how scared and anxious I was until now. I'd taken a gung-ho attitude to fight my cancer, but I wasn't made of steel. I had to let it all out with the one person who shared my fears with me beyond even Matt.

We embraced until we calmed our tears and drew back from each other. Slipping her arm through mine, we started walking again. "Thank you," I said. "I didn't know before we got here how much I needed that."

"I know you did," she replied. "That's why I pulled you away from your crew. I knew you would never show them how the cancer's affecting you deep down inside. You're a natural leader."

"How did you know?"

"I'm your mother." She glanced at me and laughed. "And you're so much like your dad. Strong and sensitive." Her smile vanished. "I thought Avelus had a plan to cure you."

"He does, sort of. It's complicated."

"How so?"

I exhaled the last of my tension. "There's a sigil, *restore,* that would be able to stop the cancerous cells and turn them back into healthy ones."

"That's great news," Mom said.

"It would be, except the only known example of the sigil is etched into the inside of Keep's skull."

"What? Did you say, *inside*? How is that even possible?"

"I don't know. Apparently, his wife worked with sigiltech. She figured out how to do it and used him as a guinea pig. Then she died."

"And he doesn't know what the sigil looks like."

"No. He never actually saw it. And we can't exactly crack his skull open to take a look."

"And they don't have technology to see the inside of someone's skull in the Spiral?"

"I assume not or Keep would have suggested it."

"That must be frustrating. Having an answer so close, but still so far."

"Part of the reason why I needed a good cry, I think."

"What about his wife's records? Or lab? Or whatever she had? Maybe she left notes."

"He said it was all destroyed during the war."

"What about other sigils? That can't be the only one."

"We haven't found anything else yet that we can use. And there's still a problem. Apparently, I'm allergic to the catalyst. Or as Keep puts it, the catalyst is allergic to me. Pretty much any time I use it I can wind up paralyzed temporarily. It's painful and scary."

"And also frustrating. To have access to that power but to have a barrier in using it has to be maddening."

"It is, but if we found a healing sigil at least Keep could use it on me like he does with the one we do have, *calm*. It would help. Anything would help."

She smacked her lips the way she always did when she was thinking hard about a problem. We made it all the way down to the barn before she spoke again.

"What about that mining company? The one you said was a front for one of the bad guys? Suck-ass?"

I laughed. "Matt calls him Suck-ass too. It's Succaath. We blew up the company and the guy who owned it. We destroyed everything."

"Are you sure?"

"Yeah, I was there when we wiped their servers, and Keep said he went to Dellacqua's house just to make sure he hadn't hidden anything there. That route's a dead end."

"Are you sure?"

The way she asked gave me pause. I eyed her curiously. "Yeeeeesss," I said slowly. "Why?"

"I've been doing some digging."

"You? Digging? Mom, you're not a detective. You're not even good at the Internet."

"Maybe I just never had the right motivation before now," she replied. "It also helps that I'm working one job now, not three, thanks to you. I've become pretty adept at the Internet in the last few weeks. Did you know Alonzo Dellacqua had another child?"

I could feel my mouth gaping open at the news, my heart rate jumping. Not so much because it might be a lead to healing sigils, but because it might mean Sucaath's connection to Earth hadn't been completely severed.

"By your reaction, I can see you didn't. His name is David Morgan. As near as I can tell, Alonzo had him with a woman born here on Earth, not whoever he had his daughter with. It could be that David doesn't know anything about the mining company or sigiltech. Alonzo and his mom were never married and never shared an address, so they might have had nothing to do with one another. Anyway, David's some kind of genius. Eighteen years old and set to graduate cum laude from Stanford in a couple of months. He's also one of their top student researchers in their Bio-X program."

I shook my head in disbelief. "I don't know what that is."

"It's a biosciences institute whose main goal is to unlock the secrets of the human body through a blend of biology and technology."

"Did you get that from their website?"

She nodded. "I paraphrased it a little though." We both laughed.

"And you think that this kid might know about sigiltech?"

"He's only three years younger than you, Ben. He's not a kid."

"When he's nearly been swallowed by a black hole formed by a candy bomb, I'll stop calling him a kid."

"Huh?"

"Long story. I'll tell it during the barbecue."

"Like I said, he might know something about sigiltech. He might not. I don't think it would hurt to go talk to him. I had planned to go in a few weeks. I didn't know if you would ever come back or what your situation would be like if you did come back, but I thought it would be better to have as much information as I could ready for you just in case. But I'm sure David would be a lot more likely to talk to you than he would me, and—"

I cut her off by wrapping my arms around her and squeezing tightly. "Mom, I love you." Just the fact that she had gone through so much effort when she didn't even know if I would ever come back to make use of it reaffirmed how much she cared.

"I love you too," she replied. "Will you go?"

"I'll see what I can do. We only have a couple of days, and we can't afford to lose any more time if we want to get *Head Case* back."

"If you can go, you should. Don't leave any stone unturned."

"I agree. If at all possible, I won't. And if we have to leave again before I can go see him, I'll do my best to come back for that." I put my arm across her shoulders. "Let's go back to the house. I think I smell the burgers on the grill. Even with the molecular scans, Asshole still can't make food taste as good as the real thing."

"It's probably too perfect," Mom replied.

I paused before nodding. "You know, I hadn't thought that. But I bet that's exactly what it is. Maybe I could write a program to add some variability. I bet Gia could help with that. Don't tell her I told you this, but she's a superstar singer in the Spiral." I paused and made a face. "And her music is awful."

Mom laughed. "Is she rich?"

"Very."

"Maybe you should marry her, then."

"She's almost your age."

"What? She doesn't look a day over thirty, if that."

"She's rich," I repeated as an explanation for her youthful appearance. "But I'm not interested anyway."

"Is it her music?"

We both laughed again. "No, Mom. I have too much going on right now to think about getting involved with anyone. Besides, I wouldn't want someone to get that close just in time for me to die on them."

Her smile faded. "You aren't going to die."

"My crew and I are trying to stop a war out there," I replied. "I could die anytime, and not from cancer."

"But you won't," she insisted.

I shrugged mentally, deciding not to press the issue. It was one area where she wasn't ready to cope without denial. I breathed in deeply. "I definitely smell burgers. Come on."

CHAPTER 7

Bill had set up the barbecue on the front porch of the house, where shade and overhead fans helped blunt some of the summer heat. My belly was filled with two burgers, a pair of hot dogs, and too much potato salad by the time George, Gloria, and Kyrie arrived, pulling up in the new truck they had bought with the money Keep had given them. I introduced them to the rest of my crew following our joyful reunion, happy to see George making good progress with his physical therapy. Of course, Shaq was a huge hit with Kyrie. She and Sally hand-fed him bites of raw ground meat before getting into a game of hide and seek with him in and around the house. He had a much more playful nature than I'd ever realized and seemed to really enjoy interacting with the two girls.

With everyone together, I gave a quick account of everything that had happened to us after Keep and I left Earth. Matt and Alter helped fill in some of the details of what happened onboard *Head Case* while we were on Earth, giving everyone a full picture of our adventure.

The adventure of a lifetime, for better or worse.

I dropped into the seat next to Keep as the hastily

assembled party wound down. Mom, Marie, Druck, and Alter were in the house cleaning dishes, while everyone else sat quietly on the porch, sipping drinks and enjoying the cooling evening air.

"Better than being captured, right?" Keep asked. He had dark circles under his eyes and sweat running down his forehead. He looked like shit, and I told him as much. "I tore open space and time a few hours ago; what do you expect?"

"You did the same to bring us to Caprum to see *Head Case,*" I replied. "You didn't seem tired then."

"What do you think the hat is for? It kept my face in shadow and sucked up the perspiration. I was ready to call it a night before you plopped down and started hassling me about my appearance."

"I need to talk to you about something," I said.

"I know. You've been giving me that look since you came back from your walk with your Mom. She's not in trouble, is she?"

"No, she's fine. But I do appreciate your concern."

He shrugged. "I like her. She's a good woman."

"Wait. You don't have a thing for my mother, do you?"

"No offense, kid, but she's too young for me."

I laughed. "Everyone's too young for you."

"In all seriousness, when Priya died, I swore I would never love anyone else. And I meant it."

I drew back in surprise. "You're kidding, right? A thousand years, and you've never been with anyone else?"

"Nope. Not kidding. She was the one. My one and only."

"That's actually really sweet," I replied.

"Heh. What? You didn't think I had it in me?"

"Not really."

"It's always about the promises I make, kid. Because I don't make them lightly."

"I respect that."

He nodded. "Now, what is it you want to talk about?"

I leaned in closer and lowered my voice. I didn't want to drag anyone else into this, at least not before I ran it past Keep. "So, it turns out my mom's gotten pretty good at Googling. She discovered that Alonzo Dellacqua had another child with a different woman."

Keep's forehead perked up and he straightened in his seat. "What?"

"Yeah, that's what I said. His name is David Morgan. He's an eighteen year-old genius who's about to graduate from Stanford with a doctorate in biosciences when he should still be in high school. He's already the head researcher. Mom thinks we should go talk to him."

"We?" Keep said. He shook his head. "Not me, kid. I plan to sleep it off for the next eight hours or so, discharge the Star, and then go back to bed for another six to ten hours. After that, we'll be back in business. We can't afford to linger here forever, and you don't have time for a side quest."

"What if he knows about sigiltech? He could be the key to finding a sigil that'll help me with my cancer."

"I get it, Bennie. The bad cells are spreading and you're becoming more desperate for a way out of that fate. You know I want the same thing, but the odds this Morgan kid has the answers aren't all that good. Your best chance is for us to get back to the Spiral as soon as we can."

"He's Alonzo's son. How could he not know anything about what his father was doing?"

"Were they close?"

"I don't know."

"They weren't close," he stated. "It was a rhetorical question."

"How do you know?"

"Because I already searched Alonzo's house. I never

found anything mentioning a son. Even if he really does have one, I don't think they stayed in touch."

"Unless Alonzo didn't want anyone to know about David. Maybe he was trying to protect him."

"You're reaching, Bennie."

"Come on, Keep. It would mean a lot to Mom. She put in a lot of hours tracking David down."

"Sorry, kid." He pushed himself out of his chair. "I'd love to do a solid for her, but I really need my beauty sleep." He put his hand on my shoulder, looking me in the eye. "And we really need to get back to Atlas, asap. Chasing after a weak lead is just too risky, capiche?"

"Yeah, I capiche," I replied, doing my best to hide my disappointment.

"You came to me because you wanted my opinion, because you know I'll never disrespect you by telling you what you want to hear. So just hang tight, okay kid? Twenty-four hours from now we'll be back on the other side of the universe."

I exhaled sharply and nodded. "Okay."

"Okay," he agreed. "I'll see you tomorrow. Don't do anything stupid."

He headed into the house while I stared out at the cornfields. I didn't know how many minutes had passed before Matt replaced Keep in the chair next to me.

"Hey bro, you okay?" he asked.

"Yeah," I replied flatly.

"Seriously? Don't bullshit me. I've known you too long for that."

I looked over at him. "Mom found out Alonzo Dellacqua has another child. She thought I should go talk to him to see if he knows anything about sigils. Keep thinks it's a waste of time."

"Another kid, huh? Interesting. What do you think?"

"I think he's probably right. The odds this guy knows

anything are likely somewhere between slim and none. At the same time, I just can't shake the feeling that I should follow-up. That if I don't go I'll regret it in the future."

"That seems like a pretty easy choice to me."

"Except then I think that if I do go and something happens to me, it could affect the whole crew. We have a responsibility to more than just ourselves here. I feel like I'm being selfish."

"Hold on a sec," Matt said, leaning over and looking under the seat.

"What are you doing?" I asked.

"I'm trying to find my crystal ball." He straightened up and glanced at me. "You don't have one on you, do you?"

"You think you're funny," I said.

"Hilarious," he replied. "But I'm not joking right now. We have no way of knowing what future outcomes hinge on decisions we make now. You can decide to stay and meanwhile David's got a photocopy of the sigil inside Keep's skull at the bottom of his underwear drawer. In fact, if you want to look at it that way, we're here now, able to go after this information, assuming it exists, because of what we chose to do, going after the blueburn. Maybe we're meant to go see this David kid to see what he knows."

"Yeah, I know. Which is why I'm torn on what to do."

He considered the equation for a few seconds. "I'll tell you what. Give me this David guy's address and I'll go. If you leave without me, then you leave without me. Don't wait up."

"Matt, no," I said.

"Ben, yes," he countered. "If there's even the slimmest, lamest, more insane chance in the universe that I can do something that might save your life, then I'm taking it. Whether that means standing up to a Gilded or going to have a convo with a nerd." He jumped to his feet. "What's the address?"

"I haven't gotten it from Mom yet," I replied. "But you can't..." I stopped talking. Matt was already on his way inside to find Mom and get the address. "Matt, wait!" He didn't slow, disappearing into the house. "Matt! Damn it." I should have known he would seize the moment. Then again, maybe I did know. Maybe I just wanted someone to make the decision for me. "Matt!" I hurried into the house, not catching up until I reached him in the kitchen.

"Ben, what's going on?" Alter asked as I entered.

"We may have a lead on someone who could possibly help him with his cancer," Matt said. "Or at the very least might know some things about sigiltech that could help us."

"It's not likely," I added.

"It's extremely unlikely," Matt agreed. "But there's still a non-zero chance. He doesn't want to look into it and risk delaying our return to the Spiral, so I'm going to go for him." He turned to Mom. "Mrs. Murdock, can you give me David's address please?"

"I'll come," Alter said.

Matt and I both froze in response to the comment. "Alter, you do know if we don't get back in time we might be stuck here for a while," Matt said. "Or even forever. You'd lose your home."

"Some things are more important than a pile of sand, Matt," she replied. "If I can be of help, I'll come."

I stared at her, dumbstruck by the comment. "You'd give up *Head Case* for me?"

"Wouldn't you give up *Head Case* for me?"

"Well, yeah. Or Matt. Or Shaq. or Quasar."

"Or me," Druck interjected from the sink, where he was scrubbing dishes.

"I guess so," I answered, though internally I couldn't confirm it.

"So why is it any different for me?" Alter said. "Before,

my home came first because I didn't have a family. Now, my family comes first. End of story."

"Keep doesn't think we should go."

"Keep isn't in charge here," Matt said. "Technically, since we're on terra firma, I am. And I'm going."

"Here, Matt," Mom said, handing her phone toward him. "The address is in the contact list. This way you can call if you need anything."

He accepted the mobile. "Thanks, Mrs. Murdock."

"Matt," I said, intending to continue the argument.

"I've got the addy, Ben. There's nothing you can do now."

"Mom, how could you?" I asked.

"It seems to me the only person here who isn't doing everything they can to keep you alive is you," she replied. "And maybe him." She motioned to Druck.

"What did I do?" Druck asked.

"If we leave now, we can be there by morning," Matt said. "Ben, how long did Keep say he needs to recover?"

"Forget it," I said.

"Not your call," Matt repeated. "I have the address. I don't need to know the timing."

"No. I mean forget worrying about what might happen. It's my life we're talking about, and Keep won't leave without me. I'm in."

Matt smiled. "You're making the right choice. And Keep can't leave without us. We're taking the Pony."

CHAPTER 8

We were on the road within half an hour. While everyone on Team Hondo wanted to come along, I didn't think stuffing the Mustang with an entire entourage and overwhelming David was the best approach. Since Alter and Druck were in the kitchen when Matt and Mom convinced me to make the trip, I gave them first dibs on the rear seats, which they accepted. Of course Shaq had badly wanted to come, but after what happened the last time I was here I wasn't about to leave the farm or my family unprotected again. Between him, Keep, and Quasar, I had no worries that anything could happen to Mom, Sheri, or the Ackermanns while I was gone. It was an important job. More important to me than tagging along to visit a more likely than not dead end lead. I knew Shaq would defend all of them with his life.

Already sound asleep, Keep had no idea we left. I knew he would be upset when he awoke to find both me and the catalyst gone, though I wasn't completely sure which he would be more agitated about. I understood that it would only take a simple fender bender to complicate our trip back to Atlas. But I also had faith in Matt as a driver. He was fast but never outright reckless.

Besides, he had been looking for an excuse to drive the Mustang, and watching him visibly loving every minute he spent behind the wheel of the car made the risk worthwhile. If he was tired, he didn't show it, and we made good time traveling up I-5. Druck's mouth kept going for a good part of the drive as he shared stories about his time in the military and afterward, both before and during his incarceration. He very obviously skipped over the events that had led to his imprisonment on the Persephon Penal Satellite, dismissing it as a misunderstanding. Matt and I told some stories too, reminiscing about our childhoods to his benefit and Alter's, but mostly just enjoying one another's company for the first time in what felt like forever. We hadn't spent a ton of time together on *Head Case*. There always seemed to be some task that pulled us in opposite directions. The car ride gave us a chance to hang out again, talk about whatever, and for a few hours, forget about everything we had left a universe away.

It was two in the morning when Matt pulled the car to a stop along the curb on the opposite side of the address Mom said belonged to David Morgan. He quickly turned off the ignition and headlights to reduce the risk of either waking the neighbors or David himself. In the back seat, Druck's woodcutting snore broke off and he let out a soft groan and wiped drool from his chin.

"Are we here?" he asked, groggy scratchiness in his voice. He cleared his throat.

"Yeah," Matt replied. "His house is right there."

Druck leaned across Alter to get a look. "Quaint. Simple. Like the rest of this planet." Sitting back again he inhaled some phlegm from his sinuses. "So what's the plan? Do we go in, drag him out, and make him talk? Or are we sending Enigma in to deal with him?"

"We don't even know if he's alone in there," Matt replied. "He might live with his mother or some other students. Most college kids can't afford to rent their own house, especially in an area like this."

Druck looked at the home on our side of the street. "You're saying this is a nice area?"

"It's a whole lot nicer than where Matt and I grew up," I replied. "I'll just go up and knock."

"And say what?" Matt asked. "It's two a.m. and none of the lights are on. He's probably asleep. I thought we would at least wait until morning."

"We don't have time to wait for him to leave for school. I'll figure something out." I reached for the door handle, pausing when Druck held a blaster, grip first, between the two seats.

"Take this," he suggested. "Just in case."

"I'm not going up to his door with a gun," I said.

"I'll come with you," Alter said.

"It's better if I go it alone," I replied. "You're my backup. Keep an eye on me."

Druck pulled the gun back, reversing his grip on it. "I'm ready."

I pushed the door open and climbed out, closing it softly behind me. I glanced at Matt through the windshield as I passed in front of the car to cross the street. He looked tense. Did he expect trouble or was he worried this whole field trip would turn out to be a wasted trip? And a dangerous one at that? I knew how much he wanted David to have answers that would help me. More than even I did. I really wanted this to work out, for his sake and Mom's as much as my own.

I hesitated on the sidewalk, just ahead of the path leading up to the front door of the house. Alter kept her eyes glued to the home, narrowed slightly as though she had seen something in a second-floor window. I steeled my nerves with a deep breath and headed for the door. It wasn't that I feared David or the situation. I just felt kind of guilty about waking him or anyone else up.

A Ring doorbell was installed next to the doorframe, and I looked directly at the small camera as I raised my hand to knock, figuring it would be more quiet.

"Can I help you?" a stiff voice asked from the doorbell's speaker before I could hit the door.

"Uh, yeah, maybe you can," I replied. "I'm looking for David Morgan."

"Do you know what time it is?"

"Two twelve a.m.," I replied. "I know. I'm really sorry. I need to talk to him right away. Is this his house?"

"You aren't a cop are you?"

"Do I look like a cop?"

He laughed. "You look like the last guy I played at the MTG World Championship."

"MTG?" I asked, confused.

"Magic: The Gathering," he answered. "I thought maybe you're a little too toned to be a geek, but the Han Solo duds made me reconsider. Now I'm not sure what to believe."

"I know what Magic: The Gathering is," I said. "I didn't know they had tournaments, that's all."

"Brrp. Geek card declined. What do you want with David?"

"Well, I uh…I knew his father."

I tensed my jaw, unsure of how the guy on the other end of the doorbell intercom, who I assumed was David Morgan, would react to the statement.

"Did he leave me any money?"

"What?" I replied. That definitely wasn't the reaction I expected, but maybe it should have been.

"I said. Did. He. Leave. Me. Any. Money?"

"Do I look like the executor of a will to you?" I answered. "I assume that means you're David Morgan."

"Look, whoever you are. My father was an absent piece of shit who never did anything for me or my mother. So if you aren't here to give me some inheritance I never expected him to leave me, you can sod off. Okay?"

I stared at the doorbell, heart sinking. My longshot hope crashed and burned at the word absent. "Okay," I replied. "I'm sorry to bother you. I thought you might know something about sigils. Thanks, anyway."

I turned away from the camera and started back down the walkway toward the car. A light went on behind me, and I heard footsteps rushing down stairs inside. I slowed my pace, ready when the door swung open to reveal a suddenly interested David Morgan.

"Wait!" he snapped. I spun back around. David stood on his front steps in a pair of Sailor Moon boxer-briefs, his round stomach overhanging the elastic, a second chin rounding below the first. At least part-Asian, with serious eyes, a small nose, a mop of dark hair, and a sedentary physique, he trembled where he stood. "Did you say sigils?"

"Yeah," I replied. "Your father—"

"I know," he said, cutting me off. His gaze slipped over my shoulder toward the Mustang, and he suddenly looked fearful.

"It's okay," I said. "That's my ride."

A pair of headlights flashed on toward the end of the street, jerking my attention to a dark van. It peeled away from the curb, coming our way. I heard Matt start the car.

"What about them?" he asked, pointing at the van.

"No. Not them," I replied. I reached into my pocket, slipping a sigiltech ring onto my finger and clicking the needle into my skin. Every time I used it was a risk, but sometimes that risk needed to be taken. Especially with a black van speeding toward me.

The sigil activated, glowing brightly as I *pushed* the van. The force of the action lifted the vehicle and threw it sideways where it crashed loudly onto a lawn and slid to a stop. Almost immediately, houses around the scene began lighting up.

"Oh shit," David said, staring at the ring. "I'll be right back." He disappeared inside.

"Where are you going?" I shouted, my eyes on the van as the back door dropped open and a Sucaath SWAT team started climbing out. Of course not all of them had been killed at the processing facility. And of course they were surveilling David.

"I need to get my laptop!" he shouted back. "Don't let them murder me."

Sirens blared in the distance. Across the street, Alter and Druck exited the Mustang and moved across the lawn toward the attackers while Matt did a U-turn to park in front of David's house on this side of the street. The front passenger side door swung open.

"Seriously," Matt shouted at me. "Five minutes, and we're already in trouble?"

"I actually don't think that's a record," I replied.

Druck found cover behind a smallish tree trunk, crouching as six bad guys moved toward us, rifles aimed mostly at me. They didn't notice Druck at first, their standard gunfire crackling over my head. I dove to the grass. Druck's counterattack lighting up the street as his energy blasts brought one of them to the ground.

Alter sprinted toward the van closer to the houses, using their landscaping as cover to make her approach. I leopard-crawled toward David's front door while Matt opened the driver's side door, using it for cover.

"David, what the hell? Get your ass down here!" I shouted as bullets kicked up dirt in front of me. Matt laid down a barrage of cover fire, buying me a few seconds to dive through the open front door, while our suckass attackers took cover behind the hedge across the street. Constant fire from Druck and Matt was successfully distracting them.

"I needed my laptop," David explained from the top of the stairs. He had a backpack slung over his bare shoulder and a pair of Converse All-Stars on his feet. He hadn't wasted time putting on the clothes he held in a ball under one arm. "I knew I was being watched. I just freaking *knew* it!"

Matt unleashed another stream of plasma bolts, hitting one of the shooters in the arm. The police sirens were getting closer. "Move it, David. We don't have time for a powwow with the cops."

He hurried down the stairs, seeming more pleased with the astuteness of his observation than he was worried about being shot. "You didn't really know my father, did you?"

"Yeah, I did. I killed him," I replied, ducking back as fresh rounds struck the doorframe. David froze halfway down the steps, and for a second I thought he might bolt back up them.

He recovered quickly, resuming his descent. "Cool."

CHAPTER 9

"That's it?" I stared at him in surprise. "You think it's *cool* I killed your dad?"

He shrugged. "I met him and my half-sister once when I was four. My mother took me to his place to try to get him to acknowledge my existence. He screamed at her, told me I was his biggest mistake, and then called the cops on us. He also decided to press charges, which put my mom on probation and me in foster care for almost a year. So, yes. Cool."

I had no words for him, so I acknowledged his explanation with a nod and activated my embedded comms. "Come on, guys. Cops are getting close. We need to get a move on."

"I'm almost there," Alter replied.

"Whoa," David said, reaching me just inside the front door. "That gun of hers is *not* firing bullets."

I grabbed him, pulling him back just before a few rounds whizzed past where he had just been standing. "Their guns are. Stay back."

The attackers leaned out from behind both ends of the hedge. One of Druck's rounds caught one of them in the helmet, piercing his headgear and killing him, leaving three still upright.

"Your ring," David said.

I glanced down at it. The glow had faded but the sigil remained visible. "What about it?"

"My father was into those symbols. I spent the first six months since I first saw them convinced he was part of a Satanic cult."

"Yeah, he sort of was," I answered. "But these are a lot more than symbols."

"I always had a feeling, but I never believed it until now. You threw that van like it was made of styrofoam."

"I didn't throw it. I pushed it."

"What's the difference?"

I ignored his question as flashing lights reflected off one of the houses.

Matt saw the lights too. "Alter, hurry!" he snapped. "Druck, fall back to the Mustang. Ben, grab David and let's go."

I glanced at David. "We're making a run for the car, got it?"

He clutched his balled up clothes in both arms. "I'm ready."

The gunfire from the van stopped suddenly as Alter finally reached the shooters. "Come on!" I growled, grabbing David's arm and urging him toward the Mustang. Druck joined us there as Matt climbed behind the wheel and pulled his door closed. David ducked into the back while I took shotgun in the front. We peeled away from the curb into another U-turn as Alter finished off the last of the attackers. She dropped him next to the car as Matt stopped and opened his door for her to slip into the back seat.

The first squad car rounded the corner ahead of us, followed by two more. Glancing at the rear view mirror, I saw a second batch of police coming to squeeze us from behind.

"Shit," Matt said, slamming down on the pedal and peeling out. He went about twenty feet before turning into an empty driveway.

"Are you *parking*?" I accused.

"Shut up," he replied, accelerating toward the fence at the end of the line.

"There could be another car on the—"

"Let's hope not," he said.

We smashed through the fence, emerging onto a slice of lawn before mowing down a small rhododendron and bouncing up onto one end of a circular driveway in front of the house behind David's. Fortunately, there was no car parked there. Tires screaming, we barreled out into the street. I heard more squealing tires as the cops followed us through the hole in the fence, hoping to close in on us.

"Hey," Druck said, apparently to David. "Nice panties. Who's the anorexic chick all dolled up like Gia?"

"What?" David replied.

"Hold on," Matt barked, swinging us around the next corner. The momentum threw Druck into David, while Alter managed to grab onto the back of Matt's seat to keep from piling on.

The Mustang roared as it accelerated, shooting down the street leading out of the residential area. A police car came around the corner in front of us, sliding across the road to block us in.

"Ben!" Matt shouted.

"Distra," I said softly, ring glowing as I thrust my hand at the police cruiser, flinging the back end out of the way. We raced past, leaving the officer behind the wheel stunned and confused.

"Nice," Matt said.

"The girl on your undies," Druck continued. "Who is she?"

"I wish you'd stop looking at my crotch," David replied.

"Come on, man," Druck pressed. "I'm just curious about the origin of the cartoon character. She looks just like a friend of mine."

"Your friend is a cartoon character?"

"No, I mean the outfit. I've seen her wear something just like that in one of her videos."

"You don't like lollipop," Alter reminded Druck. "If you watched her video, it was only to see her in that scanty outfit."

Druck grinned. "Can you blame me?"

"Can you all shut up back there!" Matt yelled. "I'm trying to outrun the cops!"

They quieted down as Matt skidded around the corner onto a wider street. Fortunately, the early morning hour meant the roads were mostly deserted, allowing him to peg the gas pedal to the floor. The road ahead was clear of cops, but police cars began filling in behind us, trying to keep pace with us.

"Ooh, yeah," Druck said. "That looked really hard, Boss. Took a lot of concentration. Now..." He returned his attention back to David. "...back to your underwear."

"Help me," David said, looking at me.

A bright spotlight hit the car, shining down from a chopper as it swooped in overhead.

"Shit," Matt cursed. "You were saying, Druck?"

"I didn't say anything," Druck replied.

"We need to ditch the car," David said.

"We can't ditch the car," I shot back.

"We go into a parking garage, we ditch the car, and we escape on foot," he repeated. "I saw it on old episodes of Cops on Netflix like a hundred times."

"Oh, and how'd that work out for the perps?" I asked.

"Okay, but they couldn't catch *everybody*."

"We don't ditch the car, and we don't split up," Matt said. "That's final. Ben, I need—"

"It's dangerous," I replied, already well aware of what he wanted. "My hand is numb. I could be paralyzed."

"I know, but what else—"

A whoomp from the back seat preceded the plasma bolt that arced up toward the chopper and slammed into the rear stabilizer. The chopper peeled away, the pilot losing control.

"Druck!" I shouted. "What the hell?"

Leaning past David, he pulled the plasma rifle back in through the window. "Just solving the problem," he answered, David looking like he wanted to die with the soldier of fortune pressed against him. "Or maybe it's the new way. You said that sigil stuff is old tech, right?"

I heard the echoing crash as the helicopter hit the ground. Looking back, I saw the pilot climbing out of the wreckage, the copilot flinging the other door open and hopping out, both thankfully unharmed. "You could have killed those cops!"

"So?"

"So they're not the bad guys."

"They're chasing us."

"Because they think we're the bad guys."

"Well, why does everybody always think we're the bad guys?"

"Oh, I don't know. Maybe because we keep shooting people?"

"Bad people. They shot at us first."

"The cops don't know that. We might have been able to weasel out of this before. No chance now."

"Then I guess we shouldn't get caught," David said, surprising me. "Pick a direction, hop on the Interstate, and keep driving."

"Are you serious?" I asked, looking over the seat at him.

"There are six dead guys on my neighbor's lawn, and I just aided and abetted someone who shot down a police helicopter. I assume by your recklessness and total disregard for anyone's sleep that you have experience with this sort of thing and somewhere to hide."

I opened my mouth, flabbergasted by his outpouring. "Well, uh..."

"You also used that ring to *push* two things out of the way, which confirmed everything I suspected about my father but seemed too crazy to believe. Not to mention, that gun fires freaking plasma bolts. Whatever it is you're doing here, I am so totally in."

"I appreciate the vote of confidence," I admitted. "But how do you know we're *not* the bad guys."

"You said you killed my father, right?"

"Yeah."

"That's good enough for me."

CHAPTER 10

We drove for over an hour, clearing well out of Palo Alto, passing San Jose and finally pulling into the parking lot of a Fairfield Inn in Hollister, California. We had all remained mostly silent during the drive, save for a short conversation between David and Druck where David explained the history of Sailor Moon to the soldier of fortune. Druck found the whole thing pretty ridiculous. As far as he was concerned, a very real Gia looked a lot better in a short-skirted sailor outfit than a cartoon. I had to agree.

Thankfully, we didn't cross paths with any more police, though I was one hundred percent certain they were already looking for us and would get our description out to other departments within the next couple of hours. I figured every PD in the state would be on the lookout for the Mustang by the time the sun came up.

But we couldn't go all night. We were all exhausted, Matt especially, though I wasn't far behind. Using the ring hadn't paralyzed me, but the effort still drained my energy and left an opening for my other symptoms to make a stronger appearance. I was dizzy, lightheaded, and physically weak. We needed a short break.

"Just give me a minute," David said as we got out of the car. He stretched out on the back seat, quickly pulling on a pair of sweatpants and a Spirited Away t-shirt, along with a pair of velcro sandals.

"Seriously?" Druck said. "That took you fifteen seconds. You couldn't do that back at your house?" He glanced at me. "I think he likes walking around in his Gia underpants."

"Fifteen seconds is a long time during a firefight," David replied. "You said you were a soldier. You should know."

"Maybe, but how do *you* know?"

"Fortnight."

"Is that a famous battle or something?"

David laughed. "No, it's a video game. Where are you from, Mars?"

"A lot further than that," Matt said. "Come on, we have two hours tops." He paused as he got a good look at the front panel near the tire. At least a dozen bullet holes marred the formerly perfect surface. "My poor baby."

"Look on the bright side," I said. "It really is the Wick-mobile now."

"How long have you been waiting to say that?"

"Since we started taking fire."

"Funny," he huffed as Druck got out, slinging his plasma rifle across his back. "Come on, Druck. Let's leave that here." He pointed at the rifle and started for the rear of the car, keys jingling in hands as he picked out the trunk key.

Druck grunted his displeasure as Matt lifted the lid. He dropped the rifle in the trunk and slammed the lid shut. We headed across the parking lot and through the front doors to the front desk.

Matt took the lead. He was the one with the credit card. "Can we get a room, please?" he asked the attendant, an overweight older woman with silver hair secured in a tight bun.

"One room?" she replied. "For all of you?"

"Yeah. Can we do that? I can't afford two rooms."

"Maximum occupancy in a room with two queens is four adults, with children it's six. I'm sorry."

"Druck's like a child," David said, drawing a stern look from the woman.

Matt exhaled painfully. "Please, ma'am. It's been an awful night. We're on our way to a funeral for a good friend from college. We already broke down twice. And I'm almost totally broke. You could completely save our lives if you bend the rules a little? I promise we won't make a lot of noise. We're just going to crash for a couple of hours and then be on our way."

She stared at Matt before her eyes flicked to the rest of us. I did my best to look sweet and innocent. So did David. Druck couldn't look innocent if he tried, and Alter seemed kind of shifty.

"I should probably ask the manager," she answered at last.

Matt sighed again, feigning an even deeper level of exhaustion. He played it well. "Please? It's two hours. No more."

She bit her lower lip, hesitated, and nodded. "Okay. But one complaint from anyone and you're out, no refund."

Matt picked his head up and smiled. "Deal."

He went through the check-in process, scoring a room on the ground floor close to the exit. I guess the hostess was pretty sure we would garner a complaint and she didn't want to have to walk too far to kick us out. Entering the room, Matt immediately went into the bathroom and relieved himself while Druck jumped onto the bed closer to the door, dumping his head on the pillow and closing his eyes.

"Nighty-night Team Hondo," he grumbled.

Matt came out of the bathroom and pulled down the blankets on the other bed before taking off his shoes and climbing in. "Are you all going to stand there, or are you going to sleep?"

"Sleep," Druck announced without moving or opening his eyes.

"I don't require sleep," Alter said.

"What?" David asked. "You don't sleep?"

"No."

"How is that possible?"

"It's a long story," I replied.

"I've got a long story for you, too," David said, shaking his backpack. "I know you're tired, but I feel like I need to tell someone before the cops or those biker-ninja goons show up again."

I glanced at the spot next to Matt on the bed. I was beat, but David was right. I had gone to him looking for information, and it seemed like he had something he wanted to share, though I had a feeling it wasn't what I was hoping for. "Okay. I want to hear you out. Alter, can you keep an eye on these two? I'll contact you if there's any trouble on our end."

"You want me to just sit here?"

"Yeah. Boring, I know. But necessary."

"It's not a problem, Ben. Just be safe."

I nodded and led David back out of the room. We wandered to the closed dining room, where I took a couple of chairs off a table and placed them close enough to one another we would both be able to see the screen of his laptop. He had just put the computer on the table when the hostess approached.

"I'm sorry," she said. "The dining room is closed."

"It doesn't look closed to me," David replied before I could answer, waving his arm toward the entrance.

"There's not even a door or a rope or anything to indicate closure. I understand you aren't serving food right now, but this seems like a perfectly good peaceful and quiet place to sit and have an intellectual discussion about quantum physics, multi-dimensional chaos theory, and anime. Possibly in that order. You're welcome to join, if you're interested."

She stared at him, unable to come up with an easy response to his argument.

"Besides," I added. "If we're out here, the room only has three in it. No occupancy problem." She frowned at me and walked away without another word. I looked sidelong at David. "Who are you?" I asked.

"Who are you?" he replied. "I mean, you're the one with the plasma rifles and the magic ring."

"Yeah, but I think you have some idea who we are. You suspected your father was into some things, and now you know those things are real. What does that tell you?"

"That there's a more than even chance that you're from another part of the universe," he replied. "And that is so amazing I can barely stop myself from freaking out like a fourteen year-old at a BTS concert."

"Well, at least you have clothes on now," I replied. "Believe it or not, I'm from Earth. So is Matt."

"Oh, I believe it. You've got the pop culture down. Those other two? No way."

"You're right about that."

"But they're human, right?"

"Druck is."

"Alter looks human to me. But she said she doesn't sleep. Do all aliens look just like humans?"

"No. I have a friend that looks like a cross between a flying squirrel and a sloth. He's also venomous and blue."

"Does being blue denote that he's poisonous, or are the two features unrelated?"

"Unrelated. You'll meet him once we get back to the farm. I can tell you everything about us later, but you wanted to make sure your story doesn't die with you, so…"

"Right. Yeah." He opened the top of his laptop and turned it on. Of course, his background image was from Macross.

"You really like anime," I said.

"I do. That was last in my list of discussion topics though." He closed the lid again, confusing me. "I should probably give you a quick backstory before I show you my work. If you can picture all of this happening in the style of *Into the Spiderverse*, it'll sound a lot cooler."

I wasn't sure how to respond to that, so I kept my mouth closed, waiting for him to talk.

"Right," he continued, once he realized I wasn't going to acknowledge that request. "Here goes."

CHAPTER 11

"Wait," I said, before David could get going with his story. "You aren't going to start where your mother gave birth to you or your first memory, right? We don't have time for that."

He smiled. "Don't worry. I'm going to give you the short version. Really, not much is all that interesting until about three years ago. Before that, I was just the only child of a single mother. I didn't even know who my father was outside of the money he deposited in my mom's bank account every month."

"I thought you said you met him when you were four?"

"If you want to call it that. I told you, he called the cops and made our lives miserable. I was too young to remember what he looked like or where he lived or anything like that."

"Okay, but you aren't *just* an only child. You're at least six years accelerated in school. Ready to graduate Stanford University at eighteen. A part of their bio lab. That's impressive."

He shrugged. "Maybe it sounds impressive from an outside perspective. For me, it became a means to an end."

"What end?"

"To solve the unsolvable equation." He laughed. "At least, I thought it was unsolvable until I saw you use your ring. Somebody already figured it out."

"You're talking about how to create a sigil?"

"I might be. I'm still starting in the wrong spot in the timeline. Let me back up. Picture this. I'm fifteen years old, already out of high school and a junior at Stanford undergrad. Whoop dee doo. It was my mother who wanted me to go there. She said with my intelligence the only things I needed to succeed in life was a good school on my resume to get my foot in the door and the motivation to keep it there. She managed to convince me of the first thing, but you know the second was a little harder to come by. Not because I couldn't handle the curriculum. I don't want to sound like I'm bragging because really I couldn't care less, but it all came too easily. I didn't need to study for anything, and I found most of it boring. I was going through the motions, but what I really needed was a challenge."

"Sigiltech?" I guessed.

"Exactly. But I didn't seek it out. I guess you could say it found me. One night, I'm trying to order the newest season of Attack on Titan and the payment is declined, so I go down to ask my mother about the issue and happen to catch a glimpse of her entering her login credentials for her bank account. After she fixes the account info for me, I go back upstairs and order the episodes without thinking much about it. Have you ever experienced that phenomena where your primary consciousness is engaged in one thing, and your subconscious is processing something else without you really being aware until it reaches a conclusion?"

"Probably," I answered. "Though I can't think of an example right now."

"Well, it was like that. I'm right in the middle of the episode when bam! I have this sudden urge to login to my mom's bank account. Not to steal from her or anything. I would never do that. But I know she gets money from my father each month, so I look for the deposit in the account, and then go into the details to get the routing and account numbers. Next thing you know, I'm reverse-engineering my way into figuring out who my father really is. It didn't take me long to realize the payments weren't coming from a personal account. They were being made from a business."

"Let me guess, Exotic Mining Group?"

"Yes. They started sending the cash about three years after the incident with my father, around the same time my mother regained custody of me. She always said it was because he felt guilty about what he had done, but I never went for that. If he had felt guilty, he would have tried to initiate contact and admitted I was his kid. I don't really know why he started sending it."

"But it came through EMG?"

"Yeah. That fact of course led me right to him, especially since I could see some of my features on his face."

"So once you knew who he was, did you try to contact him again?"

"No. He already burned me once. Why would I set myself up for that again? I didn't want to fight for a relationship with him. I wanted to hurt him the way he hurt my mother."

"That sounds familiar," I said, thinking of Gia. "What did you do?"

"I learned as much as I could about computer hacking and started messing around with his company's network, looking for a weakness. Their security was better than I expected, but some old-fashioned social engineering did the trick. I got into his servers and started poking around, with an intent to destroy anything I thought was valuable. What I found was too interesting to delete."

"Sigiltech," I said again.

"Of course. Like I said, at first I thought my father was in a cult. The lines and diagrams looked like pagan symbols to my untrained eyes. Intrigued, I downloaded the data instead of deleting it, and then went on a hunt for similar sigils online. But the mainstream search engines all came back empty. Same for the darknet. The diagrams didn't exist on the internet, so I raided the college library, still coming up empty. I couldn't figure out what they were, but by that time I just had to know. So I did the only reasonable thing I could do."

"Called Alonzo to ask him about it?" I guessed.

He raised an eyebrow at me. "You're joking, right? I hacked into his home network. That's where I found the motherlode. Instead of meaningless sigils, I found symbols surrounded by mathematical equations, each line a complex calculation I needed to understand. It was right then and there that I realized I had found the challenge I was looking for. I decided that I was going to figure out what the symbols were and how they worked. And then I was going to upload them so that anyone could make a copy. Whatever intellectual property EMG was working on, I would open-source it and destroy them in the process."

I couldn't help thinking about how hard Keep had worked over the last thousand years to prevent sigiltech from falling into the wrong hands. And David Morgan had planned to plaster it all over the world wide web. "That's pretty harsh," I said.

"Yeah. Cool, right?"

"You never uploaded any of the data, did you?"

"No. The thing is, I've spent the last three years working on the equations. About a year in, I had a breakthrough where I mentally wrapped my head around the theoretic purpose of the sigils, but it seemed so crazy I couldn't believe it was true. I tried to quit then, but I just couldn't give up the chase. The problem had me by the balls. I needed to solve it."

"Have you solved it?" I asked, starting to get a little excited by the path the conversation was taking.

"No. Not completely. I mean, I have some of the math down, which I used to create a simulation program that I believe renders accurate effects. But it's a far cry from mastery. There's just something missing. A few weeks back, I decided to break into the EMG servers again to see if I could find any clues, but they were gone. Completely offline. I thought maybe the company went out of business, but when I checked the news I saw their primary mineral processing facility had blown sky high, that Alonzo and my sister were caught in the blast, and that EMG was no more."

"Yeah, sorry about that. But your father stole something of ours and he decided not to give it back without a fight."

"It's okay. I doubt the answer I needed was there anyway."

"You said you got into biosciences at Stanford as a means to an end. Where does that fit in?"

David flipped open his laptop again. "I'm glad you asked." He logged into the machine and navigated to a program titled *SigSim*. "I've been working on this for three years now, pretty much all of my free time. After I got my bachelors in Computer Science with a minor in Biology, I joined the lab because I had questions only people smarter than me could answer."

"Smarter than you?" I said. "I doubt that."

"It would be arrogant for me to think I'm the smartest student at Stanford just because I was the youngest. Age and experience still count. Anyway, I had some of the math down, but I didn't really get it, if you know what I mean."

"I don't."

"Mathematics are present in a hundred different disciplines. But without knowing specifically which one you're delving into, it's hard to model how an equation might be used to create an effect. Addition is pretty basic, but your application of addition will be different when you're counting change in a supermarket or building a supertall skyscraper. Does that make sense?"

"You're talking about context."

He smiled in a way that made me feel as if I had earned a place in the not-a-total-idiot club. "Exactly. To do anything with the equations I believed I solved, I needed to create an environment to execute them in. But what environment, and in what discipline? Turns out, there are parts of this that reach into biology. There are other parts that stretch into chaos theory and quantum mechanics. That touch the fabric of the universe itself. Whoa!"

"And you built a simulator for the universe on your laptop?" I asked tentatively.

"No, man. I'd need a supercomputer for that. I went a bit simpler. The Bio-x lab already has software to model biological systems. They use it for testing chemicals for potential use against different diseases. They also have a tool to simulate effects of using CRISPR on different parts of DNA. Pretty cool stuff, but also too heavy to run on a laptop, so I spent a year optimizing it down to a level I could use. From there, I looked at how the equations might work based on assumptions I made about their grounding in chaos."

He clicked to activate a file browser, selected a file, and opened it in the simulator. A white sigil appeared on a black background.

I nearly choked on my surprise as I pointed at the screen. "You already knew that one, didn't you?"

"No. I built it from the ones I did know, the equations I stole from my father's personal network. Why?"

I didn't answer him yet. "What does it do?"

"Remember, I'm making a lot of assumptions here. The fact that it does anything at all is mind boggling to me, to the point that until a couple of hours ago I was certain I had messed everything up and would need a lot more years to figure it all out."

He moved the mouse cursor to a play button on the top menu bar. The sigil was replaced with an animation of a human body, with vitals on the left showing high blood pressure and an elevated heart rate. The rendering of the body suggested the nervous system was in bad shape, flashing red. The sigil appeared overlaid with the body, a long mathematical equation printed out beneath it, producing a massive amount of logged data, quickly at first but slowing as the laptop struggled to run the simulation. The fan came on, whirring loudly from the back of the machine, the battery indicator in the corner draining quickly. We waited for over a minute before the blood pressure and heart rate dropped rapidly, and the nerve endings returned to normal.

The simulation reached the end and stopped, but I kept staring at it in disbelief.

"Well, what do you think?" David asked.

"I know that sigil," I replied. "That one's called calm. And it just did exactly what it's supposed to do." I turned my head to look him in the eye. "You did it. You reinvented sigiltech."

CHAPTER 12

David stared back at me, face red, embarrassed by my reaction. "What do you mean?"

"I mean your simulator works," I replied while pins and needles of excitement coursed along my arms and legs. "You created a sigil and output the right effect."

He smiled widely and pumped his fists. "Woooooooo! Yes! Yes! Yes!' He jumped out of the chair, still throwing punches of joy in the air. "Yeeeessss!"

"Shhh!" the front-desk concierge hissed, rushing over to us. "There are rooms above this floor and people are trying to sleep."

David slapped his hand over his mouth, still whooping beneath it.

"Sorry," I said. "He just made a pretty incredible scientific discovery, so he's a little excited."

"Try being excited at eight a.m., not three," the woman suggested before returning to her post.

David dropped back into his seat. "I can't believe this. When I ran the simulation I was sure it was all bullshit. But I was right on the money. Oh, I had help, of course. But—"

"Who else knows about this?" I asked, cutting him off

with the forcefulness of my question. Rediscovering how to make sigils was exciting, sure. But it was also extremely dangerous. Enough so that I wasn't sure whether or not to let Keep in on what David had learned. Would he applaud the intellect or try to murder David to keep the technology lost?

"About the sigils? Nobody. I never told the people in the lab exactly what I was working on. They just knew I was building a combined simulator that could run on machines affordable to the average student, which was more than good enough to get them to help me out."

I exhaled in relief. "So nobody else knows anything about sigiltech from you?"

"No. Well, my mom does. I told her everything back when I first hacked the EMG servers."

"You told your mother?" I growled. "Why?"

"I thought she would be happy to stick it to the old man. And believe me, she was. Don't sweat it, broski. She's not going to turn us in or anything."

I stared at him, heart pounding, nerves tensing.

"David, I don't think you understand," I said. "And I don't blame you because three months ago what I'm about to say would have gone completely over my head too. But like you mentioned, experience counts, and the experiences I've had in the last few months tell me this isn't what it seems. My spidey-sense is tingling. Bigtime."

His excitement faded. "You mean because of the goons that jumped us at my house?"

"That's a pretty big clue. They were staking you out. Waiting for something. Exotic Mining Group is defunct. Your father and unfortunately your sister are both dead. So who put them there?"

"You think my mother sicced them on me?" David said, shaking his head. "That's crazy."

"What if your seeing the bank account credentials

wasn't an accident?" I asked. "Your mother knows how smart you are. She probably knew you needed a challenge, too. What if she set you on this path toward sigiltech? What if your father wanted you to break into the company servers? To hack into his personal network? What if the goal was to get you to dedicate your intelligence to the problem because he knew you could solve it?"

David's head kept shaking. "That's nutty conspiracy theory stuff. My mother hates my father. There's no way she helped him enlist me in his research project. I can't believe that."

A new chill ran down my spine as my mind expanded on my original theory. "Okay. What if it wasn't your father's idea to set you up? What if there's someone else who wanted to get you involved? Someone who was over both your parent's heads?"

"You mean like a board of directors?"

"A singular, powerful entity."

"Elon Musk?" he guessed.

"His name is Sucaath, and he's bad news. He wants to use sigiltech to rule the galaxy. And he could have convinced your mother to set you up. Especially if he promised her you wouldn't get hurt."

"Wouldn't get hurt? They were shooting at me."

"Probably because they saw you talking to me and they know who I am. But someone had to give them the order, and there aren't a lot of people left to blame."

"My mom wouldn't do that to me. No way." He slammed his laptop closed and stuffed it into his backpack. "Look Ben, about thirty percent of this has been fun, but I don't think we're on the same page here. It's probably best if I just call a cab and hitch a ride to my mom's place. Because there's no way in hell I'm choosing you over her." He turned and started toward the front desk.

"David, if you leave, you'll be turning everything you worked so hard for over to the bad guys. You'll be playing right into their hands."

"Better their hands than yours," he replied.

I growled under my breath and walked quickly toward him, catching up before he was halfway to the desk. I grabbed him from behind, turning him and throwing him to the ground, surprised by my own strength. "David, you still don't understand."

"Hey!" the concierge said. "What are you doing? No fighting on hotel grounds."

"Oh, I do understand. I thought you were the normal one and that other guy, Druck, was the psycho. But you're all psycho, aren't you? Starships and aliens and evil overlords who want to take over the universe. Because nobody can ever invent something powerful like this and use it to help people, right? Because that kind of existence can't be possible." He got back to his feet and set himself in an aikido pose. "Come at me, man. Come on."

"That's it," the concierge said. "I'm calling the police."

"Ben!" Alter shouted through the comms, loud enough to hurt. "Where are you?"

"Restaurant near the front," I replied, still staring at David. "Why?"

"We've got incoming. We need to get out of here."

"The cops found us already?"

"It's not the police."

The sliding glass doors into the hotel slid open. A squad of black-clad goons entered in diamond formation, their guns aimed at David's back.

"Alter," I whispered. "You're too late. They're already here. In the lobby."

"I'm coming," she replied.

David slowly turned around, raising his hands when he

saw the guns. The lead bad guy moved ahead of the others, lowering their weapon and reaching up to remove their helmet, revealing the attacker's face.

"Mom?" She was an older Asian woman, with a sliver of gray in her short black hair, sharp eyes and a smile that would have looked kind in any other situation. "What the hell is going on?"

"David," she said. "Step away from him. He's nothing but trouble."

David looked back at me over his shoulder. I did my best to make an I-told-you-so-face. My whole deduction had been an educated guess, and I couldn't deny I was pretty impressed with myself for getting it right.

"What are you doing here, Mom?" he said, looking back at her. "Why are you dressed like part of a SWAT team? And who are these people?"

"I'm sorry, David," she replied. "I should have come to you sooner, but I thought we would have more time." She pointed at me. "This one is supposed to be back in the Spiral, not here on Earth. These people work for me, and I also work for someone very powerful. Someone who will give you everything you ever wanted for completing the puzzle set before you."

"You mean Sucaath?" David asked.

"Yes. He may have told you the name, but I doubt he told you the truth. Sucaath only wants to rediscover the secrets of sigiltech so he can use it to bring balance and security to the galaxy, including Earth."

"Bullshit," I coughed behind David.

"You don't speak, Ben." David's mother said as the other goons all aimed their rifles at me. "David, I want you to go outside. Wait for me there. Once I've finished with Ben and his companions, I'll answer all of your questions."

"Why didn't you tell me about all of this before? If you

and Dad worked for the same person, why did he reject us when I was a kid? And why did you trick me into helping you instead of just coming to me? Instead of just asking?"

She stared at him, hesitant. I knew it was either because she didn't have an answer that wouldn't sound suspicious or because she couldn't answer at all. David was a smart guy. Would he see it too? "David, I told you, I'll explain everything. Just wait outside. I'll be right there."

He glanced back at me, our eyes meeting. He looked pained. Conflicted. If I hadn't already told him his mother was involved before she showed up, he probably would have left the hotel without a second thought. But I had planted the seeds of doubt, and his mother was doing a pretty good job watering them for me.

"David," she pressed.

"Did Dad know I would hack into his personal computer network?" he asked, returning his attention to his mother. "Was that all part of a setup? And don't lie to me."

Her face tensed. She had to make a quick decision. She nodded. "Yes. His researchers reached a dead end. We needed someone with the intellect and drive to push through the wall. And you did, David. What you've created is incredible, and you need to finish it. By keeping our distance, you had all the space you needed to work unencumbered."

"Your people shot at me."

"It was an error. If they weren't already dead, I would kill them myself. Please, David. You don't know who Ben and his companions are, and every second we waste is another second they have to regroup. Go outside."

David still didn't move. He shook his head. "You used me, Mom. Took advantage of me. Instead of helping me reconcile with Dad, you kept us apart so I would hate him enough to try to ruin him. And he went along with it. This is so freaking twisted I don't even know how to react to any of it."

"I know you're confused. Once we get away from here, I can—"

"No," David said. "I'm not going anywhere with you. You want me to trust you, but you just gave me every reason not to. My whole life, I never knew you were working for someone like Sucaath. I never knew you were still in contact with Dad."

"David, enough," his mother snapped, trying a different tactic. "Stop being an ungrateful child and go outside."

"I'm not eight years old anymore, Mom," David replied. "You can't boss me around. You have a choice to make." He unslung his backpack and held it over his head. "Either I walk out of here with Ben and his friends or I smash all of my work on the floor. Or you can shoot me before I do."

"David, don't," his mother said.

"Make your choice, Mom," David growled.

Two of the guns on me reaffixed themselves on David. "David, I'm warning you," she said.

He laughed painfully. "I don't believe this. You would really shoot me to keep me from destroying my work, wouldn't you?"

"I have no choice," she answered. "Sucaath—"

"I don't see him holding a gun to your head. You do have a choice. Don't use him as an excuse because you're ready to make the wrong one."

"We can talk about this later. Go wait outside. You have five seconds. Five."

David glanced back at me again. He looked like he wanted to cry. I couldn't blame him. His mother wasn't who he had always thought she was. The whole idea of it hurt me too.

"Four. Three. Two."

"One," David said, swinging his backpack down.

I threw my hand out, pushing him and the backpack out of the way as Sucaath's soldiers opened fire, bullets passing through empty space where he had been a moment before. David slammed into the wall and fell to the ground, the backpack taking only a minor hit when the other goons would have turned us into swiss cheese. Their heads suddenly snapped sideways as upgraded blaster rounds punched through their helmets from the kitchen side of the restaurant. The hotel's entry doors slid open and Clown Alter bounced in, batons burning as she launched herself at the other two soldiers.

I grabbed at my suddenly numb arm, wiggling my fingers to make sure I could still move. Then I was airborne as an invisible force threw me backward, sending me smashing into the front desk. Pain radiated through my body as wood splintered and cracked behind me. I flopped onto my stomach, stunned by the sigil-powered blow, my eyes shifting to the doors, searching for backup that was late coming through them.

David's mother turned away from me, spinning around as Alter went for her. She barely had time to *push* Alter away before pivoting toward Druck, his massive form approaching from the restaurant. She raised her hand to block his blaster fire, *diffusing* it, his blasts washing over her like a rainshower, too weak to do any damage. Alter threw both her batons at her. The Archon—or perhaps she was a Gilded—*pushed* Alter a second time, sending her hurtling back through the glass doors, the glass shattering around her.

David's mother had only reacted to Alter, not the batons. They whirled through the air toward her, one of them catching her shoulder as she ducked aside. It burned through her uniform and she cried out in pain, clutching the wound.

"Don't move," Matt ordered, closing in from the

hallway behind me where I remained on the floor. Druck continued his advance as well, forcing her to choose a target or surrender.

"Don't hurt her," David said, rushing over to his mother and getting between her and Matt. "Mom, you don't need to do this. We can work something out."

"There's nothing to work out, David," she replied. "I can't leave without your work. Without you. He'll have me killed."

"We can kill you right here," Matt said, pausing to look down at me. "Are you okay?"

"I don't think anything's broken," I replied.

"Mom—"

She cut him off as she jumped to her feet, wrapping her arm around his neck and pulling him in front of herself, her body turned halfway between Matt and Druck. Gun in hand, she put the muzzle to David's temple. "I said, I can't leave without you," she seethed. "You're coming with me."

"Mom?" David said weakly, a heartbroken expression on his face.

"I'm sorry, David. This is too important to let you screw it up." One of her goons stepped through the shattered pane of the sliding door, rifle turning toward Druck. "Oh, now you show up," she growled. I held my smile as she backed past the reinforcement, dragging a reluctant David with her.

The reinforcement moved, turning toward David's mother and pistol-whipped her from behind. As she crumpled to the floor, the goon removed his helmet to reveal Alter's grinning guise. I had a feeling the helmet was the only part of the uniform that wasn't actually her.

"Oh shit," David said, turning and looking at his unconscious mom before throwing a hard look at Alter. "Did you really have to do that?" She shrugged, and he dismissed her, going down on one knee beside his unconscious mother. "Mom?" He shook her shoulder, getting no response.

"It's time to go," Matt said, offering me a hand. I took it and let him pull me to my feet. My entire body hurt, but it wasn't so bad I couldn't walk. He put his arm around me to support me anyway. "We don't get a minute of peace, do we?"

"You had half an hour," I replied. "David, are you coming?"

He looked up at me. "What about her?"

"She's down for the count," Druck replied.

"She'll wake up soon enough," I added. "But we'll be long gone by then. I'm sure the cops will have some questions for her though."

"We can't leave her here."

"We're not bringing her along," Matt countered. "We don't have room in the car, and she's dangerous."

That reminded me. I knelt painfully beside David and pulled at her uniform, trying to lift up her shirt.

"What the hell are you doing?" David snapped, trying to grab my hand.

I blocked his hand. "She used sigils against us." I pulled her uniform shirt up far enough to check her skin. She wasn't Gilded. "I need to find them."

He eyed me for a moment before I pulled back both her shirt sleeves to find a sleeve like Keep's wrapped around her left wrist. "Son of a bitch," David said. "Damn it, Mom. You should have just told me."

I pulled the sleeve off, wincing as I straightened.

"We're getting quite a collection of that crap, aren't we?" Druck said. He laughed. "And Keep thought it was all destroyed."

"Let's just go before the police get here. David? You coming?"

"Yeah, I'm with you," he replied, fresh tears in his eyes

as he looked down at his mother. "At least you gave me a choice."

CHAPTER 13

Keep was waiting for us on the front porch of the farmhouse when we pulled up to it and stopped, likely drawn out by the rumble of the Mustang's engine. His face was set in stern lines.

"Uh-oh," Matt said, glancing at me. "You're in trouble."

"Me? Do you see a giant robot head anywhere? You're in charge on terra firma."

Matt shook his head, and we shared a laugh before climbing out of the car. Keep was already on his way down to meet us. Mom appeared at the front door as he reached the ground. Bill and Marie weren't far behind.

Keep's eyes landed on the front of the car, no doubt noticing the bullet holes before they shifted to me, his upset shifting to concern. "You okay, kid?" he asked.

"I'm a little sore," I replied, still feeling the effects of being smashed into the hotel desk. "But I'll live."

"Ben!" Mom said, rushing to me when she noticed the damage to the car. She pushed past Keep and wrapped her arms around me.

I winced in response to her hug. "Not too hard, Mom.

My ribs hurt, and I tweaked my back." Her grip loosened instantly and she backed up a step.

"Do you need some ice?"

"No, thank you."

"I saw a report on the news about some kind of gang violence in Stanford last night. Right near the school. They said six gang members were killed."

I raised an eyebrow at that. "Is that what they're calling them? Gang members?"

"It was Sucaath, wasn't it?" Keep asked.

Gia, Quasar and Shaq made it to the door. Shaq leaped from Quasar's shoulder, spreading his limbs and drifting down the porch steps to me. He landed on my chest and crawled up to his perch, nestling his head in my neck, obviously concerned.

"I'm okay, bud," I replied, scratching behind his ears. "Yeah, it was Sucaath. He isn't done here like we thought. Keep, I want you to meet David Morgan."

David got out of the car, a bewildered look on his face, his eyes on Shaq. "That...that's not from Earth, is it?"

"Nope," Keep replied. He put out his hand. "David, nice to meet you. I'm Keep. Avelus Keep."

David tentatively took him up on the handshake. "Pleased to meet you, sir." His eyes shifted to the rest of our group, pausing on Gia. I thought his mouth would drop to the floor and his eyes might explode from his head like in those old cartoons. He didn't say anything to her, he just stared.

"Why am I not surprised?" Druck asked, noticing David's look. "Hey G, he's got you on his underwear."

"What?" Gia replied, confused.

"Druck, cut it out," I said. "David, this is my mother, Carol. My friends Bill and Marie, Shaq..." He patted the Jagger's back. "...and this is Quasar, and Gia." David raised his left hand in a limp wave. The others offered their own greetings on top of one another. "Sucaath's minions jumped us after I talked to David about his father." I looked at Mom. "You were right. More right than you know." I shifted my attention to Keep. "I know you're annoyed I didn't listen to you, but I think once you hear everything you'll be glad I didn't."

"Kid, I'm just glad you and the car made it back in one piece," he replied.

"Which one are you more grateful to see?" Matt asked.

"Smart ass," Keep replied. "Nothing against you, Bennie. But we're stranded here without the car."

"I agree," I answered, glaring at Matt. Sometimes he took his little rivalry with Keep too far. "How are you feeling?" I asked Keep.

"Me? I'm good to go. I took care of the Star last night. The locals are probably wondering where the random lightning came from in the middle of a drought."

"You didn't start any fires, did you?"

"Nope. It went in reverse, remember, from the ground to the sky. But you can't really tell that from a distance."

"It was pretty amazing," Bill said. "And the kids loved it."

"Kids?" I asked.

"Kyrie had a sleepover with Sally last night. They're both conked out right now after staying up to the wee hours."

"Why don't y'all come inside?" Marie suggested. "Carol and I are making eggs. We'll crack a few more."

"We need to get going," Keep said. "Especially if you had a run-in with the police."

"I think we have time for breakfast," I replied. "We need to talk, anyway."

"I'm glad you're back safe, Ben," Mom said, giving me a second, much gentler hug. "I'll see you inside."

She and Marie went back up the steps, Marie pausing

on the porch. "Bill, we could use a little more help." He responded with his signature laugh and followed them into the house. The rest of us gathered around the Mustang for an impromptu debriefing.

"So Sucaath isn't defunct here like we thought," Keep said. "That's bad news."

"It may not be as bad as you think," I replied. "David has control over what he was after."

"Which is?"

"He wrote a software program to model sigiltech," I answered, pausing dramatically. "And it works."

Keep's face contorted into a position I'd never seen before. A mixture of excitement and fear. "Can you elaborate?"

"I can show you," David said.

"We don't have time for that right now," I replied. "He showed me. Alonzo and his people were working on reconstructing the science of sigiltech. Reverse-engineering sigils they knew so they could use the equations to create new ones. They made a little progress, but David supercharged it."

"And you can create new sigils?" Keep asked.

David shrugged. "I'm not sure. What I made is a proof of concept. I didn't even think it was accurate, but Ben told me it was."

"He reconstructed calm," I explained. "Perfectly. And I assume he can rebuild others. I think the more sigils we can give him, the more he can create."

"I see," Keep said, losing some of his initial excitement as he turned his stern look on David. "Do you have any idea how dangerous that is? How dangerous that makes you?"

David flinched, apparently uncomfortable with the statement, and the idea. "I'm nowhere near that point. I made one sigil. I have so many incomplete equations. And my focus has been on the interaction of sigils on a biological basis. Effects on the body. I always thought my father was trying to cure disease."

"Like cancer?" Keep asked.

"Any disease, but yeah. Cancer."

Keep glanced at me. "I assume that's why you brought him back with you, instead of killing him."

"What?" I said as David's face paled. "Why would I kill him? He didn't do anything wrong."

"Maybe you kill innocent people, Keep," Matt added. "We don't play that game, and you know it."

"It's nothing personal, Davie," Keep said. "Being able to create new sigils would put us back to where we were a thousand years ago. The sigiltech war nearly destroyed the Hegemony. What we're trying to do is stop exactly what his brain can start."

"Or, maybe sigiltech isn't bad in the right hands," I replied. "In the hands of someone who wants to help people, not gain power over them."

"It always starts out that way, kid. The best intentions. Let me create technology to heal. It never takes long before it's weaponized."

"I'm not making any weapons," David said. "I don't even want to continue with this stuff if it's as dangerous as you say. Really, I got into it so I could stick it to my old man and ruin his company. Then I just enjoyed the challenge. But first my mother is ready to abduct me by force to hold onto this tech, and now you're talking about killing me to keep it secret. I just want to watch anime, play video games, and not be bored with everyday shit."

"We need him," I said.

"You need him," Keep countered. "Are you willing to put yourself ahead of the entire universe?"

"Forget about me," I snapped. "You don't get to decide who lives and dies because of this. Maybe that was your mission a thousand years ago, but that's bullshit. Who made you the judge, jury, and executioner? He has every right to live, every right to pursue this. Because other people have become power-hungry doesn't mean he will."

"Thank you, Ben," David said.

"You're welcome," I replied.

"Then tell me you won't use his sigil if he creates one that can save your life," Keep said. "If it's not about you."

"That's ridiculous. Did you have a stroke or something while you were sleeping?"

"Save your life?" David repeated. "What does that mean?"

"It means he's dying," Keep answered. "Bennie's got cancer in his brain and lungs."

David's face fell. "Oh, shit. That sucks." He paused. "I can probably figure it out. I just need some time."

"Yeah, I mean, we *could* save Ben's life," Matt said. "But somehow that's a bad thing, right Keep? You asshole."

Keep's jaw clenched, visibly torn between the promises he had made and the fact that he probably didn't really want me to die. "I never said saving Bennie is a bad thing. But putting him over the potential to make things so much worse may be."

"We're not killing him," Matt added. "Not today. Not ever." He looked at David. "Don't worry. You're safe with me."

"And me," Alter said.

"I guess me too," Druck chimed in.

"And me," I added, glaring at Keep. "You did it your way, and look where it's gotten you. I know it's not easy for you to accept, but maybe we should try my way for a change."

He stared back at me for a long, tense moment. Then his

face softened and he nodded. "Okay, kid. You're right. Truth is, I don't want to have to do this forever. I'm tired. We'll do it your way."

"Thank you," I said. "Let's have some breakfast and then go save the galaxy."

CHAPTER 14

We ate quickly, with the idea that the police might show up at the farm at any moment in the back of my mind. I did my best not to be angry with Keep for even suggesting we should murder David, trying to see things through his perspective. I couldn't imagine being a thousand years old. I couldn't envision participating in a war, losing my wife, or spending centuries trying to secretly keep peace in a galaxy. At least he had been open to our insistence that David be safe with us. As the only one capable of bringing us back to the Spiral, he could have put up a much bigger fight, asked for concessions, or even used his sleeve to kill David and forced us to go along with it if we wanted to see *Head Case* again.

He would never look his age, but watching him as we prepared to leave, it seemed to me he had gained twenty years in the span of an hour. The fight against Sedaya and Sucaath appeared to weigh on him more than I'd realized. Which led me to another conclusion. He needed me more than I'd thought. Despite the sigil that kept him alive and his body relatively young, he was still wearing down mentally. How much fight did he have left?

There were fewer tears when I said goodbye to Mom and Sheri this time. Even though I was returning to the Spiral in greater danger than ever, oddly enough none of us felt like we wouldn't see one another again. And if we didn't, Mom already knew I was at peace with the decisions I had made. That I was living the life I wanted to live for as long as it lasted. That while I wouldn't categorize myself as happy—who could be completely happy when the entire universe was under threat?—I was challenged, motivated, focused, and fulfilled. Which, when it came down to it, was more rewarding than outright, open joy.

David wasn't a small guy, and adding his extra mass put a strain on our ability to fit everyone into the Mustang. To maximize space, Matt reluctantly gave up the wheel of the car to join Alter in the trunk. While she couldn't change her overall mass, by reverting to her raw, alien form she was able to increase her density and decrease her size, as well as shape herself to the interior. Since half of the crew still hadn't seen her natural form and she didn't really want them to, it limited the options of who could go back there with her. I originally volunteered, but Keep wanted me available just in case he needed an extra boost on the transit.

So it was that we left the Ackermann farm a second time almost identically to how we had left it the first time. Me behind the wheel, Keep to my right. Only this time David rode shotgun, watching intently as Keep prepared to stab himself with the catalyst and whisper the focus words that would open the rift between Earth and Atlas, thousands of light years away. We'd only been gone from the Spiral for eighteen hours. Less than a full day, though I knew Keep had rushed us back sooner than he originally planned. In part because of what had happened in Palo Alto. But I also had a sense he had decided on a greater urgency before that, even if I didn't know why.

"This isn't going to be exactly like last time, kid," he said as I put the car in drive and hit the gas. "Take it slow going through the void."

"Are we going to fall off a cliff or something?" I asked, easing off on the accelerator. It probably looked funny to Mom and the others, watching us drift down the driveway at five miles per hour.

"No cliff. Just a wall. Here we go." He opened the cap on the transmission shifter and sunk his hand over the needle. Whispering his focus words, the rift into the void formed ahead of us.

"Oh, wow," David said at the sight of it. "This is nuts. Cool, but nuts."

I guided the car into the darkness, handling the weight of the transit much better on my fourth try. I was too determined now to not succumb to the momentary heaviness, too eager to return to the Spiral and continue forging ahead.

We punched through the other side, the wall closer than I expected. I slammed my foot down on the brakes, throwing everyone forward as we slid to a stop.

"You understated how close the wall would be," I complained as the car settled back on its suspension.

"You handled it beautifully," Keep replied.

"I feel sick," David said, pushing open his door and practically falling out. He took a few steps before vomiting.

"Not everyone handles it well."

I opened my door and climbed out, pulling the seat forward to let Quasar exit. Keep did the same after getting out on the passenger side.

"Where are we?" Gia asked. The room wasn't large, and at first I thought we were in a garage somewhere. Except there didn't appear to be an exit anywhere, for the car or us. It was as if we had transited into a sealed metal box.

"Welcome to Atlas," Keep said as I circled to the trunk to let Matt and Alter out.

They were pressed together as a result of the hard stop, though she had regained her Enigma persona. Their current position was a little compromising, and they rolled apart, faces red to be caught in the accidental embrace.

"Sorry about the hard stop," I said, putting out my hand. Alter took it and I helped her out of the trunk.

"At least we survived it," Matt replied as I helped him out too.

"David, are you okay?" I asked.

"Yeah," he replied, still bent over at the waist, his eggs on the floor at his feet. "I get car sick sometimes in general. That was something else. Cool and completely terrifying at the same time."

"It happens," I said. "Matt and I both puked within the first few hours we were in the Spiral."

"Really?"

"Yeah," Matt agreed. "It seems to be a rite of passage for Earthians."

"So we just traveled across the universe into a tomb?" Druck asked, also noticing the lack of an exit.

"Hardly," Keep replied. "It's a safehouse." He raised his hand slightly and a small square of the ceiling lifted and slid aside. "Badabing badaboom."

"Nice," David said.

"Yeah, it's great," Druck agreed. "Zar, can you give me a boost?"

"Sure," she replied.

"Let's grab our gear first," I said, reaching into the trunk. Our packs were shoved against the back seat, and I nearly had to climb back in to reach them, passing them out to Druck and Quasar.

"Shaq, can you do me a favor and recon the upper

floor?" Keep asked. "Just in case. It's been a while since I was here."

"Sure," Shaq buzzed. He hopped from my shoulder to the top of Druck's head, using the perch to leap up through the hole in the ceiling.

"How long is a while for you?" I asked.

"About fifty years."

"You think your safehouse has stayed empty for fifty years?" Matt asked.

"The odds are good. It's in the old city."

"What's that?" David asked.

"Quick history recap," Keep replied. "Atlas was the first planet settled by an Earthian generation ship when it fell into a wormhole and came out in the Spiral, timewise two thousand years before it left home."

"Whoa."

"Whoa indeed," Keep agreed. "Like any good civilization, it took some time to get it off the ground. But within three hundred years, the settlers had spread across a good portion of the inhabitable parts of the planet. Within five hundred, they'd multiplied to pretty solid numbers and really picked up their exploration of the galaxy. After another thousand years, around the time I was born, humankind had spread to hundreds of planets, interacted with dozens of intelligent alien life forms, and basically made the beautiful mess we call the Hegemony. Not long after that, Sashkur invented sigiltech, the war happened, and the rest is more history that brings us to where we are today. The largest battle of the sigiltech war happened in orbit above Atlas, over the capital city of Haydrun. The fighting destroyed a large portion of the capital, and when the war ended and peace resumed, the Emperor at the time decided to cover what he began to call Old Haydrun and build New Haydrun on top of it. You with me?"

"I think so," David said. "So we're in Old Haydrun right now."

"Bingo bango boingo. Give the kid a prize. Not just anywhere in Old Haydrun. This is my original place here. My home away from home, from back when I worked for the Royal Guard."

"Wait," Quasar said. "*You* worked for the Royal Guard?"

"Well, I had to do something to make a living. Rent doesn't pay itself."

"What rank were you?"

"That's not important. What is important is that I had this place here in the old city, and fortunately, it wasn't laid to waste during the war."

Shaq's head dipped through the hole. "Clear," he buzzed. "But smelly."

Keep smiled. "Nothing a little fresh air won't help, I'm sure." He motioned toward the hole. "Shall we?"

"I'll go first," Druck said. "And help the rest of you through. Zar?"

She stood to the side of the hole above her, forming her hands into a step. Druck put his foot on it and she boosted him up to the hole. He pulled himself through, his feet disappearing before he turned and reached back down for their gear. Zar passed him the packs and then helped all of the others to the upper floor, leaving Keep and me for last.

"We'll be right there," I said. "Keep can push me up."

"Okay, Boss," Druck said, leaving the edge of the opening.

"What's up, kid?" Keep asked once we were alone.

"Your story," I replied. "This room." I turned a circle, eying the smooth walls, ceiling, and floor.

"What about it?"

"A safehouse usually has supplies in it. Food and water

at a minimum. Enough to shelter in place for a while. I learned that by playing Fallout."

He smirked. "You got me again, Bennie." He lowered his voice. "Don't tell the others, but this room wasn't a safehouse."

"It's a prison, isn't it?" I asked.

His mirth faded. "Close enough. I hate to say it, but the best way to hunt archons was to get the right people talking. And nothing works as well for that as total isolation."

I swallowed hard, my whole body shivering. The more I learned about Keep's past, the less I wanted to know.

"Ancient history, kid," he said, regaining his typical personality. "Literally. Come on, we've got work to do."

CHAPTER 15

The panel in the upper floor we now stood on slid back into place at Keep's command, joining the patterned tile so perfectly it was impossible to see any seams. I looked across the rest of the space we had climbed into. Musty and covered in layers of dust, the small bathroom with the checkerboard flooring led out into a long corridor that would have looked right at home on twenty-first century Earth. Long dead electronic screens that I assumed had once shown portraits or landscapes hung from faded plaster walls that merged with deeply grained wood floorboards.. Overhead, flat round LED lights would have provided illumination if they had been functional. The open room at the end of the passageway was decorated in dark wood, a very ordinary-looking sofa facing our direction, flanked by a minimalist steel end table.

"I expected something more sci-fi," I said as Keep led me out of the bathroom. The others had spread throughout the space, doing their own bit of exploring.

"Design goes through phases," Keep replied. "When the settlers first arrived, they had to deal with limited resources and simplicity. Over time, things got more and more ostentatious until it rivaled the best, or maybe the worst, of baroque. Just wait until you see the palace. Then design swung back toward something a bit more classical, refined and understated."

"Yeah, but I mean, no weird toilets. No walls that are also screens or paint that senses your mood. No big open rooms with only one piece of furniture in it for no apparent reason. I don't know. Sci-fi."

"Some things don't need to be improved on, kid. There is such a thing as too much technology. Too much complexity, even if it looks simple on the outside."

"I suppose. I just expected a little more wow. Is New Haydrun like this too?"

"Its shell is more modern, but if you're talking about home decorating, it hasn't changed much. Some people have all the bells and whistles you can want, but it isn't the norm."

"Ben, take a look at this," Matt said from the room on my left. At first, I thought he meant the room itself, but it was empty. He stood by a filthy window, the dust wiped away from a portion of it by his sleeve. The cleared portion offered a diffused view of the world outside.

I walked over to it, squinting to look through. Keep had already said a large portion of Old Haydrun had been destroyed, so I expected to see plenty of mangled buildings, rubble, and debris. I wasn't disappointed. Broken buildings jutted like jagged stalagmites up all around us. Overhead, a spaghetti web of pipes and wiring clung to a slab of material held firm by massive interconnected pylons. t The columns dropped into the old city and continued deep into the bedrock. Incredible to look at, but also unbelievably sad. So much destruction. So much loss. What surprised me was the amount of life still present in what I had thought would be, as Druck had put it, a tomb.

There were lights on across the desolation, the spaces at the base of the damaged structures occupied, the streets immediately outside our location not completely deserted. A man in ragged clothes moved across my view only a few feet away, not even glancing in my direction as he passed. On the other side of the street, a woman in a dirty flight suit stood next to a dented and beaten hovercart half-laden with boxes of something she looked to be trying to sell to the limited passersby.

"I thought Old Haydrun would be deserted," I said, looking back at Keep.

"Nope. The poorest of the poor need somewhere to live. So do the rest of the individuals that the more civilized part of society wants to forget. Old Haydrun is a dangerous place, but not much different than the worst areas of any Earth city."

"And yet they've never smashed your windows and broken in here?" Matt asked.

"Go ahead, Mattie," Keep replied. "Try to break that window. Give it your best shot. You can even shoot it if you want." He looked at me. "You wanted sci-fi. There you go. The only thing getting through this window is sigiltech. Same for the front door."

"Is it fair to say you have your own wizard's tower?" I asked.

"Except only the first three floors are intact," he replied. "So it isn't much of a tower. But we've got the place to ourselves."

"I still don't understand why we went through the trouble of buying the starhopper and bringing *Head Case* here instead of using sigiltech to transit," Matt said. "Especially when you have this place to transit to. Even you said getting through the spaceport would be risky."

"Does this really seem like the ideal situation to you, Mattie?" Keep answered. "What if I brought you here and then we were separated or I perished? Bennie doesn't know how to transit yet, and he's liable to paralyze himself if he tries. It's a much more complex action than pushing. I would venture to say this approach is a lot more risky."

"Good point," Matt admitted. "In that case, I agree with you for once."

Keep smiled. "I'm glad we could find common ground."

We left the empty room, continuing down the main hallway. The door on the left closest to the end turned out to be the stairs, made of the same wood as the floor. It was tempting to go to the third floor to get a slightly better view of Old Haydrun, but I continued to the last room where the rest of the crew had already gathered.

"Nice place," Druck commented, helping himself to a seat on a long slab of cushion with a short back. He shifted his butt on it for a few seconds. "You could use more comfortable seating though."

"I never did entertain much," Keep replied, the statement sending a fresh shiver down my spine. He had entertained plenty, just not in the way Druck meant.

"This is so unbelievable," David said. He stared out a large window that was surprisingly clean and clear. The view from this room looked down a wide cross-street where a few dozen people were moving toward or away from our position, oblivious to us inside.

"I assume this window is mirrored?" I said, walking over to it to get a better look. A light overhead drew my attention, and a small drone zipped toward us, coming within a few feet of the window before turning and heading down the street.

"That window doesn't exist from the outside," Keep answered. "Feel free to stare as much as you want. I used to come here all the time to think. When Old Haydrun was just Haydrun, there was always something interesting happening."

"What about the upper floors," I asked, "before they were destroyed? Did you have the whole building?"

Keep laughed. "Moi? Not a chance. This was a Royal Guard barracks. Once upon a time, I had a room on the sixty-first floor."

"How tall did this place go?" Matt asked.

"Sixty-four floors."

"So you were pretty high up in the pecking order."

"I was in Special Services. More educated, better training than the rank and file."

"So, yes?"

He shrugged. "I guess so."

His reluctance to take credit for his position surprised me. I hadn't seen Keep as being particularly modest. I had a feeling it was because he wanted to spend as little time as possible talking about his past.

"Well, we're on Atlas," Quasar said. "Are we going to pick up our original plan from here?"

"With some modifications," I replied. "For one thing, we need to recover *Head Case* from the Royal Guard. For another, we've got David now."

"How does he change things?" Druck asked.

"He exists," Matt answered. "Which means he needs to be integrated into the plans."

"What plans?" David asked.

"We need to pay a visit to the Empress of the Atlassian Hegemony. That's the name of the collection of fiefs that compose each quadrant of the Manticore Spiral," Matt explained. "We have evidence that one of the dukes under her rule intends to use sigiltech to overthrow her, so we want to get an audience with her to present the evidence and warn her of the impending danger. She's not far. Up there somewhere." I pointed at the ceiling. "In New Haydrun."

"That doesn't sound so bad," David said.

"It's slightly more complicated than that," Druck said. "Because me, Zar, and those two are wanted criminals."

"Oh," David replied nervously. "You didn't mention you were criminals."

"Would you have come with us if we had?" I asked.

"No."

"There you go. We didn't actually do anything wrong, which is why we broke out of prison when we had the chance."

"So you're innocent?"

"Completely."

"Isn't that what everyone convicted of a crime says?"

"In our case, it's true."

"Isn't that what everyone convicted of a crime says?" he repeated.

I shrugged. "The point is, we need to be careful about how we get that audience with the Empress because odds are if anyone notices us we'll be arrested on sight. Or worse."

David groaned. "This is just great. I thought I was coming back here with you to continue my research in peace, without having to worry that my apparently psycho mother wants to kill me. I'm not a secret agent or anything like that, and I have no interest in getting involved in a conflict. I could have stayed back on Earth with my mother if I wanted that. I'm a geek first. A scientist second. I've never even held a gun."

"Your mother came to the hotel with an AR, and you've never picked up a piece?" Druck asked.

"No. I didn't know she knew anything about guns before that."

"You don't need to use a weapon," I said. "Just stick close and stay out of the way, and you should be fine."

"Is it too late for me to change my mind about coming with you?"

"A little," Keep answered, chuckling.

"Look, we have a plan. It got a little sidetracked but we're back in business now. Once we head up to New Haydrun, we'll be right back on target."

"Except for the part where our ship is impounded," Druck said.

"Not helping," I snapped, glaring at him. "We'll get our ship back." I turned to David. "Anyway, you're here. There's no going back. And take it from someone who knows, once you've gotten a taste of what this place has to offer, you probably won't want to go back."

"I hope you're right," David replied.

"So, how *do* we get to New Haydrun from here?" Matt asked.

"That's the million dollar question," Keep replied. "If you recall what I said about the type of individuals who live down here, you understand that the residents of New Haydrun do what they can to keep the residents of Old Haydrun out of their city. At the same time, they want the wrong kind of individuals to move down here so they're out of sight, which means they can't make travel from one to the other illegal." He walked over to the window and pointed down the street. "You see that big pylon in the middle of the city?"

I found the massive round support structure in the distance. It looked to be nearly thirty feet in diameter. Even from here, I could tell it was coated in a layer of fungus, slime, and grit that had to be anything but healthy. "It looks like a sewage pipe."

"And to most of the population upstairs, that's a reasonable description. There's an elevator in the center of that support pylon. Everything and everyone moving between the two cities goes through there. A security station scans faces and checks identification at the top. I don't need to tell you why that's problematic."

"There must be other ways to the surface," Matt said.

"Of course," Keep admitted. "How else would that Sythian on the corner sell Popjoy?"

I looked for the source of his comment, finding a small reptilian alien huddled against a large piece of crumbled skyscraper, a dozen vials of bright purple liquid laid out on a ragged blanket. "Let me guess? Drugs?"

"Bingo," Keep replied. "Gangs smuggle everything through old access tunnels and shafts left over from the lid's original construction that they don't want the authorities to see. It's dangerous and dirty, and there's always a chance law enforcement will raid the access and temporarily shut it down."

"Why not permanently?" Matt asked.

"Come on, Sherlock. You're letting me down. The City Guard raids the active access and either keeps the merchandise or pockets some nice bribes. They close off the tunnel with barriers they know will be breached sooner or later, and then rinse and repeat."

"You're right," Matt agreed. "I should have known that."

"And you can get us through one of these access points?" I asked.

"Presumably," Keep replied.

"What does that mean?" Druck asked. "You live down here. What about your connections?"

"I haven't been here in fifty years. My connections would all be dead or retired. But don't fret. Old Haydrun isn't a complicated place. Money doesn't just talk down here. It sings love songs. It shouldn't take too long to make contact with a gang who has active access to the new city."

"What're the risks?" I asked.

"Primarily, that the gang leader will recognize you and turn you in for the bounty. We aren't dealing with the most upstanding citizens on Atlas. It's a good idea to always watch your back, your front, and both sides for that matter. Badabing badaboom."

"I don't like the sound of any of that," David said.

"You're welcome to hang out here," Keep replied. "We can come back for you later. Maybe. We have a bad habit of leaving things scattered across the Spiral."

"Like my Avenger," Druck said.

"My Avenger," Matt corrected. "The Mustang's stuck now too, unless you sigil it out of here."

"I told you we'll protect you," I said to David. "You're safe with us."

He nodded, but didn't look convinced. I couldn't really blame him for that. We had pulled him directly into an even worse situation than I'd anticipated.

"I know some of you didn't get any sleep last night," Keep said. "There are bedrooms on the third floor. If you're tired, you can hit the sack up there for a few hours. After I tuck Bennie in, I'll go check in on a few places I used to know and see what's what. Alter, I wouldn't mind a bodyguard if you're up for it."

"Sure," Alter replied. "I'll come with you."

"I want to go, too," I said. "I'm not that tired."

"Sorry, Ben," Matt said. "Keep's got it right. You need to stay here and let him *calm* you so your body can recover."

"What? Who put you in charge?" I asked incredulously.

"Are we on *Head Case*?" he countered.

"No."

"Then you did," he replied with a smile. "Fifty-fifty, remember?"

I made a sour face and sighed. "Damn it. Fine."

"Can I watch you use the calming sigil?" David asked. "It'll help me tune my simulation."

"It's kind of embarrassing for me," I admitted.

"Dude, I'm a scientist. It's all clinical."

I hesitated before caving. "Okay. You can watch. Let's find a bed and get this over with."

CHAPTER 16

Keep's *calm* put me to sleep for nearly six hours. I awoke refreshed, realizing how tired I'd actually been before resting. I was starting to get used to the fatigue. Maybe too used to it. With the cancer slowly spreading, my energy didn't hold out the way it had a few months ago.

Shaq was curled up against my head, fast asleep until I stirred and sat up. He stretched adorably before quickly licking his paws clean and then cleaning his face. He caught up to me just ahead of the stairs, leaping from the floor to the wall and then to my shoulder, where he clung near my ear.

"How are you?" he buzzed.

"The rest helped," I replied. "You?"

"Perfect."

Quasar and Druck had left our gear in the room next to the bathroom where we had entered the house. I found my meds in one of the packs, along with emergency rations and water bottles someone had smartly grabbed before we left *Head Case*. Bill and George's gift was in there too, still wrapped and waiting to be revealed. I nearly opened it then, my curiosity almost more than I could stand. But the outside of the tag read FOR YOUR EYES ONLY, and I was hardly alone right now. I heard Matt and David's voices echoing from the ground floor living area, and someone's footsteps on the stairs.

Making my way down the corridor, I paused, startled when a door to my left opened at the end of the adjoining foyer. A wave of warm air washed in, along with Keep and a more concentrated version of the musty smell that permeated what remained of the building.

Keep pulled to a stop, surprised to see me there. "Bennie, you're awake," he said. "Perfect timing."

Alter stepped out from behind him, carrying a large, worn duffel bag that was faded and covered in patches. "How do you feel?" she asked, obviously concerned.

"Better than before," I admitted. "I take it you found someone to smuggle us topside?"

"Easy peasy," Keep replied. "Turns out one of my old contacts had a kid who's heading the Sludge."

"The Sludge?"

"There are four primary gangs down here. The Sludge is one of them. They're named after the fungus that grows on the support pylons. Because it's slowly taking over Old Haydrun."

"The fungus is called the Sludge?"

"I'm sure it has a scientific classification, but who uses that? Anywho, pack your bags, kid. We're getting out of here."

"We never unpacked our bags," I replied. "How much is this costing us?"

"A cool million. I know it sounds like a lot, but considering the alternatives..."

"Do you think we'll ever be able to get the Mustang back?"

"As long as I survive or you learn how to transit, plus

either another million electro or your bounty's rescinded, sure. Why not?" In other words, it wasn't likely.

I activated the embedded comms. "Attention all hands. Keep and Alter are back. Let's regroup in the study."

"Copy that," Druck said, responding for everyone.

We made our way down the hallway to where Matt and David were on the sofa. "Look alive," Keep said as Alter dropped the duffel in the middle of the floor. "We picked up some destination appropriate outerwear while we were out. There's something for everyone."

"What's wrong with what I'm wearing?" I asked.

"Nothing," Keep replied. "Except everything. If we want to get close to the Empress, we need to look like we belong in the palace. There's a change of clothes for me in there too."

Alter knelt over the bag and unzipped it, starting by pulling out threadbare coats and dirty cloaks.

"Did you pick up the wrong bag?" Matt asked, looking at the duds.

"That's to blend in down here," Keep replied. "You'll shuck the top layer when we exit the tunnels."

Druck and Quasar entered the room, eyes falling to the clothes as Alter continued removing them from the bag.

"You found something in my size?" Quasar asked.

"Believe me, it wasn't easy," Keep replied. "Fortunately, Vango's enforcer is your size. You'll have to settle for menswear, though."

"Wouldn't be the first time."

"How come underground gang leaders always have names like Vango or Kingo or Kano?" David asked. "So cliche."

"Why don't you tell him that when you meet him?" Keep replied. "I'm sure he'll appreciate the feedback."

"I'm not wrong though," David insisted.

"You're not wrong," I agreed, amused.

Gia shuffled into the room, eyes still heavy from sleep. Seeing her just out of bed, her long hair frizzy and tousled, her face puffy, I would never have pegged her as the same woman I had seen up on stage before Alter's pillow fight. Not that she looked bad. In fact, I found her natural appearance more appealing rather than less.

"Didn't you sleep at the Ackermann's?" Matt asked.

"Not really," she replied. "The bed was a bit harder than I'm used to. I slept better here. Too well, maybe." She rubbed her eyes. "I thought we might have more time. I could really use a shower."

"No time," Keep said. "Vango gave us an hour, and the deposit is non-refundable."

"What are you talking about?" Gia asked.

"Vango is the gang leader who agreed to smuggle us to New Haydrun," I summarized. "But I guess we're on the clock. How much was the deposit?"

"One hundred percent," Keep replied.

"You gave him a million electro in good faith?" I asked, my eyes widening in shock. "How do you know he won't turn us in and collect the reward on top of that?"

"Honestly, kid? I don't. Except I didn't announce who I was bringing topside. Just that we needed access as a group. Hopefully she won't know who you are." He shrugged. "I told you that was a risk. It's not like we can afford to walk away and not buy passage."

"We're so screwed," Druck said.

"Ben, this is yours," Alter said, throwing me a shrink-wrapped bundle of clothes. "Matt, here." She threw him a similar bundle, passing out the others to the rest of the crew.

"How come you don't have one?" David asked when she had finished.

"I don't need it," she replied.

"Why not?"

Alter stood up, her current outfit pulling back into her form until she stood naked in front of us, clearly female though her breasts and genitals lacked definition. In that state, she looked more like a mannequin than human. David watched in fascination as new clothes formed from her flesh, molded like clay until she wore a pair of loose black trousers and a long black microfiber coat over a frilly black blouse.

"Ready," she said.

"Wow. That is so cool!" David exclaimed.

"Wait a second," Druck said, seeing her change for the first time. "You…that…I…huh?"

"Seriously?" Quasar quizzed him. "You still hadn't figured it out?"

"I…No."

"When we all evacuated *Head Case*, a simple headcount should have given you a clue."

He shrugged. "I didn't really think about it. I'm not a math person." He looked at Alter. "How do you do that?"

Quasar face-planted. "I don't believe this. She's an alien, you idiot."

"Since when?"

"Pretty sure she was born that way, Druck."

"I'm glad you're embracing what you are," I said, smiling at her. "There's no reason to hide it with us." I glanced at Druck. "But if you say anything to anyone else about this—"

"I won't," Druck said, mind still reeling. "So wait. You're Enigma?"

"Yes," Alter said.

"And that's why nobody could ever catch you. Because you just poof, turn into somebody else to get away."

"Yes."

"Damn. How did I miss this the whole time?"

"I already told you, it's because you're an idiot," Quasar

said. "A good soldier, an incredible mech pilot, but otherwise a moron."

"Takes one to know one," Druck commented.

They both laughed.

"Moving on," Keep said, unbuttoning his shirt to change into his new clothes. "There are plenty of empty rooms if you're shy."

Gia took her bundle out of the room. So did David. I thought about going somewhere private, but I didn't need to strip naked to change and wasn't that shy about underwear. I thought Quasar might go to another room, but maybe Alter's visible reconfiguration convinced her to undress to her undies in front of us. I did my best not to look at her, but I couldn't help noticing the colorful tattoos that ran along her back and upper arms. I wasn't sure if I should mention them or not. Druck took care of it for me.

"Love your tats, Zar," he said, not shy about giving her the once-over. He had some artwork on his skin as well—a large snakelike creature wrapped around a mech that occupied his entire right calf.

"Thank you," she replied. "I got them done after I was accepted to the Royal Marines. They're done in special ink only available to service members. The shade changes depending on the light." She turned her body to pose like a swimsuit model. The tattoos seemed to come alive when she did, the color flowing like water.

"That is really cool," I added. "Did it hurt to have it done?"

"Oh yeah, lots," she replied. "But it was worth it."

We finished dressing. Our outfits were all riffs on the same look Alter had reformed into, with dark trousers and coats over fitted shirts. Mine also came with a red vest, Matt with a yellow one. Keep's jacket differed from ours, longer and larger, and he also wore a black beret.

"This is fashion?" Druck said, looking down at his

clothes. His shirt had a frilly front like he was a Flamenco dancer or something. "I feel like I should be standing on a street corner hitting on soldiers on Graviti." He pointed at Quasar. "How come she gets the cool threads?"

Her jacket was sleeker and more leathery, closer to the dragon-scale coat Sephiroth had worn on Furion. I had tried to get Asshole to make me a coat like it, but the materials on hand didn't allow for a suitable replica. Her shirt was dark blue, her pants more finely detailed. They were men's clothes, but they looked good on her, without taking away her femininity.

"Jealous?" she asked, obviously feeling good in the clothes.

"A little," he admitted.

David returned to the room first, his clothes a little tight. He didn't seem to care about that part of it. "Don't they have t-shirts and shorts on this planet?" he asked. "Or is this galaxy too cool for that?"

"We're trying to get into the Empress' palace," Keep replied. "You don't do that wearing shorts."

"They don't have tourists here?"

"Not American tourists."

"Ouch," Matt said. "Low blow."

Gia returned a few minutes later. She had taken the opportunity to clean herself up a bit more, combing her hair and wrapping it into a ponytail and adding makeup I didn't know she had. She still didn't look like *the* Gia, but she did look younger and less tired.

"Ta-da," she said unenthusiastically. "Who picked the sizes for these threads? The blouse is pinching me in all the wrong places."

"Sorry," Keep replied. "I did the best I could purely on memory."

"We brought a bunch of guns with us," Druck said.

"What are we supposed to do with them? There's no way we can bring them into the palace."

"We never planned to bring them into the palace," I said. "We aren't going there to start a fight."

"Since when do we go anywhere without a fight starting?"

"I'll book a room at the Galaxian when we reach New Haydrun," Keep said. "We'll drop our equipment there before moving on to the next part of the plan. Are you jabronis ready to go?"

"Ready as I'll ever be," David said.

"Since when are you in charge?" Matt asked.

I cringed at the exchange. I knew he had some kind of weird rivalry going on with Keep, but he was taking it too far.

Keep shrugged, unbothered by the question. "Okey dokie, Mattie. They're all yours."

"Zar, Druck, grab our gear on the way out," Matt said. "Alter, do you still have the Star?"

"I do," Alter replied, part of her form turning clear to reveal it.

"Wait, you can carry stuff in there too?" Druck said. "I didn't know we had a pack mule. Can you do guns?"

"Why do you think we all have empty holsters?" Alter replied.

"I don't have an empty holster," David said.

"You don't know how to use a gun," I replied.

"Yeah, but still."

"I don't have a holster either," Gia said.

"Really?"

"I'm not about to start shooting at Royal Guards. For any reason."

"And you think we are?" Quasar replied. "Not on my watch."

"The guns are in case Sedaya's goons show up before

we move on the palace," I said. "They know that we know about the space dock. They might anticipate us trying to reach the Empress."

"You should have said that sooner," Gia said.

"We discussed this during the first briefing on our way here," Matt explained. "Where were you?"

"I guess I wasn't paying complete attention. Is it too late to get a holster?"

"Yes," Matt and I both said at once. "We need you to focus on the technical side, anyway. Your neural link is our best tool to pinpoint both *Head Case* and the Empress."

"Neural link?" David said. "Is that a mind-machine interface?"

"Yes," Gia confirmed.

"Wow. That's so cool. What can it do?"

"You two can talk neural links later," Matt said. "It's time to go. David stick close to Alter."

"Okay," David said.

"Everyone grab a dirty coat or cloak and let's move out."

CHAPTER 17

I turned around as soon as the last of us cleared the door and Keep used his sleeve to shove it closed with a deep thud. It wasn't like any front door to a skyscraper I had ever seen before. More like the entrance to a bank vault, even the frame around it and the architecture beyond that looked menacing and impermeable. Apparently, the Atlassian Hegemony had taken the standard Atlas depiction of a man holding Earth on his shoulders and updated it slightly. Instead, Atlas held multiple galaxies, all joined together by a tight ribbon that reminded me of the scarf Sedaya used to choke me. The icon was plastered over the heavy door, along with an inscription:

Royal Guard Barracks #31

Looking higher, I saw the jagged edges of twisted superstructure, which told the story of how the rest of the building had toppled sideways, crushing the smaller building beneath it. The shells of both remained locked in an eternal, terrifying embrace beneath the heavy lid of New Haydrun.

"Horrifyingly mesmerizing, ain't it, kid?" Keep asked.

"Yeah. How many people died during the battle?"

His expression darkened. "You don't want me to answer that. Come on."

He hurried to join Alter at the head of our group, while I stayed near the back with Quasar. We made our way along the wide avenue just outside the study's window, and I glanced back a second time to confirm that outsiders only saw a wall there. If we had more time, I would have gone back to knock on the solid masonry to see if it felt more like stone or glass.

"You feel okay, Ben?" Quasar asked. I could tell she was on edge, uncomfortable with her weapons being out of immediate reach in the backpack she carried.

"Well enough," I replied. "You?"

She shrugged. "I don't want to kill the mood. But I've got a bad feeling about this."

"I think we all do. Except David, maybe." He had already drifted away from Alter to get closer to Gia. Probably to ask her more about the neural link. It seemed his interest in the technology exceeded his puppy-dog crush shyness toward her.

"He just doesn't know any better," Quasar answered.

"Have you dealt with gangs like the Sludge before?"

"Every Royal Marine starts their career with a year-long tour on Atlas, serving different needs in different population centers. The Marines with potential are usually assigned to New Haydrun, primarily because of the gangs. Everything Avelus said about the tunnels and bribes is true. But he left out how dangerous these groups really are, especially to one another. They all have spies in each other's ranks, and word will spread fast about our trip topside. If a single faction even thinks they know who we are, and by that I mean fugitives from Persephon, they'll make a move to grab us for the bounty."

"Why do I suddenly feel like a little possible just jumped to pretty damn likely?"

"Yeah, my sentiment exactly."

"Does Keep know?"

"If he's really a thousand-year-old former agent, there's no way he doesn't. Which tells me he's trying to keep things calm because he knows this is our only choice to get up there undetected."

"We'll definitely be detected if we get into a scrape with the gangs down here."

She shook her head. "Not really. The Royal Guard won't get involved in anything that happens down here, no matter how violent. As long as you keep a lid on it, you're good."

"Is that an official slogan?"

"It might as well be."

"So we should be packing the heat in that bag, not transporting it."

"Probably, but we'd never get close to the tunnels that way."

I looked down at my right hand, where two sigiltech rings rested on my fingers. *Push* and *light*. Not the most impressive sigils, but they'd have to do. And Keep was much better equipped.

"I'm sure Avelus already warned Alter," Quasar continued. " With Avelus' magic and yours, and Alter in the mix, it should give Emil and me time to open the packs and load up."

"Let's hope so."

We continued down the street, my attentiveness taking on a new dimension as I scanned for potential threats. In a place like this, where everyone looked downtrodden and dangerous, those threats were everywhere. Passing dark alleys and shady groups of individuals loitering in front of dimly lit buildings, with lobbies open to the outside, my sense of dread increased. Every set of eyes that landed on us was another potential enemy, or at least a rat that might squeal to a much more dangerous predator. Sure, we were more than capable of defending ourselves, but I wanted all of us to make it to the surface in one piece.

The central pylon and the sludge growing up it came into clearer view ahead. An icky-green, primordial muck, the material oozed along the thick beam, off-gassing in bursts of dark brown farts that sent its putrid sulfurous smell across the underground. My eyes had already started watering by the time we made a right turn at the next intersection. We forged ahead, taking a street thick with all kinds of debris, from the rusted shells of vehicles to bent girders and an accumulation of other junk that had joined the original destruction over the many years since. An obvious path had been cleared through the trash heap, an invitation to an ambush if I had ever seen one.

We had just started down the avenue when a group of armed men and women dressed in homemade body armor stepped into our path from behind some of the rubble. Behind us, a second gang moved into position, aiming their weapons at Quasar, Shaq, and me.

"Relax, Ben," she whispered beside me. "This isn't it. These guys are part of Vango's crew."

"How do you know?"

"Because they haven't started shooting yet."

We came to a stop surrounded by debris and fighters. David and Gia looked most nervous, while Keep seemed totally relaxed. I decided as long as he remained unperturbed then there was probably nothing to worry about.

Nearly half a minute passed before anything else happened. A big brute of a man moved out from behind the first debris pile, just ahead of a young girl. They stopped in front of Keep.

"This your group?" the girl asked, looking us over as

best she could from her vantage point. I realized she wasn't a child but an adult dwarf woman, with a hard face, bright eyes, and short golden hair.

"It is," Keep replied.

"They look weak."

"Weak?" Druck whispered in front of me, offended.

"Precisely why they need to get back to New Haydrun."

I noticed Keep was speaking to her with a more refined accent, coming across more like a British noble than a mafioso.

"Why did you say they came down here again?"

"Ahh, Vango. You should know better than to ask questions like that."

She laughed, so Keep smiled. Her face hardened instantly, a pistol appearing in her hand, pointed up at his face. "This is my city, Avelus. I ask whatever questions I want."

Keep put up his hands. "Of course. But you know as well as I do, too much knowledge isn't always a good thing."

She lowered her gun. "I do know that. The crossing's been arranged. This way." She made it three steps before shots rang out. Hit in the back, her bodyguard fell on top of her, the other fighters in her group spinning away from us, three more of them going down before they could find cover.

"Get down!" Quasar shouted, pulling me close to a large chunk of stones bound with mortar. She unslung our space pack and unzipped it, grabbing one of the plasma rifles and thrusting it at me. "Told you," she said as the rest of my crew scattered.

I held the weapon close to my chest as rounds zipped overhead, targeting Vango's gang. Her bodyguard, who appeared unharmed from the round to his back, remained with her as they scrambled to cover, winding up right next to Keep.

"You set us up," she growled, blaming us for the ambush.

"Hardly," he answered. "There wasn't enough time. They were waiting for you to come into the open. There are snipers all around us."

I looked out at some of the taller wreckage, catching a muzzle flash that ended with another of Vango's gang members falling and rolling down the garbage pile they had climbed up to return fire.

I activated my comms. "Keep, what do we do?"

"We already paid Vango," he replied, softly enough she wouldn't hear him over the gunfire. "Better to get on her good side."

"How do we handle the snipers?"

Quasar popped up from cover, aiming quickly and firing a plasma bolt at one of the sniper positions down the street. I couldn't tell if the round connected or not, but Quasar seemed to think she'd gotten him.

"Scratch one," she said when that sniper didn't shoot again.

Not to be outdone, Alter rose to her feet, holding a rifle from Druck's pack. She scaled one of the rubble piles, ducking low as rounds blew up chunks of brick and mortar. Resuming her ascent, she fell prone next to a dead gang member, aimed and fired. This time, I saw the bolt hit the shooter, who fell from his perch nearly forty feet up.

"Scratch two," Alter said. She slid back down the pile. "I think an entire gang is coming our way."

The gunfire intensified, both sides exchanging shots as we hunkered down amidst the junk and debris. A few more of Vango's fighters were killed, their bodies falling down the rubble piles and coming to rest nearby. Quasar and

Druck hit two more snipers, but the tension on the Marine's face told me things still weren't going our way.

"This is bullshit," Druck said, expressing the same thought. "We're sitting ducks down here. Vango led us right into a damn kill box."

Quasar and I looked at one another at the same time. My gaze shifted to the unharmed Vango and her bodyguard. "Keep, it's a setup," I decided. "We've been double-crossed."

"Why am I not surprised?" he replied. Immediately, something launched Vango's bodyguard away from her, slamming him into a garbage pile and impaling him on a piece of bent rebar.

"Namo!" Vango shouted, stunned by her man's death. "What—" She was cut off as Alter grabbed her by the throat and pinned her to the ground.

"Call them off," Keep said, looming over her. He had dropped his proper accent, reverting back to his usual speech pattern. "Now!"

"What?" she gagged. "I didn't—"

"This street had trap written all over it," he continued. "But I gave you the benefit of the doubt. I thought to myself, there's no way she jumps us here. It's too obvious. I'm not afraid to admit when I'm wrong. What about you?"

"It's not me," she hissed out, barely audible through Keep's comms.

"They were waiting for us," Keep repeated. "Your bull got shot in the back and didn't flinch. You did a pretty good job making it look authentic. You even let them kill some of your own."

"I didn't," she continued to insist.

"Bullshit," Druck spat.

"Call them off," Keep said again.

"I can't." She began to writhe, running out of oxygen.

"You said we were weak. That was your go phrase,

wasn't it? Weak enough to take on. You never considered what kind of people escape from a place like Persephon. You never thought about how dangerous those types of people might be."

She made choking sounds, still convulsing on the ground beneath Alter's steel grip on her throat. "Please."

"They're closing in," Quasar said. "We need to resolve this now."

I noticed how Vango's eyes shifted to my rings as they started glowing. I'd already decided on my move if it came to that. There's a lot of debris all around us. Bad news for anyone caught in its path if it became dislodged

"Call them off," Keep said a third time.

"I...okay."

"Yes, you'll call them off?" Keep asked.

"Yes. Yes."

Alter let her go. She sucked in air, heaving for the first few breaths.

"Okay, I set you up. Made a deal with the Jokers. You know what the bounty is on that one?" She pointed directly at me. "Duke Sedaya's offering thirty million just for him, another thirty for the rest of you."

"Sixty million?" Keep asked, as if the amount would lead him to reconsider our partnership. "That's insane."

"The deal's done. I can't cancel it. I can't call them off. Now I'm going to die here with you."

"You must have had leverage. Something to assure they wouldn't shoot you."

"Ivor turned over his daughter as collateral. The deal goes bad, she gets dead."

"So call them off. He won't risk that."

She laughed. "He might." She turned over her hand, revealing a small transmitter. "I already tried to stop him. They're still coming."

Quasar shifted and opened fire, sending plasma blasts

up the nearest garbage pile as the first wave of Jokers crested it, taking them down before they could shoot. "Too late," she said. "They're here."

CHAPTER 18

I didn't get to *push* the rubble surrounding us. Keep beat me to it, raising his hand and spinning in a circle, the glow of his sleeve visible beneath the tattered cloak he wore over his more formal attire. He really did look like a wizard in the outfit, especially as he twirled around, the piles of rubble shifting and moving beneath the feet of the Joker gang members trying to gain the high ground over us. They immediately started losing their balance, throwing off the aim of those who tried to open fire and sending wayward rounds zipping past. We hunkered down again, all of us except for Keep and Alter. She stayed close to him to ensure nobody managed to cut him off while he worked his spell.

Large stone blocks, bent and twisted girders, old vehicles and more lifted from the ground and flew away from us, carrying our attackers with it as it smashed into the surrounding buildings. Other residents of Old Haydrun scattered from the maelstrom like rats fleeing a sinking ship, desperate to escape the descending debris. The entire city rumbled and shook, dislodging centuries of accumulated dirt and grime, the sludge on the pylons giving off more gas than usual. Despite what Quasar had said, I couldn't believe this wouldn't attract the attention of the Royal Guard in the city above.

It was over in less than a minute. Keep lowered his hand. His sleeve stopped glowing. The debris settled wherever it had moved to during the massive *push*. Staggering, he stumbled to his knees and would have face-planted on the street if Alter hadn't caught him. Beside him, Vango stared at the end result of the defense, mouth agape, shaking with fear from what she had done.

"Keep!" I shouted, running over to him.

He smiled as I approached, sweat running down his brow, face pale and tired. "I couldn't let you have all the glory, now could I, kid? Though you would have handled the effort a lot more easily."

"And probably ended up paralyzed and numb from the effort," I replied. My attention shifted to Vango. "If someone had tried a little straight dealing, it wouldn't have been necessary."

"I should have known sixty million wouldn't be as easy as it looked," Vango said in her defense, still in awe of what Keep had done.

"That was so awesome!" David exclaimed, coming over to us. "The stuff the sigils can do, it's just…mind blowing. I can't wait to get back to my research."

Keep glared at him. "You make a single sigil that isn't defensive, and I'll kill you myself."

David's excitement fled. "Yeah, of course. I don't want to hurt anyone."

"People did just get hurt," Gia said.

"Bad people," Druck added. He glanced at Vango. "But we missed one."

Shaq growled at her, shifting his weight on my shoulder. She looked up at him, biting her lower lip. "Is that a Jagger?"

"Yeah," I replied. "And he's not very happy with you right now."

"The bounty didn't say anything about a Jagger," she said. "Damn Sedaya."

"Now you're getting it," Gia agreed.

Druck whistled. "Sixty million. That's a lot of electro. What's the Royal Guard offering?"

"Ten million," Vango said.

"Not bad either."

"Yeah, but why's Ben worth thirty?" Matt asked. "The same as the rest of us *combined*."

"Because Sedaya hates me the most," I replied. "I don't really know why. I didn't blow up his space dock."

"You're the one who keeps getting away," Keep answered. "That's a big deal to a man like him." He turned to Vango. "Let's go."

"What do you mean?" she replied.

"We still have a deal. Your double-cross failed, so you might as well earn the million I already gave you."

She seemed confused. "You still trust me to smuggle you through the tunnels?"

"Trust you? I never really did. But you didn't plan for us to live this long, so you couldn't have arranged another ambush there. And even if you did…" He pushed back his cloak and jacket, revealing the sleeve. It glowed as he activated the sigils.

"You need to tell me how you use that," David said. "Oh, man, I have so much to learn."

"Sure, Davie. Later." Keep stared down at Vango. "Well? Do we still have a deal, or should we kill you straight away?"

She smiled. "We still have a deal. Come on."

We resumed our trek through Old Haydrun, turning right again at the end of the formerly debris-filled street and moving closer to the stone perimeter surrounding the remains of the city. The wall appeared to be made from a dark brown clay. Over the years, aspiring artists had sculpted hundreds of incredibly detailed forms in the material, everything from a cartoonish dragon to a near-pornographic depiction of a man and woman entangled in each other's arms.

As we drew nearer, I could see how the older designs were more filled in by the brown clay, becoming fuzzy compared to the sharpness of the newer work. The clay seemed to be accumulating even now.

"What are the walls made from?" I finally asked.

"Sludge poop," Vango replied, drawing an immature laugh from Druck.

"What are they really made from?" I questioned.

"I'm not joking," she answered. "The off-gassing releases tiny spores, which are carried across the city by the air currents that sweep in from overhead, pushing them around the perimeter. Eventually, they stick to one another and add to the walls. From what I've heard, Old Haydrun has shrunk by nearly thirty percent since they shored up the outskirts and built the lid. And they expect that within a few thousand more years it'll be gone completely."

"That's incredible," David said. "And disgusting."

"You'll notice the smell is worse the closer we get to the wall. I hope you don't have delicate stomachs."

"I already feel sick," Gia said.

As we walked, I noticed the other residents of the city had changed their attitudes toward us. Before, they had stared as we passed, sizing us up with no hint of fear. Now, they scattered at our approach, ducking down the dark alleys or into the buildings, doing their best to stay well away from us, innocuous and out of sight. Watching them flee made it hard not to feel superior and smug toward these people. Sigiltech made it so easy to become arrogant and drunk on the power it provided. That Keep had stayed relatively grounded after so many years said a lot about his true nature that lay beneath his sometimes harsh exterior.

Or maybe it spoke to the hurts he had endured and the horrors he had seen.

"In here," Vango said two blocks later, leading us up three small steps to the front of a stone building that appeared a lot older than any of the other construction around it. A faded inscription over an open door frame read ARCHIVES.

"What was this place?" David asked as we entered. A steel cage surrounded the immediate entry, a pair of checkpoints set up to check entrants before allowing full access. The guard stations were occupied by a pair of men dressed similarly to Quasar, wearing the clothes of Vango's now-deceased bodyguard.

"A public datastore," Keep answered. "All the knowledge of Earth and the journey across the galaxy was kept here once, a history appended with each passing day."

"Kind of like the sludge poop," Druck commented.

"Miss Van Gogh," one of the guards said, eyes flicking to us, clearly confused by our presence. "Is everything okay?" The other guard's hand slowly moved toward the pistol on his hip.

"Van Gogh?" Matt said. "Keep, why did you pronounce it Vango?"

"An honest mistake," Keep replied.

"Bullshit."

He shrugged. "I thought if I called her Van Gogh you might be more inclined to trust her."

"Because she has the same name as a famous artist?" I said.

"No offense, kid, but I'm willing to bet you've trusted people for less."

"You aren't wrong," I admitted. "But that was before coming to the Spiral."

"Bron, move that hand from that piece before you wind up impaled on the chandelier," Van Gogh ordered. "I'm fine. Everything's fine. Just forget I ever mentioned making a quick sixty million.'

"Yes, ma'am," the guard replied as Bron's hand fell away from his gun.

"Our agreement was to make sure this group gets to New Haydrun," she continued. "Is the shipment ready to go?"

"Yes, ma'am," he said again. "Klavin's downstairs. He's got everything set up already. He wasn't expecting to smuggle organics, though."

She glanced back at us, uncomfortable with the constant reminder that she had intended to see us captured or killed. "Yeah, well, plans change." She waved us toward the openings in the steel cage. "Shall we?"

The two guards made sure to keep their hands where we could see them as we passed into the Archives. The narrow lobby led to a set of four openings, each flanked by marble columns. Beyond them, a large room had once offered dozens of computer workstations to access the datastore. Unfortunately, the roof had collapsed on the space, crushing most of the terminals and leaving everything covered in rubble and dust. A tarp was erected over the hole, preventing further water damage inside the building.

"This way," Van Gogh said, leading us toward a normal wood door on the left. She pushed it open as we approached, pointing us to a stone stairwell leading into the building's basement. "All the way to the bottom."

We kept going, ending up in a hallway lit by overhead strips of LEDs, with large, open rooms on both sides. Every room had the same contents. Large, dark machines sprouted from a perforated metal floor, wires bundled and snaking away beneath the grating. Dark and lifeless, but I still recognized them as data servers.

"Those came from Earth," Keep said. "They were on the colony ship when it arrived in the Spiral."

"Do they still work?" I asked.

"They might, but all the data they kept here was transferred to the Hypernet. Now, it all fits on a chip the size of your finger."

"The power requirements are too heavy for what we're able to siphon from the overhead conduits," Van Gogh added. "Now they're gravestones. The past is dead."

"The past is coming back from the dead," I said. "The same power that caused all of this. You already got a taste of it."

"Ben," Keep said in a warning tone.

"What do you mean?" Van Gogh asked.

"The sigils," I replied, holding up my hand and activating the rings. "The destruction of Old Haydrun came from these. Sedaya offers sixty million for our heads with one hand, while doing everything he can to make full use of the power of the sigils with the other. You think you're getting rich, but you're digging your own grave."

"What about you?" she replied. "Why do you have them if they're so bad?"

"Because we wouldn't stand a chance without them," I answered. "Like you just saw."

She nodded. "Why are you telling me this?"

I shrugged. "We need all the friends we can get."

"She isn't your friend," Keep said.

"But maybe she could be," I responded. "Because staying alive is more valuable than sixty million electro."

Van Gogh laughed. "Only just. But I hear you. I'll keep what you said in mind if you ever come back to my domain."

We reached the end of the hallway, passing through

another door into a large storeroom. A bare-chested, muscular man stood in front of a long metal wagon, currently empty. Just beyond that, a metal grate covered a small hole in the wall, three feet in diameter.

"You've got to be kidding," Druck said when he saw the grate. "I thought we'd at least be able to stand."

"How are we going to make it to the surface without getting filthy?" Gia asked.

"Miss Van Gogh," the man said, eyes sweeping over us. "Jackson is ready on the other end. He gave the all clear."

"Thank you, Klavin," she replied, turning to us. "Speaking of graves, here's how this works. You all need to pile into that cart there. If it doesn't fit, it doesn't go. As soon as you're in, Klavin's going to drop a lead cover over the cart. It's thick and heavy enough to block any potential scans from the Royal Guard. Tracking organics is one of the primary methods they use to locate active tunnels. Any questions?"

David raised his hand. "How long will we be in there? I'm not claustrophobic, but I don't like being so close to other people."

"If everything goes well? Thirty minutes, tops."

David's face paled, but he nodded his acceptance.

"You can lose the rags to save a little space," Van Gogh suggested.

"Good idea," Matt said, slipping out of his threadbare coat. The rest of us followed suit.

"Who wants the bottom?" Druck asked.

"We're going to have to Tetris this one if we want everyone to fit," I said.

"If I had known this would be in my future, I might have eaten fewer donuts," David said. "Nah, probably not. It's a good thing for you all that I happen to be a Tetris master." He walked over to the cart, looking in before looking at us. "Zar, you're on the bottom, on your right shoulder."

"Damn," Quasar said. "Here goes nothing." She climbed into the cart, laying on her side.

"Gia, Ben, you're next. You both need to lay flat facing one another, heads to the sides.

"I can take Ben's place," Druck volunteered.

"Ugh," Gia commented.

"It has to be Ben or Alter to create a flat plane to build the second."

"I don't know if my back can take the pressure," Gia said.

"You can stay here," Keep remarked.

"I'll go on the bottom," I said. "To cushion you."

She nodded, still not thrilled. Neither was I.

I climbed into the cart next to Quasar. Gia lowered herself slowly onto me, putting her face next to mine. It would have been kind of intimate if we weren't about to be crushed under the weight of the others.

"Shaq, slip in beneath Gia's feet," David said.

"Mmm-hmmm," Shaq buzzed. I felt his weight on my ankles a moment later.

"Druck, Avelus, you need to make a C-shape on top, slightly on your sides. Matt, you and I will get into the remaining space. Sorry, man, but you'll have to spoon me."

"Awesome," Matt said.

"Alter, you'll go on top. We'll have to leave the packs behind."

"There isn't enough room for three layers," Klavin said.

"Yes there is," David replied.

"David, there's a box in Zar's pack," I said. "It needs to come with us."

"I'll grab it," he said.

"Well, I guess you get a million electro plus a nice haul of guns," Keep said before climbing into the cart. "Don't even think about trying anything because we're in this sarcophagus. I can blow this thing open without much effort."

"I believe you," Van Gogh said. "No tricks. I just want you out of here."

Keep and Druck took their places in the cart. David joined them, holding my box. His weight pushed most of the air out of my lungs, making it harder to breathe. Matt climbed in after him, forced to wrap his arms around the other man and squeeze in close. Alter climbed in on top of them.

"The lid won't seal like this," Klavin said.

"Just lower it onto my back," Alter said.

"Alter, are you okay with this?" I managed to squeeze out.

"It's the only way," she replied.

Klavin grunted as he picked up the cart's lid, muscles flexing to position it before lowering it onto Alter's back. With less light getting in, I couldn't see her release her persona, reverting to her raw, alien form. I felt her tentacles snaking down to my legs as she flattened out.

"There's not a lot of air in there," Van Gogh said. "So breathe as lightly as you can. Good luck up there. I mean it. And thanks for the guns and the funds."

She was still laughing as the cover finished settling over us.

CHAPTER 19

"Are we almost there yet?" Druck whispered, his voice strained by the pressure of having us all crushed inside the cart.

"Shut up," Quasar replied. "You're using up our air."

"What air?" David said. "I can barely breathe."

"Exactly," Matt responded. "All of you zip it."

Silence fell back over the inside of the cart. I had kept my eyes closed since we lost the light, doing my best to ignore the sensation of being pressed down like the bottom of a hamburger bun. It had worked for the first ten minutes or so, until my muscles started aching and my brain kept telling me I needed to move, if only a little. Except I couldn't move. None of us could. To make things worse, it was starting to get hot, our combined body heat contained in the airtight container. I kept reminding myself this was the only way to get out of Old Haydrun and move the plot forward. No matter how uncomfortable we were. No matter how much it hurt, we had to endure it.

A few more minutes passed. My breath was already strained. I could only take in small gasps of thinning air, not even enough to satisfy my increasingly burning lungs. I tried to pull in one more, only to find that there was none left. The others gasped around me, experiencing the same thing.

We needed to get out of here. Now.

"Keep," I managed to squeeze out, wondering as I did if it was a bad idea. I knew he heard me because his sleeve began glowing, providing just enough light through the spaces between our bodies for me to make out Gia's ear in my peripheral vision, and Matt's shoulder overhead. One of Alter's tentacles squeezed into the space as well, the translucent material diffusing some of the light.

He might have tried to speak his focus word. All I heard was a light hiss repeated a few times. My lungs were on fire by then, my body desperate to convulse. I felt Gia's muscles quivering on top of me as she reacted the same way. Sudden panic threatened to overwhelm me. I thought I could tell the cart was moving through the vibrations in the bottom, but now I wasn't so sure. What if Van Gogh had closed the lid and just left us there to suffocate? But she knew we could break out, so why would she do that?

Now I wasn't so sure we could break out. If Keep or I couldn't speak a focus word, we couldn't *push* the cover off our tomb. But that didn't make any sense. The focus word was supposed to be a helper. We weren't actual wizards casting spells that required incantations. The spoken part was performative. Procedural. Keep had to know that. Didn't he?

Two more soft hisses from him suggested to me that maybe he didn't. In all of his thousand years, he had probably never used sigiltech without vocalizing what he wanted to do. The connection between his brain, body, and the catalyst probably didn't work without that missing piece.

There was no air. We were all dying. The cart remained sealed.

I was the only one who could fix it.

I did my best to calm down. I could get us out of this. There was no reason to worry. The ring with the *push* sigil lit up. Closing my eyes again, I visualized the cart's lid, creating a clear mental image of it. My hand tingled, telling me the catalyst was active and ready. Instead of speaking a focus word to execute the action, I pictured the cover being shoved off my mental image of the cart.

At first, I didn't think anything had happened. I still couldn't breathe, and when I opened my eyes the cover was still in place. But my ring was glowing brightly and I sensed the energy coursing through my blood, feeding the sigil through some kind of quantum chaos, as David had described it. Gia shuddered on top of me, convulsing as she suffocated. Quasar twitched beside me, and I worried that Shaq, with his smaller lungs and faster heartbeat, might already be dead.

A woody groan interrupted the friction of our clothing as we writhed. It gained in intensity, building up slowly, as though I was turning a dial on the *push* instead of blasting it out full bore. Keep had told me that was impossible. Then again, he also believed he couldn't use the technology without the focus word. Maybe he didn't know as much about the sigils as he thought he did.

I fought to intensify my focus on the push, increasing the power a little more. The groaning increased in volume, the cover pulling at its anchors, trying to escape them. A little more force. A little more effort. I could almost feel the strain as though I were physically pressing on the lid, muscles straining to remove it. Only there was hardly any strain. My hand tingled but wasn't going numb. The power flowed freely, out of the ring and up at the barrier blocking us from life-giving air.

I turned the dial a little higher. Maybe a seven out of ten. One side of the cover popped and my efforts to breathe were rewarded. Cool air flowed into the cart and we all sucked in the oxygen, gulping it down. Instead of pushing harder to remove the cover, I held steady, keeping it raised enough so we could breathe without removing it completely. I could hear the cart's wheels now too, rolling smoothly along the tunnel.

"Did you do that, kid?" Keep asked.

"Yeah," I replied. "I still am."

"How?"

The question brought a smile to my face. "I guess imminent death is a better teacher than you are."

"Sink or swim, eh Bennie?"

"It seems that way."

I continued holding the *push* with a level of control I had never even approached in the months since Keep and I started training. It felt so easy. Almost too easy. Every second that I used the catalyst was another second I could find myself paralyzed. I didn't worry about it as much because Keep was right there. He could *calm* me if I had another episode of sigil sickness.

A few more minutes passed. The corridor began to brighten, a literal light at the end of the tunnel. I pushed slightly harder on the cover, lifting it a little more. "Alter, you should shift back now."

One of her tentacles brushed my cheek gently before retreating, her central mass thickening again as she remolded herself like clay, transforming back into her Pilot Alter form. She had just about completed the metamorphosis when the cart came to a stop. I immediately dropped the *push* as a hand grabbed the edge of the lid, lifting it away.

"Hurry up," a deep voice urged. "It looks like the seal on the lid broke during the trip up. If the Blues were watching, they'll be here any minute."

Alter jumped out of the cart, helping Matt and David

out while Keep and Druck spilled out on their own. I was relieved when Shaq scampered free, hopping onto my shoulder, and Gia picked herself up off me.

"Was it good for you, Captain?" she asked playfully before taking David's hand. It seemed the lack of oxygen had made her a little punch-drunk.

"Yeah, great," I replied flatly, accepting Matt's offered hand and climbing out of the cart.

Quasar turned flat onto her back, remaining there for a second to enjoy the freedom to draw a few deep breaths.

"Come on," grunted the man who stood nearest the exit. Tall and lean, there was something about him that made me wonder if he was fully human. "Spotters say the Blues are headed this way. Unless you want to be arrested, you need to clear out."

"We definitely do *not* want to be arrested," Druck said as Quasar crawled out of the cart.

"Then go," he said. "And get as far away from here as you can. When they see the empty cart, they'll know we smuggled people. They won't be happy to come away empty-handed, and they'll be looking for you."

"Don't worry about that," Keep said. "I know where to go."

We followed Keep out the door and down another short passageway to a stairwell. More of Van Gogh's people were stationed there, and they waved us past, guiding us up the steps, along a few more hallways and out into a back alley between a pair of buildings. I looked up as we exited outside, happy to see daylight.

"This way," Keep said. "Shaq, you need to get out of sight. Jaggers are incredibly rare here."

"Okay," Shaq buzzed. He left my shoulder, disappearing beneath my jacket and moving into my sleeve. His body flattened along my bicep, creating a slight bulge that I didn't think anyone would notice.

Keep led us along the alley, away from the closest street. Glancing over, I spotted dozens of people walking past, dressed in a wide assortment of styles that wouldn't have looked out of place in LA. The only thing that really drove home that we weren't in Los Angeles was the Jiba-ki that crossed with them.

"Cool," David remarked, no doubt getting a glimpse of the catlike alien at the same time I did. "I guess we aren't too far from Pandora."

I looked back a second time just as we reached the end of the alley, about to join the other pedestrians along what appeared to be a much smaller street. A Royal Guard aerial personnel carrier landed at the other end, two full units of Guards pouring out from doors on both sides. One unit headed for the front of the building we had just left; the other started down the alley.

"Don't look at them," Quasar snapped, getting my attention. "Act like you live here."

I turned my gaze away from the Guards, sticking tight to the others as we entered the flow of foot traffic. The wider thoroughfare offered a much fuller view of New Haydrun, and it took all of my willpower to keep my eyes straight rather than gawking at the surrounding buildings like a tourist. Even so, I couldn't help noticing them in my peripheral vision. All glass and supertall, a lot of them vanished into the clouds thousands of feet above.

Flying vehicles of all kinds maneuvered around the structures, following flight patterns and rules of travel I didn't immediately understand. Everything from small, single-person, rotor-driven boxes to huge freight vehicles zipped back and forth overhead, though their routes seemed intentionally designed not to block the sun from the ground. The resulting strobe effect flickered through the pedestrians. Compared to the other planets Matt and I had visited, Atlas was the closest to what I had always imagined a futuristic city would look like. In fact, it made the other worlds we had visited, save for maybe Kasper and to a lesser extent Caprum, look like backwater shitholes.

Keep guided us along the street at a quick pace as more Royal Guard vehicles moved into the area. They swept overhead a few times before landing so close behind us I got the sense Keep had timed our escape to stay one step ahead of them without looking like we were on the lam.

We walked a few more blocks, passing what appeared to be a raised landing area for the aircraft on my right. Dozens of vehicles took off and landed in rapid succession, smoothly navigating tight confines and making their way into the flow of traffic. Keep slowed there, directing us into the landing site.

"How did you know which direction to go when we came out into the alley?" Matt asked him.

"I recognized the building we were in," Keep replied. "Remember Sherlock, this isn't my first rodeo. We'll grab a transport here and take it downtown, closer to the palace.

"Are we still staying at the Galaxian?" I asked. The hotel was part of our original plan, and once we reached it, we would be mostly back on track save for the need to rescue *Head Case*.

"We are," Keep confirmed.

We took an elevator up to the landing platform, joining a short queue of people waiting for transport across the city. They were mostly dressed in outfits not too dissimilar from my more typical Spiral threads. We were the only ones wearing what I took to be more formal attire, making us seem wealthy compared to them. Enough so that we drew some prolonged looks that made me uncomfortable. What if any of them recognized us?

The line moved quickly, the transports swooping in, picking up riders and lifting off again within a handful of seconds. Within a few minutes we boarded a taxi large enough, probably-not-coincidentally, to carry all of us and touched down when it was our turn. I probably shouldn't have been surprised the transport was automated, but I gawked just the same, rushing to the front of the nearly-square vehicle to look out the full-length windshield in the open front. David joined me there, and we continued gaping at the city as the transport slid smoothly in with the other aircraft.

"Amazing, isn't it?" David said.

"I've already seen some incredible things," I replied. "This is still pretty unreal."

The city was beyond beautiful. Pristine and sparkling, covered in high rises split by landing areas and plenty of parks, along with an assortment of buildings with more artistic architecture, the purpose of which I could only guess.

And then there was the palace.

It came into view shortly after takeoff, as the transport rounded one of the myriad skyscrapers. Situated on a lush property that covered at least ten city blocks, it was easily recognizable as the most classically built structure in the city. Keep hadn't been kidding when he called it baroque. In fact, the first thing that came to mind was the Palace of Versailles in France. If he had told me the Empress' palace was a straight up clone, I wouldn't have been surprised.

The biggest difference I could easily discern was in the gardens. Five of them surrounded the round instead of rectangle main building. I didn't need Keep or Quasar to tell me each outer circle represented one of the quadrants, with Atlas in the middle. The diverse flora growing in them made that clear. Even if that wasn't enough, it appeared as though the guards standing watch around the gardens were picked from the ranks of each Duke's military, their varied uniforms augmenting the colorful display.

"That place is huge," David said.

"And old," I replied. "It escaped the sigiltech war unscathed. It was built over two thousand years ago."

"Wow."

The transport skirted the perimeter of the palace grounds before turning and descending. I spotted the Galaxian Hotel as we neared another landing site. As tall as many of the residential towers in the city, its windows were coated in material that sucked in the ambient light while diodes along the structure flashed, making the whole thing look as though a small piece of outer space had been transported to the planet's surface. The effect was very cool, but also a little nauseating.

We exited the transport and returned to the street, walking two blocks to the hotel. The space effect didn't extend to the bottom floors, which sported full-length windows that allowed a complete view of the extravagant interior. Watching people come and go from the building, and looking inside, I suddenly didn't feel as overdressed. Where we had stood out for our outfits before, now everyone around us seemed similarly clothed, allowing us to blend in easily with what I assumed was Atlas' uppercrust.

"I'll get us a room," Keep said as we entered the Hotel. "Wait here. Don't stare."

"Instructions easier given than followed," David replied under his breath as Keep made his way to the front desk. I agreed, but it was hard not to be taken by the opulent excess of both the hotel's decoration and the people around us.

"Now this is what I always imagined the future would be like," Matt said. Even he failed to adhere to Keep's act-like-you've-been-here-before edict.

"I've never stayed anywhere like this in my life," Druck added.

"The room service is kind of a letdown," Gia commented. Of course she had been here before.

"How much do you think this is costing us?" Matt asked.

"I don't know, but I'm sure it's coming out of our account," I replied. Keep still had my phone, able to make payments with it at will. "At least it's only one night."

Keep returned within a couple of minutes. "We've still got a few hours before it gets dark." He motioned to the elevator. "Shall we?"

CHAPTER 20

In order to accommodate all of us in a single room, Keep had booked what the hotel called the Nebula Suite. Over four thousand square feet, it occupied the entire south side of the ninety-ninth floor, just one below the Universal Suite, which took up the entire one hundredth floor. With five bedrooms and three bathrooms, the Nebula Suite could sleep all of us with barely any doubling up, and offered amenities and perks unlike anything I had ever come close to experiencing on Earth.

Not that I would have time to experience it here. Despite the one hundred thousand electro cost for a single night, we only intended to be there for five to six hours at most. A major expense, to be sure, but it would be more than worth it if we succeeded in getting our warning to the Empress, and even more worth it if she both pardoned us for our prison escape and made sure *Head Case* was returned to us.

A long shot? Probably. But we didn't have a whole lot of options. We'd already discussed and dismissed sending her the recording of Sedaya's conversation with Neftal indirectly. There was no way to guarantee the stream would ever make it in front of her eyes, especially if the duke already had loyalists planted in the palace, ready to intercept anything that might cast suspicion his way. Other than that, as wanted fugitives, there was little else we could do to make sure she understood the danger except present it in person. And none of us were under any pretense that a live audience was guaranteed to end well.

But we had to try.

Entering the suite, it was hard not to be excited by everything it had to offer. The view was breathtaking, with full length windows wrapping around the corner of the open main living space, which was decorated in dark wood, gold, crystal, and fine rugs as though we were already inside the Empress' palace. Fresh flowers were placed on every table, perfectly arranged, and an array of delicacies waited on a tiered centerpiece in the middle of the room, along with a few bottles of chilled champagne. An equally ornate corridor led to the bedrooms and bathrooms, and Druck and David took off down the hallway, eager to see everything. The rest of us stayed behind, more reserved than the newest member of our group and the mech pilot. We had gone from rags to riches, literally, inside of an hour.

All it had taken was nearly suffocating while being crushed together in a rolling coffin

"Well, we made it," Matt said, walking over to one of the windows and looking out at the city. "A little worse for wear, and down a bunch of equipment. But we're here." He turned to me. "What's with that box you had David pull from the pack for you?"

"Bill and George gave it to me. It was a gift," I replied as Shaq squirmed out from under my coat, regaining his place on my shoulder.

"And you didn't open it?"

"Not yet."

"Why not? Someone gives me a gift, I tear right into it."

I smiled. "The tag suggested I should open it when the time seemed right."

"The right time is always now," he joked.

A wave of panic hit me. "Shit. I don't know what happened to it once we got out of the cart. We left in such a hurry—"

"I have it," Alter interrupted before I could get too upset. "I know it had to be important to you."

I smiled, relieved. "Can you hold onto it for me for now?"

"Of course."

"I think our little adventure in Old Haydrun may have worked out for the best," Keep said, his gaze shifting to me. "What you did back there. I've never seen or heard of it being done before. I don't think it's hyperbole to say you saved our lives, kid."

Shaq nuzzled my neck in gratitude.

"Yeah, nice work, Ben," Matt agreed, clapping me on the shoulder. "You saved our bacon. All of us."

"Pure self-preservation," I replied. "But I'm glad it worked out for everybody."

"Do you think you can do it again?" Keep asked.

"I'm not sure. I think so. Why?"

"Throwing all that debris around downstairs took a lot out of me. If we get in trouble inside the palace..." He trailed off, but the meaning was clear. Any emergency escape that required a more powerful use of sigiltech would fall on me.

"I could freeze up at any time," I reminded him.

"Which is why I overexerted myself against the ambush," he replied. "It's not how I would have drawn it up, but what are you gonna do about it?"

We stared at one another, a weight settling over the room.

"Y'all have to see this," David shouted, rushing back down the hallway. "The rooms are incredible. Everything about this place is incredible." His enthusiasm was an unplanned tension breaker that forced me to smile.

"I never thought I'd live like the upper crust," Druck agreed. "Even if only for a few hours. If anyone needs me, I'll be in the spa tub, covered in bubbles."

"You're going to take a bubble bath?" Quasar asked.

"Yeah, why not? We paid for all of this, we should use it."

"Aren't you a tough guy?"

"Tough guys like bubbles too."

"Ben," Gia said, her serious voice in sharp contrast to the moment of levity.

"What is it?" I replied as the others fell silent, the weight returning as quickly as it had faded.

"I haven't had access to the hypernet though my neural link since we launched our assault on Sedaya's freighter. My neural link couldn't get a signal from underground, and of course it couldn't connect inside the cart. I finally reestablished the connection."

"And?" I asked.

Her face hardened. "Apparently, at almost the same time I was being attacked on my planet, a dozen other nobles and their successors were assassinated across the Quad. None of the assassins were captured, and no one has come forward to claim responsibility. The media is calling it the most deadly day of nobility reorganization in centuries."

I swallowed hard, my heart suddenly racing in response to the news. "Geez. And you were on the hit list."

"And the only one that survived, thanks to you," she replied. "There's another piece I think you'll find interesting. One of the affected noble families was—"

"Nobukku," Keep finished for her.

"Yes," she confirmed.

"That doesn't make sense," I said.

"Sure it does," Matt said. "I think we're pretty confident Sedaya arranged the assassinations. Nobukku probably outlived his usefulness, and getting rid of him both removes the only other person who may have had a change of heart and warned the Empress about his plans. Plus, now, whatever Sedaya promised Nobukku in exchange for loyalty, he keeps."

"Brilliant deduction, Sherlock," Keep said. "Right on the money. Nobukku's death is understandable. The others, not so much. If the line of succession is broken, the Empress selects the next family to take control of the duchy. It would have benefited Sedaya more to wait until he gained control of the Hegemony before removing his primary opposition."

"But that would also be a lot more obvious, wouldn't it?" Matt questioned.

"True," Keep agreed.

"Misdirection," David said, drawing our attention.

"What do you mean?" I asked.

"Like a magician." He smiled. "Not the sigiltech kind. A traditional street magician. Misdirection. Hey, what's that over there?" He pointed into the distance. Druck fell for it and looked, and David punched him in the arm.

"Hey!" Druck said, spinning back as David put up his hands.

"I could never beat you in a fight. But if I put your attention somewhere else for a second, I can get in one good shot. That might be all I need."

"If I'm Sherlock, maybe you can be Watson," Matt said. "But what would Sedaya's one good shot be?"

"I don't know," David replied.

"You can bet he's planning something," Keep agreed.

"Or he already did whatever he intended to do," Alter said. "The assassinations happened weeks ago."

"Has the Empress named successors?" Keep asked.

"Not yet," Gia replied. "It appears she's waiting for the Royal Guard's investigation into the murders to wrap up. She doesn't want to inadvertently promote the party or parties responsible for the killings into a higher position of power."

"That makes sense," Quasar said.

"This would all be moot if the Spiral wasn't so damn draconian," Druck said.

"Don't start whining again."

"I'm not whining. I'm just saying that—"

"We know what you're saying," Quasar shot back. "You manage to make a comment against the Empress almost every day."

"Both of you, shut it," Matt snapped. They both stopped talking. "Gia, is there anything else we should know? That intel is interesting, but I don't see that there's anything we can really do with it right now."

"No," she answered. "Like Alter said, it happened weeks ago. But I definitely think it's related to all of this."

"I think we can all agree with that," I said. "I know you're going to do more digging on the topic."

"Of course." She paused. "There's something else."

"That doesn't sound good," David said.

"The Blue Burn. It didn't have any details attached to it when we chased after the ship. It still doesn't. At least not publicly."

"I sense a *but* coming on," Matt said.

"But there are rumors going around in darker corners of the hypernet. They're saying Prince Hiro was taken."

"What?" Quasar practically screamed with surprise.

"Prince Hiro?" Keep said. "Kidnapped? That can't be possible."

"Yeah, there's no way anyone could get past the palace

guards," Druck said with a laugh, since that was exactly what *we* were planning to do.

"But why would they want to?" Quasar said. "Kidnapping the heir to the throne won't get them the throne. They'll only succeed in drawing half the Royal Navy to whatever planet they try to hide on."

"Maybe that's the idea," David suggested. "If you pull half the fleet away, then you only have half left to fight. Divide and conquer."

"Which might be necessary if you're Sedaya and you just lost an entire space dock of sigiltech ships," I said.

"They're just rumors," Gia reminded us. "Not everything on the hypernet is true."

"You can say that again," Matt agreed.

"There must be something prompting the rumors though," Quasar said.

"The Blue Burn bounty was publicly broadcast to every ship in the area," Gia replied. "And Hiro hasn't been seen since."

"It was yesterday," Keep scoffed. "The kid's probably just sleeping in."

"Someone claiming to work at the palace says she heard from the maid who cleans the prince's room claims she wasn't allowed entry this morning. But again, only hearsay."

"We'll find out for ourselves soon enough," Keep said.

"What if it's true?" Alter asked. "What if Prince Hiro was taken?"

"Then I bet the Empress will give a hell of a lot to whoever brings him back," Keep replied.

"You mean us?" Matt asked.

"Why not us?"

"We still have to make it into and then back out of the palace both alive and not in handcuffs."

"And we already tried to stop the blueburn," I added. "It didn't go that well for us."

"You know what they say. Better luck next time. But you're right. First things first. We'll just keep that one on the backburner until we make it back here safe and sound. Badabing badaboom."

"Great," Druck said. "Well, if that's all we've got right now, there's a spa tub filled with lavender scented suds calling my name."

"You have an hour," Matt said. "And then I want everyone back here so we can go over the plan. Got it?"

"Copy that, Sarge," Druck said. "David, you're welcome to join me if you like bubbles."

"What?" David said, face flushing.

"Gotcha," Druck teased, cracking up as he left the room.

"Ugh," David said once he was gone. "How do you stand that guy?"

"He's a good fighter," Matt replied. "And an even better mech pilot."

"Too bad we don't have our mech," I said.

"If you'll excuse me," Gia said. "I'm going to find an empty bedroom and continue my data crawl. I also need to check in on the automated systems back home and make sure everything is still running smoothly. I'll be back in an hour."

"Let us know if you learn anything valuable."

'You know I will." She hurried past David and down the hallway to one of the rooms.

"Damn, she was supposed to tell me more about the neural link," David said. "If anyone has a Thunderbolt adapter, I can plug in my laptop and do some tinkering with the simulator."

"We're on the other side of the universe," Matt said. "I doubt they still use Thunderbolt here."

"What? You've never heard of backwards compatibility?"

"Like two thousand years backwards? No."

"Sorry Davie," Keep said. "No Thunderbolts here."

"How am I going to charge my laptop? My work is useless if I can't actually work on it."

"Alter can make you something compatible when we have more time," Keep answered. "I'm going to take a quick nap, recharge a little." He left the room too.

The spread of food near the middle of the room caught my eye. "I know how I'm going to spend the next hour."

CHAPTER 21

All of us except for Gia and David exited the Galaxian at eleven o'clock local time, stepping out onto a street much less crowded than when we had arrived. Atlas' sun had set two hours earlier, leaving this section of the city illuminated by warm yellowish light from narrow poles that rose out of the edge of the sidewalk at thirty foot intervals. The air traffic had thinned out considerably as well, and the setting of the sun had allowed for a wider flow across the entirety of the streets, making it appear even more sparse.

It was a beautiful night. Idyllic, if not for the reason we were on the planet and walking toward the outer perimeter of the palace grounds. This place was everything an Earth city should be, and maybe would be in the future. The colonists had left Earth four hundred years from now, and this is what they built after they arrived. Would Earth follow the same path?

"Hey Keep," I said, sidling up alongside him.

"What is it, kid?" he replied.

"I was just thinking. The original settlers of the Spiral came from my Earth, four hundred years in the future, right?"

"That's how the story goes."

"So there must be information about what Earth was like when they left. Videos? Photos? Written history that goes beyond my present?"

He glanced over at me, expression tight. "Look kid, there's a lot of complexity to the whole wormhole through spacetime thing. And considering you're even asking the question now, I assume Alter warned you about all of that already."

"She just said *Head Case's* datastore doesn't carry any information going that far back. And honestly, I never gave it that much thought before now. We've been so busy running toward or away from danger, it hasn't been top of mind."

"We're still kind of busy right now."

"I know, but looking around at this place, it feels like you could just drop it on Earth and it wouldn't feel that alien at all. Kind of like Paris." He smirked at my joke. "And it's incredible. Clean. Well lit. No apparent sign of crime or homelessness. So it got me thinking about the colonists and why they left in the first place, if Earth was anything like here."

"Also like an American tourist in Paris, you're only seeing the highlights," Keep replied. "Lots of places look great on the surface. You've gone deep enough to see the blemishes and you're still falling for it."

"You mean Old Haydrun?"

"Bingo. The point is, Atlas is far from perfect. You've already seen that the Hegemony at large is far from perfect. But when you're talking about hundreds of planets, trillions of life forms, perfection isn't attainable. Even pretty good is a rough go. The goal is to keep the peace. To give every individual in the Spiral a chance to live a decent life. If Sedaya has his way, he'll throw this place into such turmoil, the whole thing will fall into chaos. With sigiltech, he'll come out ahead in the end, but I guarantee it'll be bloody and awful for everyone. And for what? So he can go to bed in there at night?" He pointed to the palace, stunningly lit in the darkness.

I remained silent as we reached the twelve foot steel fence that surrounded the palace grounds. A guard on the inside marched along the perimeter, dressed in a mustard yellow uniform with dark plates of body armor over it and carrying a thick rifle. The outfit was functional but also ceremonial, reminding me of a Samurai. He didn't shift his gaze from straight ahead as he passed us, keeping a perfectly steady gait.

Keep was right. I had already dismissed Old Haydrun as though it was a totally separate world like Furion. It was especially easy to do since we had traveled from there to here in total darkness and nearly died in the process. I wasn't sure if the way the city handled the darker aspects of society was the right one or not. Like Keep said, on the surface it sure seemed so. But I wasn't ignorant enough to think there weren't layers of nuance I didn't have the experience to see.

"Okay, but that doesn't answer my original question," I said. "Is there information about Earth's future stored somewhere? Like maybe in the original archives in Old Haydrun and transferred when it went offline?"

He shrugged. "Probably. To be honest, nobody here thinks that much about Earth, if at all. There's a good chance the intel exists, but it's probably stored in a central location and hasn't been accessed in a long time. I don't really know."

"So you don't know what happens in Earth's future?"

"Nope. Don't care, either. And neither should you."

"What if by bringing Matt and me here, and now David, you changed the future so that the colony ship never left?"

"You watch too many movies, kid. Anyway, everything

that's happened has already happened. It can't unhappen. And even if you knew what the future held for Earth, and that future remained on the same course that sent the original settlers into space, what good would that do you? If the news is bad, then you have to live with the knowledge of what might be. If the news is good, whoop de-doo. You aren't alive then to enjoy it anyway. You're alive now."

"Yeah, I guess you're right," I decided.

"I'm glad you agree."

We made our way along the perimeter. Two more guards passed on the other side of the fence, with the same perfect march and blank expressions as the first. Each time, Keep pushed back his sleeve to check a cheap *I heart New Haydrun* wrist watch he had picked up in the Galaxian gift shop. Reaching the corner, we continued following the fence, passing two more guards.

"When I give the word, we go," he said through our embedded comms, alerting the entire crew at once. Nobody responded to the statement. We had gone over the plan multiple times back at the hotel. We all knew what to expect.

The next guard walked past on the other side of the fence. He was about twenty feet away when Keep gave the signal.

"Now," he hissed over the comm. Immediately, his sleeve glowed beneath his coat, lifting Alter into the air and *pushing* her up over the fence. Dressed in one of the Samurai-like uniforms for a cover story just in case someone spotted us, she was still in the air when Keep's push hit me, sending me over the fence right behind her. Even expecting the boost, my heart pumped in nervous excitement, and my stomach dropped as I hit the top of the arc and started falling.

It took effort, but I managed to land on my feet, stumbling forward a few steps to keep from falling and dirtying my pants. Oddly enough, such a simple thing was one of the most important parts of our deception. Matt came down behind me, also staying upright. Quasar and Druck followed us and then Keep.

As soon as he landed, he pulled the sigiltech glove from his coat and slipped it on, tucking his hand beneath his jacket to hide the glow from both the glove and his sleeve. *Absorb* and *negate* canceled out the environment surrounding us until it faded into darkness. The lights closest to our position went dim, the two sigils shrouding us as we dashed across the open space toward the rear gardens. I looked both directions as I ran, spotting the next guard as he reached the corner of the property.

Keep had the timing down. He deactivated the sigils, allowing light to flow through the area once more just as we ducked into the garden, hidden there by the foliage. The guard noticed the change in light and slowed a couple of steps, confused by it. Shaking it off, he picked up the pace for a moment to regain his expected position and continued on without raising an alarm.

"We're in," Keep said. "Badabing badaboom."

"Gia," I said. "Any hints we've been spotted?"

"Negative," she replied. She couldn't listen in to the encrypted chatter on the guard's comms with her neural link, but she did have a means of measuring the traffic. If anyone had reported anything out of the ordinary the volume of communication would pick up as well.

"We're go for Phase Two," Keep said, checking his watch. "Alter, thirty seconds."

She nodded just before she ditched her Samurai-clad persona. Left in her bland humanoid form, she reformed into Enigma, all in the required thirty seconds. Without a word, she turned and sprinted away from us, darting toward the palace and quickly vanishing from sight.

I didn't need to tell Druck and Matt they were up next.

They waited for Keep's go-ahead. When he gave it, they headed away, cutting across the garden to get into the palace through a service entrance. We had already concocted a story for them to use if anyone tried to prevent them from entering, and if that didn't work they could head out through the front gate. Getting onto the grounds was the challenging part. Getting back out would be easy.

"I'm in," Alter announced over the comms.

Keep and I glanced at one another, our eyes passing the same message to one another. Already? She had slipped into the palace almost a minute ahead of schedule.

We waited for the perimeter guards to clear before Keep gave Quasar and me the go-ahead. I locked eyes with him momentarily before we headed away from him at a normal walk, arm-in-arm as if we had come out to the garden for a stroll. He would move on the palace last and on his own, ducking in through a maintenance door.

"I thought this would be a lot harder," Quasar said as we made our way along a meandering path through beds of flowers, colorful trees, and other exotic vegetation.

"A good plan, well-executed, should seem a lot easier than it really is," I replied imitating Keep's voice. He had said the same thing at least a dozen times while we were going over the plan. "Badabing badaboom."

Quasar laughed, which only helped sell our dalliance as another couple came into view further down the path. A younger man and a woman in a maid uniform, sitting on a bench together. They looked our way as we neared.

"Nice night, isn't it?" I offered.

"It is," the maid replied. "And a perfect time to be outside and away from the tension."

"Krissa, mind your tongue," the man warned, glancing at us. His eyes narrowed. "I haven't seen you around the palace before."

"We're visitors," Quasar replied. "Emissaries from Kolten."

"Emissaries? I thought all of the meetings were canceled through the week, on account of—"

"Who needs to mind their tongue, Bertru?" Krissa said, cutting him off. "Excuse him. He's been suspicious of everyone these last few days."

"I've heard rumors that the Empress' son was taken," I said. "Even if it isn't true, just the idea would put one on edge, I would imagine." I clenched my jaw after channeling my best Bridgerton formality, worried I was trying too hard.

"No doubt," Bertru replied. "Enjoy your walk sir, madam.'

"And you, your leisure," I replied.

Matt and Druck reported they made it into the palace as Quasar and I continued on, bypassing a few more palace employees out for a stroll on our way across the garden. I decided not to speak to any of them just in case they questioned our credentials again, and they didn't try to speak to us either. In fact, everyone we passed seemed uptight and nervous.

"Something's definitely happened here," I said. "Whether the prince was kidnapped or not."

"Yeah, everyone we pass seems like they're walking or sitting on eggshells," Quasar agreed. "Canceling all meetings through the week? That's unheard of."

"I'm in," Keep announced over the comms.

"Damn, how are we last?" Quasar asked.

"We took the scenic route," I replied.

We reached the edge of the garden. A pair of large wooden doors a short distance away led into the palace proper. A pair of Samurai guards flanked it, heads up, eyes forward.

"Act like you belong here," Quasar said.

"I was about to tell you the same thing," I replied.

She kept her arm wrapped around mine as we approached the door. It began swinging open on its own when we neared. Neither guard moved a muscle. I only realized I had been holding my breath once we entered an insanely grand corridor and I finally exhaled.

"We're in," I declared over the comms. "Phase Three is a go."

CHAPTER 22

The massive corridor that followed the perimeter of the palace interior managed to make the exterior seem bland by comparison. Decorated in gold, marble, and dark wood, it was lined with massive portraits of the Hegemony's rulers dating back to the founding over two thousand years earlier. Looking down the length of the passage made our search for the Empress' location feel like an impossible, needle-in-a-haystack task. I had to remind myself that we had three other teams scouring the palace for her, and now that we were inside we didn't need to worry as much about time. As long as we could roam freely within the walls of the gigantic building without drawing undo attention, we didn't need to stress about how long we spent wandering.

Quasar and I turned left from our entrance point without pausing, walking as if we knew exactly where we wanted to be. With the late hour, only a few other palace guests and employees were in the hallway with us. Consumed with their own thoughts, they didn't pay us any mind as we crossed paths.

My gaze drifted to the portraits as we traversed the passageway, taking in the faces of each of the former rulers.

A nearly even mix of men and women, they all had the same thick, dark hair, various shades of olive complexions, and big, bright smiles. The oldest person in the portraits looked to be in his sixties, the youngest no more than twelve. It was amazing to me that a single family could maintain their grip on power for so long, until I considered how they had nearly lost it during the first sigiltech war, and now they were under threat to lose it again if Sedaya got his way. How many other close calls had there been over the years? Over the *centuries*? Undoubtedly, remaining in control for that long hadn't been easy.

Did their reign benefit the Spiral or hold it back? It was an argument Quasar and Druck had fought over more than once since they'd joined the crew. I still hadn't chosen a side and didn't think I ever would. Life was too short to spend it worrying about stuff like that. Especially for me. It wasn't like the Spiral and any of the issues within it were up for a democratic vote.

We left the grand hallway through an archway leading into another corridor that took us toward the southern corner of the palace. Still large compared to what would be considered standard but tiny compared to where we had just been, the textured plaster walls were broken up by more framed paintings and photographs. It appeared each had been taken on a different planet, intended to reflect what made the location unique.

The goal of Phase Three was to locate the Empress, with each team following a predefined path to the places she was most likely to be at this time of night. Alter was on her way to the Empress' personal quarters, while Quasar and I were headed for what outsiders called the throne room. By the looks of it, it was more like a military operations center where she would receive constant flows of information from her many advisors. According to Keep, a lot of people believed her role was mostly ornamental and ceremonial.

They didn't realize how much time and effort the Royal Family really put into keeping the Hegemony running as smoothly as it did.

Keep was on his way to the Empress' private offices, not that far from where we were going. His separate route would help reduce the chance we might miss her along the way. Matt and Druck would recon the underground gym, swimming pool, motor pool, and hangar—all places she might be if she was enjoying a little bit of leisure time before turning in for the night. Outside of finding her ourselves, we had our eyes and ears open for clues we might pick up, either from the movements of individuals including the Royal Guards, or from any other actionable tip they might give us. Fortunately, Keep knew the interior of the palace like the back of his hand, and he had taught each of us our paths from a memory which turned out to be spot-on.

Quasar and I followed our route, maintaining a look of tense annoyance, as though we were late to wherever we were headed. We went up three flights of stairs, past a number of intersections, made a few right and left turns, and kept going to another staircase.

Nearly twenty minutes later, we neared a pair of Royal Guards standing outside one of the doorways, slowing to listen in on their conversation as we passed.

"...forced overtime this weekend," one of them said softly to the other.

"Understandable, with everything going on," the other replied.

"How long does she think she can keep this quiet?"

"Long enough, I guess. Orlan claimed she hired Enigma through a Dark Exchange."

I nearly came to a stop on the far side of the guards when I heard that. As it was, I turned my head and stared at the artwork, slowing down and trying to hear the other guard's reply.

"Enigma? I heard she was back running jobs. She's no bounty hunter, though."

"That's just what Orlan said. You know her. She likes to exaggerate."

Quasar grabbed my arm, pulling me away from the painting. "Too obvious," she whispered.

"They didn't notice," I replied as we continued on. "It sounds like the Empress hired a bounty hunter for something."

"The Empress doesn't use the Dark Exchange," Quasar replied.

"How do you know?"

"Why would she when she has Marines?"

"Do the words plausible deniability mean anything to you? Depending on what she needs, it might not look good for her to send Marines to do it. Like assassinating nobles."

Quasar nearly froze in place. "What?" she hissed. "Are you suggesting—"

"Shh," I warned. "She can't legally remove dukes from the pecking order, right? So what if she really, really hates one of them?"

"Then Sedaya would have been dead a long time ago."

"Good point. But that doesn't mean she hasn't or would never use a DEX. Especially if the rumors about her son are true."

"Team Hondo," Keep said softly through the comms. "No go on the private offices. I chatted up one of her admins. She hasn't been here in two days."

"Before the blueburn," I said as softly as I could, leaning toward Quasar to make it look like I was sharing a secret or joke with her.

"Bingo. I'm going to double-back and head down toward Mattie and Emil."

"You're closer to us."

"Yup, but you won't need my talents if you get in a jam."

"Copy that."

"We've reached the fitness center," Matt added. "Seems deserted down here. No guards, no employees. Nobody. We're making our way toward the motor pool now."

"On second thought, maybe I will rejoin you near the throne room, Bennie," Keep said.

"I wonder what Alter's up to," Matt said. Her lack of communication wasn't really a concern. If she was in a sensitive spot, she couldn't exactly stop to announce her status.

"She'll let us know if she spots the Empress," Keep replied. "She's the last person we need to worry about."

"Agreed," I said.

Ten minutes later, Quasar and I passed a pair of intersections between us and the hallway we took that led us to the throne room. A pair of gold-leafed doors flanked by another set of palace guards signified the entrance to the command center. Under their watchful gaze, we cautiously approached the doors from over fifty feet away.

I wondered absently why Gia was the only one who used robots as protection. Certainly, the Empress could afford machines that didn't get tired or daydream. A robot also couldn't be bribed or bought off. It seemed to me that if someone had really kidnapped Prince Hiro, they had to have had help from the inside. A situation maybe a robot could have prevented.

The answer came to me as we reached the farthest intersection, passing it without slowing. I caught a glimpse of Keep out of the corner of my eye, coming down the adjacent hallway from about twenty feet out, ready to fall in behind us. While a robot was a more perfect guard, the use of machines sent the wrong message to the rest of the

Spiral. It showed weakness and distrust, as though the Empress knew people were out to get her and could easily infiltrate her inner circle. She didn't simply refuse guard-bots. She had hand-picked fighters from militaries throughout the Spiral serving here. The best the Hegemony had to offer on loan from every noble. Not only the best organic fighting force available, but also a show of fidelity from her subordinates. Which worked really well on a lot of levels

Until it didn't.

"Empress Li'an."

Alter's voice, sounding as if she were greeting the ruler of the Hegemony, nearly brought me to a sudden stop.

CHAPTER 23

I could picture Alter down on one knee, bowed before the most powerful woman in the universe. We had to keep walking, but Quasar and I both slowed down.

"Who are you?" A light voice replied. "What are you doing in my private quarters?"

I cast a sidelong glance toward Quasar. She did the same to me. We'd already passed the corridor where Keep approached, losing sight of him again, but I was sure he was just as surprised as we were by the broadcast over Alter's comm. She'd set it to transparent mode to be sure we would be able to eavesdrop on the conversation. What surprised me most was the lack of fear in the Empress' voice. She didn't seem concerned that Alter might be an assassin, especially ironic since she was wearing Enigma's persona.

"I'm sorry to intrude, Your Majesty," Alter answered. "I came a long way to warn you about a threat from—"

"Warn me about a threat?" the Empress snapped, interrupting her. "You're too late. A threat already visited my house. A threat already tore the heart from me."

"Your Majesty?" Alter said. "Are the rumors true?"

"What business is it of yours? You don't belong here. These are my private quarters. My oasis from a universe that's seen fit to take from me what I value most. Leave me at once, before I call the guards."

"Your Majesty, I understand you're upset, but there is a greater threat against you. Not only you, but the entire Hegemony."

In listening to the conversation, my heart was already pumping. All signs pointed to the rumor about Hiro being true. I felt bad for the Empress, and worse for the little boy. According to Gia, he was only eight years old. Too young to become a pawn in these kinds of games.

"Upset? You don't know anything. Get out at once."

"I can't leave," Alter insisted. "I spent too long and fought too hard to be here. I lost people I cared about to bring you this warning. You need to hear it."

"If there's some danger to the Hegemony, you can take it up with General Nattic through the proper channels, not by barging in on me when I'm grieving my loss."

"This isn't getting us anywhere," Matt cut in, listening to the conversation.

I missed the next part, distracted when I heard multiple pairs of feet approaching from behind us.

A loud voice barked at us. "Step aside for General Nattic!"

Quasar and I split to each side of the corridor, lowering our heads respectfully. It took everything in me not to look at the second or third most powerful person in the Hegemony, the commander of the Royal military. A unit of Royal Marines preceded him, intimidating in their full armor, all of them nearly as large as Quasar. They didn't pay us any mind as they passed.

But Nattic did.

A lump formed in my throat when the General came to a stop between Quasar and me. Even as he turned my direction, I kept my eyes facing his broad chest, his dark green uniform jacket heavily laden with hardware. He was a big man, signs of his formerly muscled physique still visible beneath the age and comfort of commanding battles instead of fighting in them.

"You," he said sternly. "What are you doing here?"

"Sir, my name is Kalkan," I said, the words coming out too softly.

"Look at me," Nattic ordered.

I raised my eyes to his face. He looked just as tough and mean as he sounded, his large square jaw ready to chew bolts, his massive skull bald and scarred. He stared back at me, seemingly surprised by my age.

"Sir, my name is Kalkan," I repeated a little more firmly. "I'm an emissary from Kolten. In the Fertile Quadrant."

"I'm aware of Kolten," Nattic replied. "Why are you here?"

"I came to discuss the grain situation with—"

"No. I mean, why are you thirty feet from the throne room when the Empress has canceled all meetings and audiences for the foreseeable future?"

"I…I was hoping to convince her to speak with me. The situation on Kolten is—"

"We're well aware of the situation. In fact, your last delegation was here less than three months ago. The Empress doesn't appreciate pressure tactics, Kalkan."

I lowered my head. "My apologies, sir. I'm simply following the orders I was given."

He put his arm on my shoulder, his voice softening. "Then you're a good, loyal subject," he replied. "But you won't receive an audience with the Empress any time soon. Return to your quarters in the guest wing. Inform Duchess Kinata we're considering options to send aid, and return to Kolten in the morning."

I nodded. Caught before we made it to the throne room,

but it was okay. We didn't need to go in there anymore anyway. This was working out for the better. "Yes, sir," I replied. "I'll pass your message along. Thank you, sir."

He smiled kindly before facing forward again. "Let's go."

The Marines in front of him moved in perfect sync, leading him to the throne room. I exhaled silently, the relief of his weight lifting off me as my concentration returned to Alter.

"As you can see, Your Majesty. Duke Sedaya is plotting against you, and he intends to use banned and incredibly dangerous technology to overthrow you and claim control of the Hegemony," she said.

I had missed it, but apparently she'd convinced Empress Li'an to at least let her play the message we were all carrying.

"How do I know this is authentic?" the Empress asked. "And not a plot by one noble to take down another? There seems to be more of that going on these days than I can stomach."

The Marines finished filing past Quasar and me. We glanced at one another before turning away from the throne room, starting down the hallway.

"I have the metadata that prove the recording was made when and where I claim and hasn't been altered in any way," Alter replied. We had expected Li'an to doubt the authenticity of the message, but the extended data Gia had captured from the space dock made the evidence irrefutable. A lot of time and effort had gone into creating the system to prevent fakes of all kinds. "Please, Your Majesty. This threat is real and growing. You need to send a Royal Sentry to arrest Duke Sedaya at once."

Keep stepped out from the intersection as we reached it, wordlessly falling in directly behind us.

"Do not presume to tell me what I need to do," Li'an

snapped at Alter. "Duke Sedaya is not the most…savory… of my subordinates. But his family has never shown an inclination to go outside the boundaries of our laws in his hunger for power. If this is as you say, I need more evidence than a single mention of building a fleet against us, or another, more trustworthy entity to corroborate your claims."

"What?" Alter spit. I nearly said the same thing out loud, and I heard Keep and Matt both react the same way over the comms.

"I don't have faith in your so-called evidence or your motives," the Empress continued. "It is a coincidence that my son was taken right out from under my nose less than forty-eight hours ago, and here you are warning me of a nefarious plot by one of my nobility? Perhaps you're part of the scheme, sent to direct my attention away from the real danger."

"Shit," Matt snapped. "This isn't going the way I thought it would."

"You! Stop!" The shout came from behind us. I maintained my pace away from General Nattic.

"I said stop!"

I winced and came to a halt with Quasar. Keep bypassed us as if we weren't together.

"Turn around."

"What is this?" I whispered to Quasar.

"I don't know," she replied. "But I have a bad feeling about it."

We turned slowly, keeping our heads down.

"Pick up your heads," General Nattic said.

We did as he said, watching him approach with two of his Marines. The one on the left removed her helmet as they neared.

"Oh hell," Quasar cursed under her breath. "We're screwed."

Shaq shifted beneath my coat in response to her comment, ready to make a move on my say-so.

"Your Majesty," Alter said, more of her exchange with the Empress coming over the comms. "You have to believe me. We're trying to help. We're trying to save the Hegemony."

"If you want to help me, if you want to prove yourself, then you'll find my son," Li'an replied. "Bring my sweet boy back to me alive, along with the head of the person or people who took him, and you'll gain my trust."

"Hey Quasar," said the Marine who had removed her helmet. "It's been a long time. I didn't recognize you right away without your armor."

"Helen," Quasar replied. "Not long enough."

I bit my inner lip. They knew who she was. Screwed was probably an understatement.

"You must be Benjamin Murdock," General Nattic said, glaring at me. "A wanted fugitive sneaks into the Imperial Palace less than two days after another criminal sneaks out. With a disgraced former Marine and fellow fugitive along for the ride. Coincidence?"

"Actually, sir, it is a coincidence," I replied, hearing Keep moving back toward us. "We entered Atlas space around the same time the kidnapper was leaving. We tried to stop him.

Nattic stared at me. "One, I never said anything about anyone being kidnapped. So how do you know about that? Two, we did confiscate a derelict that was hit with one of our torpedoes and matched the description and identifiers of your ship. But you weren't on it. How did you get here?"

I stared at Nattic, unsure how to respond or if I should say anything at all.

"Excuse me, General," Keep said, slipping around my left side.

"Who the hell are you?" Nattic growled, turning his glare on Keep.

"Nobody of any importance," he replied. "But I'm afraid we're in a bit of a hurry, so if you'll please just walk away, it'll save everyone a lot of unnecessary effort."

Nattic's brow furrowed, eyes furious. "Who the hell do you think you are?" he bellowed in Keep's face. "You don't tell me what to do. Marines, grab them and hold them for questioning." The Royal Marines further down the hallway immediately sprang into action, running back toward them.. "I'm especially going to enjoy questioning you," the general grunted at Keep.

"It's tempting," Keep replied. "But I'm afraid I'll have to politely decline." He raised his hand, glove and sleeve both glowing.

"What is that?" Nattic asked, just before Keep *pushed* him and the two Marines with him down the hallway. They flew backward through the air, crashing into the others.

"Alter, Matt," I snapped over the comms. "It's time to go!"

CHAPTER 24

Keep, Quasar, and I sprinted away from the throne room as General Nattic and the Marines behind us untangled themselves and returned to their feet. We rounded the corner just before they could get a clean shot, Keep leading the way. Bounced around by the run, Shaq emerged from his hiding place under my jacket, moving to my shoulder and digging his claws into the fabric of my coat.

"Mattie, how close are you to the motor pool?" Keep asked over the comms.

"We're already here."

"Ever steal a car before?"

"No. You?"

"That's a story for another time. The keys are in a locked box inside the control room. Can you see it?"

"Yeah. There's an attendant sitting inside."

"I'll take care of him," Druck said.

"No killing," I interjected.

"Fine, I won't kill him," Druck replied. "A nice bump on the head will do the trick."

"Alter, where are you?" I asked.

"On my way outside."

"Meet us at the motor pool exit," Keep said.

"Copy that."

A palace guard came around the corner ahead of us, heavy rifle already in hand but pointed to the side. He tried to swing it toward us, only to be yanked violently in our direction, soaring through the air. He surprised me by not losing his cool. He still tried to aim the weapon until Keep pulled him roughly to the floor, his armor cracking against the marble. Quasar kicked him in the side of his helmet on the way past, knocking him out cold.

"Keep," Matt said. "Are you sure you want a hovercar?"

"What do you mean?" Keep replied. "We need to get out of here somehow. On foot isn't going to get it done."

"I mean, the hangar's right next door," Matt answered. "There's this pretty sweet looking star hopper down here."

"You don't have a pilot," I said.

"I can fly it," Druck said. "Not well, but good enough to get it to you. Maybe."

Keep cringed at the thought of Druck piloting a spacecraft. My expression probably looked the same. "Is this sweet star hopper blue and gold with a huge Atlas emblem on its side?"

"Yeah, that's the one."

"That's the Empress' personal transport. If you can grab it, grab it. Alter—"

"Hanger exit," she interjected. "Got it."

"Gia, how do things look out there?" I asked.

"Comms are going crazy," she replied. "They're clearing civilian air traffic from around the palace. And if I'm not wrong, they're scrambling defense forces from the spaceport. I think this is going to be a repeat of what they were doing just before we got here."

"Except we don't have the prince in tow," I replied. "Maybe they'll go a little easier on us."

"And look incompetent a second time?" Keep said. "I highly doubt that. Get down!"

I reacted without thinking, throwing myself into a forward dive. Quasar did the same, and blue bolts of energy flashed over us, crackling and dissipating when they hit the wall ahead.

"Stun rounds," she said. "They mean to take us alive."

"I'm not sure that's a good thing," I replied.

"Me neither."

The shooting stopped almost as quickly as it started. Keep stood over us, using the glove to *absorb* the stun energy, the blue bolts warping as they were pulled into the catalyst. That didn't stop the two Marines who had caught up, though they did stop firing their rifles, reaching instead for their sidearms.

Keep released the absorbed energy back at them, catching them off-guard. The blue blasts hit them both in the chest, the energy crackling through their armor with enough force to bring them down a few feet behind us. Quasar raced back to them, plucking their rifles out of their frozen hands while they looked on.

"Whatever happens, tell Nattic we aren't the bad guys here," she said. "You'll figure that out sooner or later. Hopefully sooner."

She ran back to Keep and me, passing me the other rifle. Just in time. Another pair of palace guards fired on us from the intersection ahead, using the corner as cover. Keep pulled them both into the open, and Quasar and I hit them with enough stun energy to bypass their armor, freezing them up.

"We've been spotted," Matt snapped. "A freaking army just poured into the motor pool."

"What about the hopper?" I asked.

"Too close for them to stop us. But how do we get the garage door open?"

"It should be automated based on identifier," Keep replied. "It'll open for you. If it doesn't, blast it."

"With what? I thought starhoppers weren't armed?"

"Come on, Sherlock. This is the Empress' personal short-range starship. And you think it isn't armed?"

"Right. What was I thinking?" Matt answered.

We reached the stairwell, pushing through the door. Immediately, stun blasts came up at us, and we barely fell away from them in time to avoid being hit. We had entered recklessly and nearly paid the price.

Like before, Keep *absorbed* the initial burst of energy, *dispersing* it back at the palace guards on the stairs. He only managed to take out one of them as the others ducked behind cover.

"Not this way," I said, diving back out into the hallway with Keep and Quasar behind me. The rest of the Marine unit turned the corner as I got to my feet, sidearms ready to fire. I turned my head away and activated the *light* sigil, creating a flare of bright illumination between us that blinded them, giving us a chance to slip around another corner. "Which way to the underground hangar?" I asked.

Keep pointed ahead. "Not far, but we're going to have to take the emergency exit."

"What emergency exit?" Quasar asked.

"I've reached the hangar exit," Alter said. "I haven't been spotted yet."

"We're coming to you," Keep said. "Be there in a jiffy. Mattie?"

"On our way as soon as Druck figures out where the thruster start is. Good thing this ship is armored."

"And then some," Keep said. "It's the push button on the right, just past the yoke."

"I knew that," Druck said. The whine of thruster ignition came through his comm. "We're in business. See you soon, sweethearts."

"I'm reading a boatload of orbital defense fighters moving in on the palace," Gia announced. "And it looks like three Royal Sentries are positioning themselves overhead. I don't think you're getting out of this one. Maybe you should surrender."

"Why the hell would we do that?" Druck answered before anyone else could. "We're just getting to the good part. I think someone here is looking out for their own hide."

"What?" Gia said. "No, that's not it."

I had to admit, her tone was incredibly unconvincing. "Sounds like that's it to me."

"Fine. You know I can't afford to be caught aiding and abetting you. I'll lose everything."

"Sedaya already tried to kill you once," I replied. "If he gets what he wants, you'll still lose everything."

"Bennie, we turn right up ahead," Keep said. "Fifty feet."

I looked ahead. "There is no right turn fifty feet ahead."

He glanced back at me with a smirk. "There will be."

"Gia, if there's anything else you can do to help us with that neural link of yours, now's the time," I said. "If you'd rather take your chances with Sedaya, at least help David get to the hotel roof."

"Damn it," Gia cried. "I never should have gotten involved with you in the first place. What the hell was I thinking?"

"You were thinking it's the only reason you're still alive."

"Okay, I'm still with you. We'll meet you on the roof. Shit. The Empress is going to take my planet for this. My career is over."

"Respect," I said. "You're doing the right thing."

"Here we go," Keep said, his sleeve glowing.

The entire building started shaking—at least the part of

it closest to us—sending rumbling vibrations through the floor. Keep threw his hand forward like he was punching the wall, and the *push* blasted away the stone, exploding it outward into the Grand Corridor.

"Mattie, you need to catch yourself and Quasar," he announced as we changed direction. The Marines reached the hallway behind us, gunshots screaming past as we broke for the hole.

I activated my sigiltech ring, eyeballed the number of steps to the edge of the newly created opening, and closed my eyes.

In my head, I imagined Quasar and I reaching the edge and jumping off, the push from the floor catching us both and subsiding slowly, lowering us almost gently.

The fear drained from my body as I sensed the energy flowing through the ring. My feet lost the floor, but I didn't panic. What I saw in my mind's eye was exactly what would happen.

I opened my eyes, looking down as we dropped toward the floor, supported by an upward force that made it feel as though we were going down a slide rather than free falling.

"Woooo!" Quasar shouted beside me, enjoying the ride.

Keep landed first, turning and *pushing* the Marines back as they reached the hole. Quasar and I landed on our feet near him, a door out of the palace right in front of us.

I started toward it until a wave of dizziness overtook me, dropping me to my knees.

CHAPTER 25

"Not now," I whispered, down on my knees and trying to stop my head from spinning. The catalysts felt cold on my fingers, and my hand refused to move. It was like the sigil sickness, but it hadn't hit my whole body or stopped my breathing. Why? Because I had used only a portion of the power available to me. Either way, I struggled to get back on my feet. To continue moving toward the motor pool exit. "Not now," I repeated when my legs refused to push me all the way to my feet.

"Keep!" Quasar shouted, looking back at me and getting his attention.

"Bennie," he cried, seeing me down on one knee. "Zar, pick him up."

I shifted my eyes, unable to get any words out through the weakness as Quasar scooped me up from the floor and slung me over her shoulder like a sack of grain, leaving me looking down at her ass as she carried me through the door.

"Stop right there!" a guard shouted, and Quasar pulled to a quick stop. "Drop your weapon."

I saw Keep's feet move, bringing him toward us.

"You! Halt!" Another voice shouted. "Hands up! Don't try anything or we shoot."

"Okay," Keep replied, stopping. "You got me."

A vibration from the ground ran up Quasar's legs and small pebbles on the pavement outside the palace started shifting. I knew without being able to see that the shaking came from the underground hangar door sliding open.

"You're all—"

It was all one of the guards managed to get out before falling silent. A thud, his body hitting the pavement, followed. Gunfire rang out, and I would have flinched if I could have. Except it wasn't aimed at us. A second thud of bodies dropping preceded a third. Quasar shifted, firing her stun rifle over and over. I spotted the reflection of Keep's sleeve on the pavement, lighting up as he used it against the guards. The glow faded a few seconds later, the threat temporarily neutralized.

"Thanks for the save," Keep said to Alter as she joined us near the motor pool door.

"Let's move," she said, the shifting thrum of the starhopper's thrusters getting louder. Displaced air washed over me, followed by the lighter whine of an extending ramp and the hiss of an opening hatch. Quasar darted forward, rushing up the metal ramp and into the ship, Keep right behind her.

"Get Bennie strapped in," he said to Quasar. "Alter, take over for Druck."

"Ben," Matt said, rushing over to me. "Is he okay?"

"He's having an episode," Keep said. "Not sigil sick or he wouldn't be breathing. I'll calm him once we're out of here."

"I'm okay," I croaked out. "Rings."

Matt dropped into the seat beside me, taking my hand and tapping on the sigiltech rings to release them from my skin. Almost immediately, a wave of relief passed through me. I tried to exhale, only to find myself coughing roughly, doubling over from the effort. At the same time, the starhopper's ramp retracted, the hatch closed, and I felt the G-forces despite the counter-inertial tech as Alter launched us away from the palace.

"I managed to force clearance for the Empress' ship through orbital control," Gia said over the comms. "But they'll figure out it's been hacked soon enough. And they'll figure out it came through my servers at some point. David and I are headed for the roof. You'd better pick us up there."

"I've got you," Alter replied.

I stopped coughing, looking down at a bit of blood that had sprayed onto my hand. Glancing at Matt, I knew from his pinched expression he knew as well as I did what it meant..

"Just hang in there," he said.

I released the restraints on the seat. I wanted to get up front to help Alter. The dizziness had subsided, though I still felt sore in the back of my throat.

"Where are you going?" Keep said, strapped into the seat on the other side of the wide aisle. He thrust his finger toward the rear. "Bathroom's that way if you need to puke."

"Co-pilot," I said, pulling myself forward.

"You can barely stand, kid."

"Co-pilot," I repeated, fighting my way to the flight deck. Druck had switched to the co-pilot seat, and he looked at me over his shoulder as I entered.

"Captain, are you okay?"

"Yeah," I replied, though that was only about thirty percent true. "I've got it."

He didn't argue, abandoning the seat so I could replace him. I dropped into it and quickly strapped in, looking out of the forward transparency. The starhopper approached the roof of the Galaxian just as Gia and David came out of a service access door. Further in the distance, plenty of flashing lights maintained the perimeter around us, tricked into allowing us to leave. On the holographic sensor display, an incredible number of military ships maintained an ever wider position around us. Whatever Gia had done, she had either managed to convince everyone chasing us that the Empress really was on this ship or that we weren't the droids they were looking for.

I lowered my head as the rooftop split in two, my mind still spinning. I didn't understand what had just happened, other than there was some strange new interplay between my cancer and the catalysts. It brought my mind back to the third component of my situation. Nurse Alter had said my blood was different in ways she couldn't explain. Was the interaction between mutated cancer cells and the catalyst causing that? Or was it the other way around? Did that have anything to do with my newly discovered control over sigiltech? Or would I gain control over the strength of an action only to be rendered unable to use it without suffering symptoms of both afflictions?

It was a strange line of thinking considering the situation. Alter dropped the starhopper onto the hotel roof, the sound inside the spacecraft changing as the rear hatch opened to let Gia and David in. On the grid, the configuration of defensive ships around us began to reorganize, the once hesitant orbital control starfighters coming at us in a straight line.

Whatever Gia had done had bought us about thirty seconds, and was over now.

"We're buckled in," Gia said. "Get us out of here."

Alter lifted the starhopper off the rooftop and hit the throttle, shoving me back in my seat as the nimble spacecraft shot up and away from the Galaxian. The aggressive movement seemed like a signal to the ships giving chase.

Warning tones blared across the flight deck as missiles launched from the defenders, streaking toward the rising starhopper.

There was no panic in Alter's reaction. She tapped on hand and thumb controls on the yoke, sending flares out behind the starhopper as it gained altitude. The projectiles hit the decoys and exploded, leaving us unharmed. For now.

"We need to get to hyperspace," Matt said. "And get out of here."

"No," Keep countered. "This ship has limited range. They can send Royal Sentries to every planet we can reach and catch up to us before we can refuel. Not that anyone would be dumb enough to refuel the Empress' personal ship."

"So what are we supposed to do?" Druck asked. "There's no point running away if we're just going to get caught again."

"Gia, you said *Head Case* is still on the Sentry that collected her?" Keep asked.

"That's right," she confirmed.

"Are you crazy?" Quasar said. "How are we supposed to even get into the hangar of a Royal Sentry like this, never mind take a *different* starship back out?"

"I'm still working on that part," Keep admitted. "Alter, just don't let them destroy us. Gia, link to this ship's computer and mark the target."

"This isn't going to work," Gia replied.

"It has to," I said, backing Keep up. He was right. There was no going back. If we surrendered, they might not even put us back in prison. They might just kill us outright. I was at peace with that for me, especially following my bloody coughing fit, but not for the rest of the crew.

"I'm marking the target," Gia said. "Alter, it's up to you to get us there."

"I will," she replied, just as she sent the starhopper into a sharp change of direction that yanked me against my restraints. Ion blasts flashed past, missing wide. A quick glance at the grid showed more starfighters coming in from orbit, preparing to drop straight down on our heads.

She would try, but seeing the sheer volume of defenders moving to stop us I didn't like the odds. Then again, this was the Empress' personal starhopper. To underestimate its capabilities would probably be a mistake.

Alter must have had the same thought, because she didn't try to maneuver away from the oncoming starfighters. She tapped buttons on the yoke, and one of the screens on the dashboard changed, showing a schematic of the starhopper and the sudden deployment of a bunch of guns all around the vessel.

"Ben, are you well enough to shoot?" she asked, glancing over at me. "The system sees everything around us as friendly."

"Even though they're shooting at us?" I replied.

"It's not a smart system," she pointed out.

"Yeah. I've got it. But how does it work without augmented reality?"

She reached over and tapped on the command screen beside the yoke, flipping through menus. A big, red *ARE YOU SURE?* popped up on the screen. She tapped *yes,* and a second holographic projection displayed in front of me, with the starhopper in the center and Atlassian defenders all around us.

"I don't want to kill them," I said. "They're not doing anything wrong."

"It's us or them, Ben," Alter answered. "Do you want it to be us?"

"No," I replied. "But these are ion cannons."

"So?"

"Gia, can you access the power output of the ion cannons?"

"Let me see. Yes."

"Cut it in half."

"What are you doing?" Alter asked. "You'll still disable them. They'll still crash."

"Not before the pilot has a chance to punch out," I replied. "I'm not killing good people for doing their jobs. Not if I can help it." It bothered me that she was arguing. I thought we'd come to an agreement on that.

"Have it your way," she said. "Select targets by tapping on them on the projections. The targeting computer will figure out the rest. Based on full power weapons, anyway."

The grid was filled with enemy ships, but the most important targets were the starfighters bearing down on us. I reached out to select one, my hand disturbed when Alter changed our direction again, throwing me off target. I used my left hand to stabilize my right forearm and tried again, selecting two of the incoming fighters, then choosing two behind us, taking advantage of the ship's array of guns.

Ion blasts poured out of the cannons, dimmer than I was accustomed to, their range reduced. As an attack, the blasts were pretty ineffective. But they did force the fighters to take evasive action, helping throw them off as they unleashed an assault of their own. We shook as some of the blasts hit the starhopper's shields. More powerful than most shield systems on ships this size, they absorbed the blows with ease.

The starfighters became visible ahead, ion blasts surrounding them as our targeting computer got a bead, sending shot after shot into them. The reduced power and their shields let them survive the barrage, and they barrelled past and slowed to come back around.

"We could have gotten two of them off our backs there," Alter commented.

"Just get us to the Sentry," I replied.

We shot toward orbit, the Sentries looming overhead, including our target, marked with a yellow outline. The ion cannons continued firing at the targets I had set, managing to disable one of them while we climbed. A heavy slew of energy poured endlessly toward us from the orbital control starfighters, who practically had us surrounded. Alter navigated expertly, reducing the number of hits against the shields, but we both knew we couldn't last out here forever. Not with our cannons using half the power, needing twice as many strikes to bypass shields. My desire not to hurt anyone innocent might cost us our escape.

If the consequences of our apprehension negated Gia's fame and fortune, that paling in comparison to what would happen if Sedaya won, did the same consequences apply to ending the lives of a few orbital control pilots? Were they expendable in the name of the cause?

I knew how Alter or Keep would answer those questions. Druck and Quasar would agree, but Matt, David, and Gia's feelings were less clear. I wasn't going to ask them now. I knew what I believed. Money was one thing. Life another. Shooting down more of the Atlassian starfighters wouldn't guarantee success. It would only make it slightly more likely, and I couldn't bring myself to trade their lives for that small percentage gain.

"Gia, can you shift more power to the thrusters?" I asked.

"If you want," she replied.

"You can't," Alter said. "You'll burn them out."

"They can burn out. We aren't keeping this ride anyway. Gia, do it."

"Done," she replied as we jolted forward.

The starhopper raced toward the Sentries overhead, tailed by dozens of starfighters with more closing on the flanks. Energy blasts shot past us from everywhere, the shields taking a constant stream of fire, but they were holding up incredibly well given the circumstances.

"We aren't going to make it," Alter said as warning tones sounded across the flight deck and shield nodes started failing. The thrusters were burning too hot as well, in danger of overheating.

But we were almost there.

"Yes, we will," I insisted, with no real cause for optimism beyond internal determination.

"We're going too fast."

"Bring us into the top of the Sentry," I said, targeting another ship with the ion cannons. "Use friction to slow us." Alter looked at me like I was crazy. "This ship's armor can take it."

She smiled, impressed with the idea even if it was easier said than done. We were still a few thousand kilometers from the target, and according to the sensor grid and the sudden evacuation of the starfighters from our vicinity, we were in for a real pounding.

" We're going to be cutting it close," Alter said.

"You can do it," I pressed.

She started maneuvering before the Sentries opened fire, a barrage of plasma bolts and torpedoes launching from half a dozen massive ships. It was kind of ridiculous, really. Our small starhopper raced headlong toward an overwhelming use of force we couldn't possibly avoid. Nattic had no intention of letting us get away. Not when the blueburn had already escaped with Prince Hiro on board.

"Ooh, that looks bad," Keep said behind me, entering the flight deck. He raised his hand, his sleeve glowing. "This is all I've got left, kid. It's on you to open the Sentry's hangar. Don't blow it."

He threw his hand forward, beads of sweat exploding on his forehead. The majority of torpedoes rushing our way hit impossible space turbulence and were suddenly thrown off course, veering away. Believing their targeting systems compromised, they self-destructed, putting up a wave of escaping energy around us and helping to hide us from the Sentries' firing solutions.

The starhopper rode on top of that wave on its way to the target, covering the distance much faster thanks to the increased thruster output. As he fell forward, weak again from using the sleeve, I grabbed Keep and held him as we changed vectors. One of the thrusters went offline, overheated, just before Alter cut the power to all of them. She brought us up to the bottom of the Sentry, like a breaching whale. The starhopper shuddered as it slammed into the Sentry's hull, sliding across it as more warning tones sounded, filling the flight deck and echoing throughout the ship. The lights flickered and David groaned, no doubt ready to hurl a second time, Matt probably right there with him.

Even with dampening, I was thrown forward in my seat, losing my grip on Keep. He would have smashed into the viewport, but he managed to activate his sleeve, *negating* the force against his body. We kept sliding until the ship cleared the hull, losing friction and maintaining course across space. With the main thrusters cut, Alter used vectoring to bring our nose around. The defending starfighters once more closed on our position, the Sentries too close to attack.

I hated to do it, but I pushed the needle of my ring back into my skin, the spot immediately turned cold. I didn't know if I would end up paralyzed or dead from using the ring again, but there was no other choice. Alter swung us in line with the hangar as a fresh round of energy blasts hit the shields, finally breaking through and scorching the hull.

I didn't close my eyes. I couldn't waste time building up power. "Distra!" I shouted, throwing my hand at the hangar bay doors. The ring glowed brightly and the metal pressed inward, tearing at the weak points and creating a massive hole into the hangar. Still pressurized, debris and unsecured items flew out of the hole, battering the front of the starhopper as Alter guided the ship inside. The Atlassian starfighters managed to get a few more shots off at us before we made it through, but none of them scored a critical hit.

Slumping forward, pain coursed through me, my right arm completely frozen. When I coughed, too much blood flew out with the spittle, splattering against my instrument panel and the transparency. The sight of it made me sick, sadness and fear sending a chill down my spine. Resolve kept me upright and focused as Alter drifted the starhopper toward *Head Case,* where it was clamped to the deck near the middle of the hangar. Lucky for us, the starhopper we had bought sat beside it, free of attachment to the hangar deck.

Pulling my phone out of a pocket with my good hand, I thumbed the controls to remotely access *Head Case.* The ship was powered up, though I didn't know what the Sentry engineers had done to bring her back to life. Either way, it had worked out in our favor. I was able to open the big grin that was *Head Case's* hangar doors.

Better than that, my experience with the phone allowed me to quickly use just my thumb to navigate to the fire control system and activate the ion cannons. I had no idea how long they might last with the makeshift power supply, but I was ready to use them if any of the starfighters trailing us shot through the hole we had made in the Sentry.

They did so a few seconds later, two of them easing into the hangar, a mistake even worse than I had initially guessed they'd make. They had to come in relatively slowly to avoid crashing into any part of the interior, leaving them tremendously vulnerable to the ion cannons of both *Head Case* and the starhopper. I only used our current ride's weapons, swinging my hand up and tapping the enemy targets on the projection. Ion blasts poured out at the craft, who hesitated to shoot back for fear of damaging the Sentry.

After nearly a dozen easy hits against each, the two starfighters drifted toward the back wall of the hangar and collided softly with the bulkhead. Momentum dragged them to the upper corner of the space where they remained.

The starhopper was barely moving by the time it eased into *Head Case's* hangar, skids maglocking to the deck as I closed the hangar bay doors and repressurized the space. "Alter, you need to get the Star plugged back in," I said through gritted teeth. We were so close to getting away it was worth the relentless pain running through me.

"On my way," she replied, shucking her restraints and practically shoving Keep out of the way in her rush to the rear hatch. She knew how badly we needed to get out of here and how quickly she had to move to make that happen.

"Bennie, you okay?" Keep asked, looking pretty exhausted himself.

"It hurts," I replied, eyes tearing. "Bad." He put his hand on my arm, ready to *calm* me. "Not yet. Not until…hyperspace."

"You don't need to fight through the pain, kid."

"I need to see this through."

He nodded. "Then we need to get to the flight deck."

I held my phone with the screen showing a visual of *Head Case's* hangar, watching for more trouble as Keep pulled me to my feet and guided me to the back of the starhopper. The rest of the crew had already disembarked, and I found them waiting immediately outside as Keep and I stumbled onto the hangar deck.

"I've got him," Quasar said, taking me from Keep. He

fell as soon as my weight was gone from him, showing how weak his use of sigiltech had made him.

"Get him to the flight deck," Keep said. "ASAP."

"Matt," I said, holding out the phone to him. "Incoming targets."

He took the device, looking at the screen. "What do I do?"

The power went out before I could answer, the remote connection to the ship lost.

CHAPTER 26

"Alter, what are you doing?" I snapped with as much force as I could muster from where I hung over Zar's shoulder.

"The dumbass Royals jury-rigged a portable reactor to the primary conduit to provide enough power to get *Head Case* down from orbit," she replied in her deeper Mechanic Alter voice. "It's a total hack-job. I had to switch off the main to unhook it and reconnect the Star of Caprum."

"There are starfighters right outside," I complained. "Our hull is made from recycled shipping containers and sheet metal. One hit and we're—" The power flashed back on. The lights seemed even brighter than before.

"I didn't have to reset everything, the batteries had enough juice for emergency power. Put the shields up and we're good to go."

"Matt, punch the shields button," I said, glancing at the phone in his hand, which hadn't actually lost connection. Only the camera feed had gone dark. "Then the top button, then the third one down."

He hit the items on the interface in rapid succession, activating the shields as we scaled the steps to the elevator.

The shield icon activated, blinking almost immediately as they registered their first hits.

"That was too close," Matt said, moving ahead of us to call the elevator down. It arrived in a few seconds and we practically fell in, joined by Gia and David. Keep remained on the floor of the hangar, doubled-over.

"Keep, are you okay?" I asked.

"I'll be fine, kid," he replied softly. "Don't worry about me. Just get us out of here."

We reached Deck Four, and Quasar sprinted down the short corridor with me in her arms. I felt awkward about having someone carry me like this, especially a woman, but this wasn't the time to exercise my male ego. "Levi, open the doors to the flight deck."

The doors slid aside just ahead of us. My muscles spasmed hard, and I howled in pain. "Ben!" she cried, slowing and nearly dropping me.

"Keep going," I urged, gritting my teeth against the agony. The spasms subsided a little as she stormed onto the flight deck and dropped me into the pilot seat. "Helmet."

She grabbed it and shoved it down on my head. Working one-handed, I started the main thrusters as the rest of the crew strapped in—Matt, Shaq, and Quasar behind me, David and Gia in the nearby jump seats.

I started coughing again, tilting my head down since I didn't have a hand to cover with. Blood splattered the front of my shirt, bile rising from my stomach. Why was I coughing up blood all of a sudden? I shook the thought out of my head, my attention better applied to the matter at hand. I would worry about it later.

It was time to go.

I pushed the throttle forward, quickly reaching for the stick as *Head Case* broke free of the maglock and moved across the Sentry's deck. Four starfighters blasted away at our shields, which were already moving into the area of rough shape. If we hadn't upgraded on the way here, we probably would have been dead already.

I focused on the hole I'd punched in the hangar doors, adjusting our vector to aim us toward it and then reaching for the throttle. Alter returned to the flight deck in pilot form, rushing to her seat. "I'll take over," she said as she grabbed her helmet.

"No time," I replied. "Hold on."

"Are you sure the hole you made is big enough?" Matt asked.

"If it isn't, it'll be the end of our escape," I replied, grabbing the throttle and pushing it recklessly forward. Pegged back in my seat from the acceleration, we rocketed away from the starfighters' assault, angling toward the jagged opening in the Sentry's side. "Alter, we need jump coordinates."

"Setting them now," she answered.

Knuckles white, teeth gritted, body tense, we reached the opening. *Head Case* shuddered violently as some part of the ship hit some part of the Sentry, but not hard enough to keep us from passing through. We exploded out of the hangar, shooting straight toward a nearby Sentry surrounded by starfighters, all of them waiting for us to emerge. Alter immediately brought up the damage report, a schematic of the ship showing I had sheared off the edges of both the robot head's ears.

"Could have been a lot worse," I said, clenching my gut to try to keep myself from coughing. We were out of the hangar, but not even close to being out of trouble.

"Coordinates are set," Alter announced. "Hyperspace computer is calculating the path. ETA thirty seconds."

"That's a lifetime right now," Matt said.

"Alter, take fire control," I said.

"I can handle both," she replied.

"No, I'm flying," I insisted.

"Half power on the cannons?"

"They should already be set. Hold on."

I guided *Head Case* into a tight turn, twisting the stick and peeling away from a flurry of ion blasts before ducking low and breaking for the underside of the nearby Sentry. Our return fire poured out of our cannons, the Star of Caprum providing more than enough energy to keep them going, especially at half power, for some time. Respecting our defenses, the starfighters spread out, trying to get safer attack angles on us.

Throttle already near max, we continued gaining velocity as I zigged and zagged beneath the second Royal Sentry, sticking close to the hull to keep the ship's guns from being able to join the fight. Starfighters trailed behind us like a swarm of bees, angrily stinging our shields while trying to avoid the rear-facing cannons sending hot ions back their way. I swung *Head Case* on a new course, guiding the ship lengthwise toward the Sentry's thrusters, counting the seconds that were passing too slowly.

A fresh pain in my lungs caught me off-guard, and I nearly let go of the stick as I bent over in a new coughing fit, more blood spilling out of my mouth as I heaved. Feeling worse than before despite my adrenaline, I fought to open the augmented reality interface to pass navigation control.

"Alter, you have the stick," I managed to wheeze out as I reluctantly made the transfer.

"I have the stick," she replied, remaining calm as I slumped back in my seat. "I'll get us out of here, Ben."

She turned *Head Case* again, passing out from under the Sentry's hull and making a sharp angle up over the top, shooting away from all of the huge ships.

"What are you doing?" I said softly as the starfighters peeled away instead of giving chase. "They're going to fire disruptor torpedoes, just like last time."

"I know. We can outrun them."

"I hope you're right."

We continued moving away from the Sentries. Only a few seconds passed before the computer buzzed warnings in my ears and the sensor grid showed the warships had attained target lock on us. Alter didn't try to break the lock, staying on course as nearly thirty torpedoes launched from the fleet.

Alter pushed the throttle all the way to max, staying on a straight line as the torpedoes approached and the hyperspace computer worked on the path, readjusting for our new heading. Thirty seconds felt like such a long time. What coordinates had she put in for our destination?

"Keep, are you clear of the hangar?" she asked.

"I'm clear," he replied.

"Ben, when I say the word, open the hangar bay doors," she said.

"Why?" I asked.

"Just do it."

I trusted her enough not to argue with her, navigating to the setting and doing my best to stay alert for her signal. Heart racing, vision blurred, stomach churning, I had a sense that once the chase was over and I lost consciousness like I knew I would, there was a pretty good chance I wouldn't wake up. Glancing back at Matt, meeting his gaze, the way he looked at me suggested he thought the same. We exchanged a simple nod. Nothing more was really needed to transmit the way we felt. My best friend, a brother to me, all I wanted was for him to make it out of here.

The torpedoes continued closing the gap, the seconds ticking away at a painful pace. At ten seconds out from the jump, the sensor grid estimated ten seconds to impact. If life were a movie, this would be the height of tension leading to the climax where we would get away by the skin of our teeth. Or maybe the film would end there, leaving the viewer on a cliffhanger waiting to see if we had really survived. Too bad this wasn't a movie. This was real, and the happy ending, or even the challenging but overall hopeful ending was hardly guaranteed.

At five seconds, Alter cut the throttle completely and threw *Head Case* into a tight spin, rotating the head around to face the oncoming torpedoes. "Ben, now!" she snapped.

I almost missed the chance, my hand shaking so much I only caught the edge of the button on my swipe at it. Three seconds later, the hangar doors slid open. Alter pegged the forward vector jets to full power, and she must have turned off the counter-inertial systems too because I was pulled roughly forward in my restraints, the straps so taut they dug into my chest, further restricting my already ragged breathing.

The universe in front of *Head Case* was filled with the brilliant blue of the many ion trails stretching out behind the torpedoes powering toward us, ready to detonate against our shields. An eclipse in the shape of the Empress' starhopper disrupted the light as space started bending around us. Pulled from the hangar by both the escaping air and the force of our acceleration, the vessel drifted between us and the warheads, the first torpedo striking it and going off, igniting the others in rapid succession. The energy of the detonations expanded like fireworks on the Fourth of July as we entered hyperspace, leaving Atlas behind.

By the skin of our teeth.

CHAPTER 27

I was getting kind of tired of blacking out and waking up in sickbay with Nurse Alter hovering at my bedside. Of course, there wasn't much I could do about it as I awoke some time later in that same familiar position, This time, however, there was a difference I didn't expect. One I would rather have done without.

Every other time, I felt better when my eyes fluttered open and Alter's warm smile reminded me I was among friends. Not this time. This time, my head still throbbed slightly and the strain in my lungs, the shortness of breath refused to subside. This time, when I glanced over at Alter, she wore a look of greater concern. This time, Keep and Matt had remained with me for long enough that both were slumped on the floor of my room in sickbay asleep, still in the clothes they'd worn on Atlas.

"Shit," I croaked. I didn't need anyone to tell me my health was failing fast, dragging me down in its horrible spiral of cancer cells cancer cells. They were growing in number more rapidly than my body was able to fight them. Had using sigiltech accelerated the process? I didn't know. Maybe. But what else could I have done? "How bad is it?"

"It's in your lymph nodes," Alter replied. "Even with Keep's efforts. In another week or two, it will probably be in your bones. That's when it'll really start to hurt."

"And there's nothing we can do?"

"Continue slowing it down as best we can, but ultimately no."

"So I have what? A month?"

"Give or take."

"Shit," I said again. I didn't feel afraid. I'd already come to terms with my final outcome. But it was happening too fast. It was trying to take me too soon. I glanced over at Matt. He looked exhausted. "Then we don't have any time to waste."

I shifted on the bed, eager to get back on my feet. As soon as they hit the floor the entire room began spinning. Alter caught me before I could fall, but the movement sent me into a fresh coughing fit that left me practically doubled-over. At least no blood sprayed out this time.

"Ben, you aren't ready to move," Alter said, putting a hand on my shoulder to push me back onto the bed.

"If I don't move now, I'll never be ready," I replied. The volume of my complaint woke Matt.

"Ben, how are you feeling?"

"Like I don't want to die before we settle things with Sedaya," I replied. "It's not how I wanted to spend my last days, but at least you're here."

He smiled sadly. "I'll do anything I can for you, bro."

"I know. Right now, you can get everyone together in the lounge. We need to figure out what to do next."

"You need to rest," he said.

"No," I replied. "Not this time. I thought *calming* would keep my cancer in check for a while. It's not working anymore. My head, my lungs, my lymph nodes. I already know the lymph nodes go everywhere. It's only a matter of time."

"There's still Keep's sigil," Matt said.

"Which is etched on the inside of his skull," I reminded him. "We already decided cutting his head open and removing his brain to get a look at it is a non-starter."

"We could revisit that."

"I heard that," Keep said, glancing over at us and drawing a laugh from everyone in the room.

"What about David?" Matt suggested. "That's why we brought him along, isn't it?"

"And because Suckass and his mother wanted him to make more powerful sigils for them," I replied. "We're lucky he decided to come with us."

"What would you have done if he had made a different decision?" Keep asked.

"What do you mean?"

"You didn't want me to do the dirty work for you. So what if he forced the issue back there? What if he forces it later?"

"I won't be here to see it," I replied. "But we can all worry about that if it happens instead of presuming that it will happen."

Keep stared at me, looking thoughtful.

"What is it?"

"Nothing, kid. Just a wayward thought. Alter, how long do you give him?"

"A month," I replied since I had already asked the question while he slept. "If we're lucky."

He shook his head. "Damn shame. What about the blood? How's that looking?"

"What do you mean?" Alter asked.

"My blood," I replied. "It's been mutating outside of the cancer."

"I can bring up a comparison." She tapped on the autodoc's screen and turned it toward me. The cells looked more round than the last time, as if they were returning to their original state. Except now there was something else embedded in them, a thicker material with a dark blue color.

"Are you sure that isn't cancer?" Matt asked. "Blood cancer is a thing, isn't it?"

"Leukemia," I replied. "Yeah, it's a thing."

"If it were cancerous, the autodoc would have flagged it," Alter explained. "The autodoc searches a universal public health datastore for matches on the genetic structure. Whatever this is, it's unique in the Spiral."

"It's also killing me."

"I know. I'm sorry, Ben."

"Matt, can you get everyone together in the lounge?" I asked a second time. "Sitting here worrying about something we can't control isn't going to help."

He nodded. "I wish we could go back to *VR Awesome!*. Rewind time so this wouldn't have to feel so real now." I could tell he was doing his best not to get emotional. It nearly made me lose control too. "Give me ten minutes."

He clapped his hand on my shoulder, offered a supportive squeeze, and left sickbay. He probably cried once he was out of my sight. I would have if the roles were reversed. Cancer had sucked from the moment I knew I had it. It had never sucked more than it did right now.

I turned to Alter. "Thanks for taking care of me."

"You're welcome."

Keep stood and sidled up next to me. "I'm sorry I don't have the sigils you need, kid. I really am."

"I believe that," I replied. "Just tell me the Royals didn't find the Grimoire."

He smiled. "The Royals didn't find the Grimoire."

"Are you lying?"

"Nope."

"Did you show it to David?"

He hesitated. "I'm not sure—"

"You just said you were sorry that you didn't have the sigils I need. David knows how to build sigils. Or at least, he's closer than anyone's been in hundreds of years. If you really want me to live, he needs the Grimoire."

"I get it, Bennie. I do. But there's more at stake here than just your life. Him recreating sigils isn't a good thing like you're convinced it is."

"I know we don't agree on that one. But I'm the Captain of this ship. I can order you to give him the Grimoire."

"You could." His body language suggested he might not comply with that order.

"I guess you need to make a decision then," I said. "You spent a long time searching for the right person to sell *Head Case* to. You believed I could help you deal with Sedaya and protect both the Spiral and Earth. How much am I really worth to you?"

He stared at me for a moment before replicating Matt's move by putting his hand on my shoulder and squeezing. "Keep fighting, kid. I'll see you downstairs."

He left sickbay, his non-answer an answer of its own. I turned my attention to Alter. "Why don't you head down to the lounge? I need a few minutes alone."

"Okay," she replied, offering a compassionate smile before slipping out of the room.

I leaned my head back and stared at the bare ceiling where pipes and wires snaked through the room. Part of me thought I should cry. Part of me wanted to. But the other side refused to waste the energy. If this was my endgame, then somehow I would find a way to put us in a position to win it.

CHAPTER 28

Everyone had assembled in the lounge by the time I made my way from sickbay. Somebody had already cleaned me up and changed me into a warm-up suit that made me feel like a member of the Tracksuit Mafia. At least it wasn't a unicorn onesie. It was actually surprisingly comfortable.

They were all excited to see me up and moving again, offering warm greetings and words of encouragement as I circled the sofa and took a standing position in front of the big television. Shaq joined me there, perching on my shoulder and nuzzling my neck. I reached up and scratched behind his ear, drawing a soft purr.

Looking out the viewport, I could see we had come out of hyperspace at some point. "Alter, where are we?" I asked.

"Nowhere," she replied with a smile.

"How far from Atlas?"

"A few hundred light years. We're safe."

"And I have access to my systems from here," Gia said. "At least for now. I've spent the last few hours running my algorithm. Looking for another juicy target we can hit. The Empress said she needed more proof. We'll get it."

"She also said that if we wanted to help then we should get her son back," Quasar said. "Have you spent any time looking into that?"

"Of course."

"And?"

"I think we can all agree Hiro's kidnapping has Sedaya's name written all over it. But tracing anything related to the blueburn back to him will be damn near impossible. As will finding the blueburn itself. Either he used his own military to carry out the mission or he hired a black ops team through a DEX. In terms of actionable intelligence, that's pretty much a dead-end. Our next best bet is to do what we did before and hope to stumble across more evidence."

"I don't think that's the way to go," Matt said. "It's time consuming, for one thing. And risky. We don't know what we're walking into."

"Locating Prince Hiro isn't a total dead-end," Keep said. "You're not thinking it all the way through."

"How so?" Gia replied.

"We saw the blueburn. Our sensors got a full read on her."

"The ship was unmarked. No identifiers."

"No doubt. And it'll probably be destroyed as soon as it drops its cargo, to make extra-sure it can't be traced."

"You said it's not a dead-end, but you're pretty much reinforcing what I just said."

"Only if you're looking forward. But history can be important too. We have the sensor readings of the ship. We can use those to work out certain details. The type of thrusters. The composition of the hull. The style of jamming chaff they used. Multiple components purchased somewhere and brought to a single place for assembly. Badabing badaboom."

"Don't badabing too quickly," Druck cautioned. "The ship was small enough it could have been brought to each planet for component assembly. Which would also make it harder to track."

"Fair point," Keep agreed. "But again, we have the composition and shape of the vessel. If we can trace it back to a manufacturer, that could give us the lead we need to get things rolling."

"Odds are they reconfigured the fuselage so it wouldn't match anything else produced," Quasar said. "So the search criteria can't be too limited."

"So you're talking about an algorithm that can scan the hypernet for visual and sensor data that matches what we collected?" Gia asked.

"Bingo," Keep replied.

"But not too strictly," Quasar added. "With some wiggle room."

"An algorithm like that will take time to figure out, even starting with existing AI packages." She glanced at Matt. "If we're concerned about time."

"We are," he replied.

"It's all about the math," David said. "The matching algorithm. You don't need artificial intelligence for this. What format is the sensor data in?"

"The sensors use a number of readings," Alter said. "Infrared, LIDAR, electromagnetic, energy-wave, to name a few. Of course, the cameras record visual data."

"But I assume those readings are translated to binary for processing by the primary computer."

"Of course."

"So we write an algorithm that matches those signatures within a specified level of variance and set it loose on the dataset. We can do the same thing with the raw image data if we have a few decent captures."

"It's a very large dataset," Gia said. "That's the bigger problem."

"So we narrow it down. Start with the simplest criteria to narrow down the set, then run each additional parameter sequentially. Instead of searching everything at once."

Gia nodded. "That could work."

"I can help you with it."

She smiled at him. "Okay. I would appreciate that."

David's face flushed and he dropped his eyes to the deck. "Okay."

"Awww," Druck teased. "Sure beats the hell out of Sailor Moon, doesn't it, Dave?"

"Huh?" Gia said as David looked even more embarrassed.

"I hate to spoil the team-up," Keep said. "But you're on your own with this one, G." He looked over at me. "David has more important work to do."

"What do you mean?" David asked. "What kind of work?"

Keep reached under his coat and produced the slab holding the Grimoire. "We intercepted this a couple months ago."

"What is it? iPad 1000?"

"Sort of," I said, staring back at Keep. He had made his decision, putting the potential to save my life over the risk that David might do evil with whatever else he learned about sigiltech. "The device isn't important. What it contains is. A compendium of sigils, with photographs. Keep can tell you what a good portion of the sigils can do. If you work together, you might be able to decipher more of the equations behind the individual lines and symbols and come up with something that could save my life."

David's eyes bugged out in response to the description of the Grimoire. "Seriously? I can totally do that."

"Can you do it in a month?" I asked.

He looked at me, face paling. "I don't know. Why?"

"Ben?" Gia said, obviously concerned.

"You all know I'm sick. It's getting worse, and I'm running out of time. No pressure, David. But this is my last shot."

He nodded. "I'll work as hard as I can on it. But I need power for my laptop."

"I can give you more than that," Alter said. "We can network your laptop to the ship's computer so you can use it's processor to run your simulations."

"The ship's computer understands Java?"

"All of this tech originated from Earth a long time ago. Java hasn't changed that much since then, though it has gotten a lot faster."

"Sweet. Orders of magnitude, I'm sure." David looked at me. "I'm going to do it." There was no lack of confidence in his reply.

"Even if he comes up with a sigil," Matt said, "you still need a catalyst. And you can't use a catalyst. Even if you could, even if you had the raw materials, we don't have anywhere to etch the sigil."

"I know," I replied. "But writing the program is the hardest part right now. While David's working on the sigil, we can start solving those other problems."

Druck put up his hand and coughed. "Can I ask a question?"

"Go ahead, Emil," I said.

"No offense, Captain. But I thought stopping Sedaya and the shadowy super suckass was our primary directive? Now we're going to drop everything on a longshot to save your bacon?"

"What the hell, Druck?" Quasar snapped. "You don't even like the Empress. I would think you'd be first on board with ditching her to help Ben?"

"I'm not saying I'm not on board. I'm just asking the question."

"Maybe you should keep your mouth shut, instead."

"He does have a point," Gia said. "If we spend a month on the possibility of helping Ben, that's a month Sedaya has to further cement his position. I don't know how I feel about that. I mean, if we could guarantee it would save his life, then I'm all for it. But on a longshot?" She looked at me. "You're a great person. And I have crazy respect for you for so many reasons. I'm sorry to put it that way."

"It's a fair point," I replied. "And maybe we shouldn't—"

"—yes we should," Matt interrupted. "Without a doubt. Without hesitation."

"You may be a little biased," Druck said.

"This may be my ship," Matt replied. "And Ben's ship. So if we say we're going to do everything we can to save his life first and deal with Sedaya second, then—"

"—then I vote against saving my life," I said.

Matt's head whipped toward me so fast I thought it might fly off. "What?"

"Druck's right," I said.

"When pig's fly," Quasar quipped.

"No, he is. This isn't about me. This is about the Spiral. And Earth. And finding Prince Hiro. That should be our priority because if we find the boy, we can not only convince the Empress that Sedaya is bad news, we can also be pardoned. Or at least, all of you can be pardoned."

"Wait a second," Keep said. "Thirty minutes ago you gave me shit about wanting to put the Spiral ahead of you. And now you want to put the Spiral first?"

"I'd just found out I had a month to live," I answered. "Cut me some slack. Even now, my selfish nature wants to solve *my* problems. But like Gia said. If the odds of everything falling into place in time are that low, then it's not fair to the rest of you, or the universe as a whole."

"Bullshit," Matt snapped. "You don't owe the Spiral anything."

"I know you always have my back. I need your support in this now more than ever."

He looked like he wanted to cry again, but he nodded. "Then you have it."

A hush fell over the lounge. We all looked at one another, unsure what to say now that I had quickly settled any argument on the matter. None of them *wanted* me to die. But we had a job to do.

"What if I could boost the odds a little bit?" Keep said, breaking the silence and drawing everyone's attention.

"What do you mean?" I asked.

He looked into my eyes, a sly smile tugging at the corner of his lips. "I may not have been completely forthright about everything I know."

"Gee, there's a shocker," Matt said.

"What is it now?" I replied.

"My wife had a lab. A secret place not exceptionally far from here. A week to get there, max."

"You said her work was lost."

"Most of it was. She erased all of the data on her experiments after she made me immortal. Good thing too, because the Royal Guard caught up to her in orbit on her way out. When she wouldn't give up the location of her lab, they killed her."

The words sent a chill down my spine.

"Wait a second," Matt said. "You worked for the Royal Guard."

"Brilliant deduction, Sherlock. So?"

"But they killed your wife."

"They thought she was on Sashkur's side. And for a long time she was. Until she saw what sigiltech would turn the universe into. By then, it was too late to save her. I tried. I warned her to leave. But she had to finish destroying her work. She had to make sure nobody could replicate what she did to me. Could you imagine if the Empress really was immortal? Humanity needs fresh blood. New people with new ideas. Without it, we would go stale, and eventually we would all die."

"But her lab is still intact?" I asked.

"As far as I know."

"And what does it have that will help?"

"Gilded catalyst. And a machine to stamp it. If Davie can build the sigil, then we can save your life. I'm ninety percent sure of it."

"That's a pretty big boost," Gia said.

"Yeah," Druck agreed. "Makes me feel like maybe you won't croak after all."

"We have to go," Matt said. He looked at the others. "Does anyone here disagree now?"

Nobody objected. My heart jumped at the revelation, though I also remained hesitant. "Why didn't you say anything about this before?"

"The situation's fluid, kid. The variables changed."

"What's that supposed to mean?"

"For one thing, the lab is supposed to stay lost. Revealing the location to all of you is a massive risk against everything I've worked so hard on for a long, long time. But that's not the only thing. Bennie, you did something with sigiltech today I didn't even think was possible. You showed a level of mastery that in a lot of ways leapfrogged you over me in terms of ability. Combined with your natural talent, that instantly makes you a very big deal. One that's too valuable to lose if we can avoid it. You asked me how much you're worth to me before. The answer is a hell of a lot. Not just to me, but to the whole Spiral."

"And here I thought you cared about me as a person," I said.

"Don't take it the wrong way, kid. After a thousand years and the loss of my wife, I don't care about anybody as a person. But as a weapon? I care about you bunches."

"So when all is said and done, this is just like the Last Starfighter?"

He laughed. "Maybe it is, after all."

"Give Alter the coordinates," I said. "Let's set a course."

CHAPTER 29

I didn't have the best week. I didn't really have any week at all. With the cancer beginning to spread like wildfire through my body and everyone on the crew buying into keeping me alive at least long enough to reach Omega Station, as the research lab had been known, I spent the entire time on a cycle of calmed sleep and waking just long enough to eat, exercise as best I could, and take my meds.

Fortunately, I wasn't awake long enough at any time to fall into too much of a depression. It was strange to me how I had been so accepting of the disease and its obvious course when Doc Haines broke the news. Now that the course neared its completion, I didn't want to finish the race.

But maybe that was the point.

Looking back at my life before Keep had come along, I had been content enough, I suppose. But in a lot of ways going through the motions. I numbed myself with video games and movies, and even though I enjoyed hanging out with Matt and playing in the band, I'd never felt completely right. Fully whole. Not that I ever dreamed of suicide or anything close to that. But hearing I had cancer and only a limited time to live had put everything in perspective. Sure, my family would miss me when I was gone. So would Matt, of course. But that would be it. No wife, no kids of my own. I would pass on, and outside of them nobody would remember me.

Now I had a real purpose. Something important to accomplish. People were depending on me, whether or not they even knew it. And I had a family that I had created myself, not been born into. Maybe we were forced together. Maybe if we succeeded some of us would go our separate ways. But the shared goal made us tight.

In the beginning, Keep had promised me the adventure of a lifetime. In the beginning, that promise had seemed impossible for him to fulfill. There had been a lot of struggle over the last couple of months. A lot of violence, fear, pain. But there had also been laughter, friendship, and some serious adventure. Plus freaking magic.

Maybe it seemed crazy, but I wouldn't trade it for anything.

I awoke this time with Matt shaking my shoulder to jog me out of my augmented sleep. My body felt heavy and tired. Too tired for someone who had spent eighty percent of their time sleeping. I glanced up at him. His expression was light, a big smile spread wide. I noticed he had shaved his head, removing his rockstar golden locks in exchange for a cleaner, more militaristic look.

"You cut your hair," I said.

"Yeah. I know you aren't doing chemo so yours isn't falling out, but I figured it was still a show of support. How do I look?"

I laughed. "Hair or no hair, you're still ugly."

He laughed back. "We're out of hyperspace, approaching Omega Station. You're still here, and we're here."

That news was enough to cajole me to a sitting position.

I didn't feel that weak physically. The calming helped a lot with that, even if it hadn't been able to control the cancer as well as we'd hoped. Though Alter had said there was a good chance I had only survived as long as I had because of it. "What about David?"

"He and Keep have been at it all week. Neither one of them has slept much. He seems to love it, though."

"Did he come up with something?"

"He says he's close."

I was tempted to lie back down again. We didn't need to arrive at Omega Station without a sigil. I decided I wanted to check in on his progress myself. I doubted there was anything I could do to help, but I could guarantee there was nothing I could do if I did nothing. I slid off the bed and onto my feet, still wearing a tracksuit. I would never have put myself in one before, but it really was that comfy, even to sleep in.

"How long until we touch down?" I asked.

"That depends," he replied.

"What do you mean?"

"Let's go up to the flight deck. You need to see this."

I nodded and followed him out of my bedroom. Shaq was curled up on the arm of the sofa in the lounge, and he picked up his head as soon as we entered, immediately launching himself to my shoulder and nuzzling my neck. He reacted the same way every time I got up, and from the impression in the couch I knew he had settled there for the long haul to wait for me.

"Hey bud," I said, scratching behind his ears.

"How are you feeling?" he buzzed. It was a more complex series of sounds, but once Alter had told me what it meant the first time I'd remembered the sequence.

"I'm upright and not coughing up blood. No dizziness. No shortness of breath. At least at the moment. I consider that a win."

"We're almost there," he replied. "You'll be okay."

"I appreciate the positive attitude," I said. "I'm going with that too."

"Where's everyone else?" I asked as we headed from the lounge to the elevator.

"Already on the flight deck," he replied.

"The whole crew?"

"Yeah. They wanted to see this place, since it's supposed to be so super secret."

"It sounds like it's worth the price of admission, since you want me to see it instead of just telling me about it."

"You'll understand when we get there." The elevator took us up to Deck Four. Matt brought us to a stop just outside of the flight deck for dramatic effect. "Levi," he said, pausing there for a few beats to drum it up a bit more. "Open the doors to the flight deck."

The doors slid aside. My eyes shot right to the forward viewport, to see what it was that made Omega Station so special.

All I saw were a bunch of rocks.

At least, that's what my mind registered them as at first glance. But as I stepped over the threshold onto the flight deck, the nascent memory began to fill in.

"That's the *Star Squadron* level," I said, recognizing the pattern of the asteroids that drifted across space ahead of us. "The one we played on." I pointed at one of the spinning rocks. "I almost flew into that one."

"Yeah," Matt confirmed. "Pretty cool, huh?"

"It is pretty cool." I kept walking forward, staring out the viewport at the asteroid field. Surprisingly, there was even a ship in the distance, dead in space with a gaping hole in its side. A battle had already been fought here a long time ago.

"Ben, you're here," Alter said from nearby. I was so enamored with picking out the details of the scene in front of us I had forgotten everyone else on the crew was already here.

I turned my attention to her, surprised to see she had erased her normal shoulder length hair, switching it out for a bald scalp. Her too? The others stood behind her, and as I shifted my gaze from her to them, I saw they had all shaved their heads, either down to a peach fuzz or totally bald. Even Gia had sacrificed her locks for me.

"This is what I really wanted you to see," Matt said, coming up beside me. "We're with you, Ben."

A few tears welled as I smiled. "I feel like I should shave my head. Thank you all. This really means a lot to me."

"It was no trouble at all," Druck joked. He had retained his typical level of baldness and hair loss. "I actually thought I should try to grow some hair to show support, but it didn't work out too well."

"It's the thought that counts," I replied. "And no matter what happens, I'll never forget it." I turned back to the viewport. "Keep, I guess you modeled the *Star Squadron* level after this place?"

"Bingo," he replied. "Sashkur built Omega Station here to make it both hard to find and hard to reach."

"But using this for the game, it seems like you planned on bringing whoever you found back to this place one day."

"Nope. I just knew the difficulty of navigating through this field. Add combat to the mix, and it bumps the challenge up to ace level. Because that's what I needed. An ace. And that's what I found. Badabing badaboom. That we're here is purely coincidental."

I wasn't completely sure I believed that, but I didn't argue.

"I'm sorry, Ben," David said. "I thought I would have the sigil by now, and hooking into *Head Case's* computer has accelerated my progress exponentially. The type of sigil you need is easy to conceptualize, but hard to execute. I'm almost there, though. I'm pretty sure of it."

I didn't really like his use of *pretty* as a qualifier for *sure*, but I nodded. "I know you're doing the best you can," I replied. "I'm not dead yet, and as long as the super secret base is as super secret as Keep says, we should have a little more time."

"Nobody found Omega Station," he said. "It's impossible."

"Avelus thought that since you've flown a simulation of the field before, you might want to fly us in," Alter said.

I glanced over at the pilot seat and smiled. "Absolutely."

CHAPTER 30

I sank into the pilot seat and pulled the helmet on, the sheet metal between me and space fading as the augmented reality system took over. I only had a limited view of the asteroid field before. Now I could see it in all of its glory. A massive obstacle course, with a prize somewhere inside.

"How do I find Omega Station?" I asked.

"Head for the center of the asteroid field, and then follow it until you see a rock that looks like a camel," Keep replied.

"A camel?"

"It's two chunks that smashed together at some point and fused. Or maybe two hit a third asteroid and they all fused. It kind of looks like Mickey Mouse's noggin too if you see it from the right angle."

"A camel or Mickey Mouse head," I said. "Got it. I guess. Everybody strap in. This is going to be a bit of a roller coaster ride." I watched the asteroids and the sensor grid, getting a feel for the movement of the rocks as the rest of the crew found seats and restraints.

"What's a roller coaster?" I heard Druck ask David from their jumpseats.

"It's an amusement park ride. You go in a small, open cart up a big hill, and then drop down the other side. Gravity builds up your speed enough to go back up additional hills and into loops and stuff."

"Sounds boring."

"It's not as fun or cool as a starship. But we make do with what we have."

"I always loved roller coasters," I said.

"You know, we can take it slow through the field," Matt said. "That's what I did in the game."

"If you want to call it that," Keep replied. "You hung out at the edge of the map for eighty percent of the time and then mosied through like a dead man slumped over a horse."

David cracked up at that, which caused the rest of us to laugh. It was a much needed tension breaker.

"When it comes to starships, I don't know how to go slow," I said at the same time I punched the throttle to max. The mains fired, shoving us back in our seats as *Head Case* launched toward the field.

"Woooooo!" David shouted from his seat.

"We're gonna die," Druck decided as the ship rapidly accelerated directly toward one of the asteroids.

I didn't change course, letting the asteroid spin away in front of us, revealing a gap ahead. Blasting through it, I twisted the stick while pulling back on it, guiding *Head Case* up and over the rock behind the first one. We hit a wider gap, adding velocity before reaching the next group of asteroids.

Twist left. Pull up, Pull back. Twist right. Fire reverse thrusters. Reduce throttle.

We shot around the asteroids one after another, diving and climbing, sliding sideways in both directions, spinning fully around. It was just like the classic Atari game, except I had a much larger field to play in and didn't have any intention of blasting the space rocks.

But I had always been good at that game.

"Ugh," Druck said. "I feel sick. If this is like a roller coaster, then roller coasters suck."

David laughed. "I thought you were a big tough mercenary?"

"I am. But I still prefer solid ground."

Checking the sensor grid, I knew approximately when we reached the center of the field's width. With the asteroids forming a wide circle around a distant planet, I knew that even staying within the middle of its boundaries, it might take hours to find Omega Station. Fortunately, Keep sat on the sofa right behind me, keeping a close eye on the asteroids as I navigated around them, searching for the secret Sashkur research facility.

A need to cough to get my breath forced me to ease off the throttle, and when Alter looked at me in concern I nodded to her, silently asking her to take the stick. I coughed while she guided *Head Case*, a dry, heaving hack that left my throat sore. At least it came up empty of blood.

"I've got the stick," I announced once I had finished the expulsion, retaking control of the ship. Alter remained more alert, ready to switch-off if, or when, I needed to cough again.

Ten minutes passed. Twenty. The density of the field relaxed somewhat, and we flew through larger pockets of open space, still keeping a keen eye out for the Mickey Mouse camel. According to the ship's computer, a full flight through the entire field would take over a day. I hoped we hadn't entered on the wrong side.

An hour passed. Two. Alter and I switched off piloting *Head Case* a few times so I could both cough and take a few minutes at a time to rest. What had started out as exciting and adventurous slowly turned plodding and boring, just like Druck's idea of a roller coaster. The constant changes in direction, thrust, and inertia began wearing on everyone. Quasar snored loudly from her jumpseat.

"Are we there yet?" Druck asked by the end of hour three, getting antsy. I didn't blame him. I felt antsy too.

"I wish," I replied. "Keep, how do you know we didn't blow past it?"

"You didn't," he answered. "I've been watching the whole time. I've been here before, remember? I'll know it when I see it."

"How do you know it hasn't been destroyed? Or changed orbits? Or collided with another asteroid?" Matt asked.

"Because Sherlock, it hasn't. Any of those things."

"How do you know?"

"It was in that orbit for ten thousand years before Sashkur hollowed it out. There's no reason to think it's moved now."

"It could have been destroyed. You said the Royal Guard caught up to your wife."

"They never found Omega Station. They hit her ship on the way out. You might have noticed it in the distance."

A cold shiver ran down my spine. That was the ship his wife died on? Was that how he knew the coordinates? It should have drifted away over so much time. It must have had enough power to stabilize before it went completely dead. Which meant she probably hadn't gone quickly or painlessly. She had probably suffocated as the hobbled ship ran out of air.

"Were you there when it happened?" I asked tentatively.

Keep sighed mournfully. "Yeah. There was nothing I could do. The Royals didn't know we were married. They didn't know what she had done to me. The experimental treatment. I couldn't stop it, and I would have been executed for treason if I had tried. That's not why she gave me the sigils. That's not what she wanted." I glanced back at him, lifting my visor. His eyes were moist, expression dour. "Thanks for helping me relive that memory, kid."

I clenched my teeth, taking the gut punch in stride. He was right. I shouldn't have asked.

His eyes shifted from me to the viewport, the sadness dropping from his face so quickly I had to wonder if it was all an act. "I know those rocks. We're close."

I returned my eyes forward, lowering the visor again. "Alter, I've got the stick," I said.

"You've got the stick," she confirmed, passing control back to me.

The sensor grid lit up with red and something smacked into our shields. Three more hits followed in rapid succession.

"I thought you said this place was unguarded," I snapped without looking at Keep.

"It's supposed to be," he replied. "Maybe somebody found it after all."

CHAPTER 31

I hit the gas, opening the throttle and sending *Head Case* jumping ahead of the sudden barrage of fire. Energy blasts zipped past, smacking into the surrounding asteroids behind us as I used the sensor grid to locate the threats. Some appeared to be stationary, anchored to the asteroids around us, while others followed my maneuvers, closing in.

"Fixed batteries and drones," Alter said, confirming my thoughts. "They've probably been waiting out here for someone to arrive."

"That makes sense," Matt said. "But for how long?"

"They could be Royal Guard inventory," Keep suggested. "It's possible they've been here since the Guard first arrived."

"A thousand years ago?" I asked.

"Closer to nine hundred," Keep corrected. "I'm nine-hundred eighty years old. Priya gave me the sigils at fifty-six. That's—"

"I don't really care about the math right now," I interrupted, swinging *Head Case* toward one of the offending asteroids, close enough to see the offending turret. Large and round, it tried to follow our course while it continued firing, its mount giving it a wide range of motion. "Alter, do you have it?"

Ion blasts launched from our cannons, slamming the turret and the rock behind it, breaking chunks of the asteroid away from the surface and sending them spinning through space. This was just like the classic game after all.

"Got it," she replied calmly. The ion cannons fired again, and another fixed turret went dark. "That one too."

"Do you think the Royals found Omega Station?" David asked. "If they did, what we came for might be gone."

"Not a chance," Keep insisted. "They might have figured out a general location and booby-trapped it, hoping to prevent anyone on the Sashkur side from returning. Since the war ended soon after, nobody ever came back."

"Why do you say that like you're guessing?" Matt asked. "Weren't you here?"

"With the main attack group. Which wasn't equipped with automated batteries or drones. This must have come later."

One of the shield nodes turned orange, hit with a pair of blasts from two drones trailing us. "It stinks no matter how you slice it," I said, twisting the stick and spinning *Head Case* into a one-eighty. Alter didn't waste any time blasting the drones with the cannons, blowing them to pieces that slammed against the shields and deflected away.

"Nice move," Druck said, watching the combat. "Why didn't you just rotate the cannons to the back?"

I swung *Head Case* back around. Alter quickly fired again, taking out another fixed battery.

"That's why," I replied.

Collision alerts blared over the flight deck's speaker, and I slammed the throttle forward just in time to avoid an asteroid that had gotten close enough that the ion trail from the thrusters left a mark on it. Four more drones tried to flank us, and I dropped the ship toward a gathering of smaller asteroids circling more quickly around one another in the gravitational dance. Being drones, the opposing ships didn't hesitate to follow.

"Roller coaster again," Druck commented. "Great."

I dove into the midst of the asteroids, ignoring my desire to cough to get more air as I guided *Head Case* around them, doing my best to get the drones behind me caught in the mess. Alter rotated the ear guns this time, firing backward at them as we passed through the rocky mess. A couple of the asteroids glanced off our shields, bumping us around a bit and throwing off her aim. She hit one of the other rocks instead, the force pushing it into one of the drones. It veered off course, smashing full-on into another in a lucky accident.

Alter caught a second a moment later, as I veered and twisted *Head Case*, bringing the ship scraping past a larger asteroid to regain the centerline of the belt. The quick turn threw off a third drone that fought futilely to adjust its course. "Gotcha!" I growled joyfully as it hit one of the rocks. Cutting the throttle, I fired the retro thrusters to reduce velocity while I made a quick hook around a larger asteroid.

The last drone flew right past us and into Alter's line of fire. She blasted it easily, leaving the field clear of targets.

"That was easy," Druck said while I guided *Head Case* through the field again, continuing the hunt for the camel.

"I just make it look easy," I replied, though in all honesty the improved shield nodes and the Star of Caprum were the only reason we had a chance against the defenses. My need to cough expanded, and I signaled Alter to take over so I could cough again. It was worse this time. The heaving for more air hurt this time, pulling the iron taste of blood up to my mouth. I swallowed it back, relaxing my breathing as fast as I could.

Calmed again, I leaned my head back against the seat

when the sensor grid lit up a second time, revealing more defenses among the asteroids. "Alter, I have the stick," I said, picking my head up to resume the fight.

Round two went a lot like round one, with Alter and me teaming up to take out another series of drones and fixed batteries while we slowly progressed through the asteroid field. Keep had modeled a level of *Star Squadron* after this, and right now the waves of drones and guns certainly felt more like a video game than reality. Would there be a larger, more powerful starship guarding Omega Station too?

Assuming we ever found the damn place.

Another ten minutes through the field brought us to the third wave of defenses. The good news about the number of drones and batteries in the area was that it upped the odds that the Royals had never actually found the station. They had either made an educated guess about its location or had somehow determined a radius and planted their traps but had never landed on Mickey Mouse Rock itself. As it was, those traps were no match for Alter and me. We disabled and avoided them, guiding *Head Case* through the chaos.

"There!" Keep shouted, nearly an hour after our first encounter with the defenses.

My gaze shot to the asteroid he had thrust his index finger at, grinning widely as if he had known exactly where and when we would locate the station the whole time.

"That doesn't look like a camel to me," I said, staring at the asteroid.

"Or Mickey Mouse," Matt agreed.

"It looks like a Milkbone," David decided.

I could definitely see the shape in the asteroid, but even that was more a matter of perspective. The rocks were like clouds that way. "Are you sure that's the right one?"

"Positivo," Keep replied. "Not my first rodeo, kid."

We still had a pair of drones pecking at us from the rear.

I guided *Head Case* through a tight loop while Alter adjusted the cannons, quickly blasting them to oblivion.

"At least there's no boss battle at the end of this one," I said, thankful my fears about a more powerful starship hadn't materialized. I adjusted course again, backing in toward the milkbone to slow our approach. "Where's the hangar? It all looks like solid rock to me."

"That's the idea," Keep replied. "Just get us in close."

After dog fighting drones for the last hour, maneuvering *Head Case* to the asteroid's surface was relatively simple. I brought us within a few miles of the terrain, which still appeared completely undisturbed. There was no sign of a base.

"Are you sure—" Matt started to ask again.

Keep raised his hand, sleeve glowing as he activated the sigils on it. The solid rock a little further ahead of us faded away, a pair of thick blast doors taking its place. Turning his wrist, he *pushed* on something that triggered the doors to slide open. He glanced at Matt. "Pretty sure."

"Very nice," David said. "So cool."

That a swarm of drones didn't come flying out of the hangar to blast us was a positive sign against the idea that the station had been compromised. Activating *Head Case's* massive headlights, I brought the ship over the bay before rotating to face it. The beams swept into the open pit, revealing plenty of bare metal and little else.

"Looks like your secret base is still secret," Druck said.

"Bring us in nice and easy," Keep said. "We'll be completely safe once we're inside. Pretty much invisible to the rest of the universe."

"What about our heat signature?" I asked.

"The bay doors and rock are too thick to penetrate with sensors, otherwise the Royals would have found this place a long time ago. When I say we're good, I mean we're good. Capiche?"

"Yup," I replied. "Going in."

As soon as *Head Case* cleared the hangar doors, Keep pushed them closed again. I killed the mains, guiding the ship across the empty hangar with vectoring thrusters. All of the ships that were once here had left during the evacuation many years earlier.

"The systems are all powered down, so we'll have to go out in space suits," Keep said. "We can bring the reactor back online from the command center." He sounded eager to step foot in the base once more, though I could only guess at the memories surfacing in his mind. Even now, he stared at the hangar bulkhead, likely reliving his last moments here. "The primary entrance is against the rear bulkhead there. You might as well bring us in as close as you can get. The less time we spend with helmets on the better."

"Okay, Team Hondo," Matt said. "Let's get a jump on things and head down to the armory while Ben brings us in."

"We won't need guns inside," Keep said. "We're the only living things on this rock."

"Famous last words," Matt answered. "I feel safer going in with a rifle."

"Me too," Druck agreed, turning his head toward Quasar. "Hey Zar? Are you going to wake up anytime soon or what?" He shouted it loud enough to draw her out of her slumber.

"Huh?" Quasar said, eyes fluttering open. "Oh, we're here already?"

CHAPTER 32

We assembled at the smaller hangar bay door thirty minutes later, all of us save Alter outfitted in space suits. She had switched to her Enigma persona, remaining in her normal black outfit. It was a powerful reminder that she wasn't human and didn't need air to survive.

Only Keep had refused to carry any sort of weapon, not that he needed it. I had a simple blaster on my hip, comforted by the weight of the weapon despite the abandoned state of the facility. Shaq wasn't with us. Without a space suit to fit his size and shape, he had to wait until we turned life support back on before he could join us.

"How far is the command center?" Matt asked.

"Not that far," Keep replied. "Ten minutes, tops to get there. Another ten max to get everything up and running again. This place isn't that big. A quarter the size of a Royal Sentry."

"Got it. Let's move out. Levi, open the minor hangar door."

The smaller door slid open, the ramp descending to the metal floor of the station's hangar. I could already see the blast door into the station proper straight ahead, about twenty feet away. We crossed from *Head Case* to it in no time. Keep *pushed* it open, releasing a blast of ancient air into the hangar. The short passageway had another door at the far end. The corridor didn't have any lights, which wasn't a problem thanks to the headlamps on our helmets. We piled over the threshold so he could close it again, preventing too much of the oxygen from leaking out into the airless space.

"Too thin to take the helmets off," Quasar announced. "I guess some of it siphoned out of the rock after a thousand years."

"The station has backup stores of air," Keep said. "It'll all work itself out when we get to the command center."

We marched down a metal-clad corridor toward a second blast door, our pace slowed a little by the required gait in our maglocked boots. Pipes and wires covered the ceiling overhead. When Keep pushed the second door open, we were met with another corridor, this one carved directly into the asteroid. It traveled a short distance before curving, and we followed it to a junction. Keep guided us to the left, and we continued deeper into the old research lab, changing direction at a couple of junctions until we wound up at an open archway leading into a small room with a pair of workstations stuffed against the bulkhead.

"This is the command center?" I asked.

"Yuppers," Keep replied. "What did you expect?"

"I don't know, something more like the flight deck, I guess."

"This is a science lab, not a starship. The command center is primarily for system control and handling incoming and outgoing traffic. It doesn't need much real estate." He settled into one of the seats and reached for the keyboard. The whole system…the whole station was dead.

"The power's totally out," Druck said. "How are you going to—"

Keep tapped the enter key. A soft hum preceded the display flashing on. "The primary controller has a battery backup in hibernation mode," he answered. "Rated to hold a charge for five thousand years. Give or take."

"Did Sashkur expect he might need to abandon this place for a while?" I asked.

"A contingency, I suppose," Keep replied. The display switched to a password screen. He typed too fast for me to see what he entered, but it allowed us into the system. He glanced back at me, smiling. "I'm not really supposed to know that." A few more taps on the keyboard, and something deeper in the facility made a loud, echoing thud followed by a soft hum. The overhead lights flashed on, and even the terminal display grew brighter. "The reactor still works. That's a good sign." He continued entering keystrokes. A hiss from a nearby air vent suggested the ventilation had come back online. Sudden weight pressing down on me told me artificial gravity was restored as well. I released the maglock on my boots, happy to be able to walk normally again.

"That ought to do it," Keep said, getting back to his feet. "The lab isn't far from here." He grabbed his helmet and pulled it off, breathing in. "A little musty, but better than the fishbowl."

I glanced at Quasar, waiting for her go ahead before removing my helmet. "Air looks good," she said, reaching for hers. We all removed our headgear, holding it in a free hand while we followed Keep down the hallway toward the lab. I also took the opportunity to use the comms back on *Head Case* to let Shaq know it was safe for him to leave the ship and find us by scent.

Keep wasn't kidding when he said the lab was nearby. About thirty feet, a left turn, and another ten feet and we were there. The door slid aside as we approached, revealing a large atrium where a projector cast a faux blue sky onto the curved ceiling, giving the impression we were outside. A number of dried up plants filled the room, split by a walkway that broke in three other directions. I imagined this room had been colorful and beautiful once. Now it was brown and drab.

Each doorway had a placard over it to help guide visitors. Science straight ahead. Supplies on the left. Assembly on the right. We walked straight through the atrium to the Science door. It too opened ahead of us.

"Nice security," Matt quipped.

"The security is outside the facility, Sherlock," Keep replied calmly. "The people who worked here didn't need to lock things away from one another."

The lab was made up of multiple additional rooms, segmented by full-length glass. The ceilings were all lined with arrays of sensors and extra ventilation, as well as what I assumed was a fire suppression system. All of the rooms contained workstations and tables. A couple of the rooms held freezers that seemed to be operational now, but probably hadn't been running for the last thousand years. One room sported a chair that looked like it belonged in a dentist's office. Was that where Keep's wife had cut open his skull and somehow moved his brain aside to etch his immortality sigil?

"What do you think, kid?" Keep asked when we reached the end of the central corridor between the rooms.

"I don't know what to think," I replied.

"I do," David said. "Where do we start?"

"We need to get you hooked into the network. We can do that through the terminal in there." He pointed at the display inside the room with the dentist chair. "That'll get you online. Then we can see if Priya left anything behind. I doubt it, but you never know. After that, we'll upload your software to the mainframe. Even though it's old, it was top of the line in its day, and still faster than *Head Case's* suboptimal processing unit. That'll help speed up your tests on the sigils."

"Cool," David answered.

"Gia, once that's done, I'll get you plugged into the network too. I know you've been working on the hunt for Prince Hiro. We don't want to forget about that."

"No, we don't," she agreed.

"What about me?" Druck asked.

Keep shrugged. "Other than Bennie, the rest of you are pretty much just here because we're here. There are quarters on the other side of the facility, along with showers, a recreation room, and some food that's probably mutated into a killer tomato by now. Go do something that doesn't include you being here for now, while the adults figure all this hee-haw out."

"You need me for something?" I asked.

"We need you to rest," Keep replied. "Stay as healthy and alive as you can."

"What do we do once you've figured things out?" Quasar asked.

"That's when we can get out of here. Track down the prince, kill the duke, save the universe. Badabing badaboom."

"For once, I like the sound of the words coming out of your mouth," Matt said.

"I want to stick around for a little while," I said. "An hour or two maybe. David, I'd like to see the progress you've made."

"Sure, man," David replied.

"Whatever," Druck said. "I'm gonna go look for those killer tomatoes. Zar, you coming?"

She shrugged. "Sure, why not?"

Shaq scampered into the room between their feet as they headed out the door, coming to me and scaling my space suit to my shoulder.

"I guess this is home for now," Matt said. "I've come close to being homeless before. I never thought I would wind up living inside a robot head and an asteroid shaped like a dog treat."

"Pretty awesome, huh?" I said.

"If everything goes the way we hope and you make it back out of here alive? Yeah, that will be very awesome."

"Come on, Davie," Keep said, the door to the lab section opening as he approached it. "We've got work to do."

CHAPTER 33

Already accustomed to living aboard *Head Case*, it didn't take long for me or the crew to adjust to living on Omega Station. The place had clearly been abandoned in a hurry. Beds were unmade. Clothes were spilled out of lockers and onto the floor. Half-eaten food had been left on tables. While there were no killer tomatoes, there was some type of fungus or mold that had prospered and spread across the floor which Druck and Quasar donned their space suits again to clean up.

The assembler was functional but ancient, only able to accept a limited number of ingredients and likewise able to produce a limited number of culinary options. For the most part, we strayed back to *Head Case* to eat. We transferred some of the water from *Head Case* to tanks on the station, which had gone dry nearly nine hundred years ago. That got the showers running again. The individual bedrooms were cozy and comfortable, the sleeping surface of my bed one of the softest I had ever felt.

Not that we planned to stay for long. Only until David created a sigil or I died. Once one of those things happened, David would turn his attention to helping Gia track down the source of the blueburn's thrusters or hull, and from there hopefully come up with a lead on Prince Hiro. I tried not to think about what I had heard about abductions on Earth. Either locate the person within forty-eight hours or there was a very high probability they would never be found. But nobody stole the heir to the Hegemony just to kill them. Whoever was responsible wanted them for a reason. They had a plan, and I didn't think that included murdering a child. That's why I firmly believed either Sedaya or Sucaath had done it, and since they were working together they were both responsible.

We could have maintained everything on *Head Case*, but it was good for morale for the others to have something to do, and they seemed to enjoy both the change of scenery and the opportunity to fix the place up. They especially appreciated the recreation room. Despite its age it turned out to have a pretty solid collection of movies, music, and virtual reality games.

I didn't get to enjoy any of that. I spent most of my time sleeping, spending maybe four or five hours a day out of bed. After the first few days, I pretty much felt like shit whenever I was awake. My appetite was just about gone, my strength dwindling, and I was getting dizzy more easily than before. While Alter had originally given me a month, I honestly wasn't sure I would make it that far.

"You should be resting, kid," Keep said as I made my way into the lab, keeping a hand on the glass walls just in case I lost my balance.

"I can't stay in bed all the time," I replied. This had quickly become our typical greeting. "Any progress?"

Keep shook his head, expression dimming. "The usual."

Which meant David was still working hard on solving the mystery but had yet to come up with a breakthrough. He had progressed to a certain point with the sigils, even going so far as to create an enhanced *calm* sigil that his simulations suggested would pretty much kill any living organism by stopping all of its bodily functions. The accidentally offensive potential of the sigil had caused Keep to gloat over his apparently correct belief that David's work was too dangerous to allow to continue. Except he allowed it because without it I would die, and he needed me in the fight. I wasn't so sure anymore that was the only reason. He seemed sincerely worried about me whenever I hobbled into the lab.

Anyway, calmed-to-death, as David called it, seemed more dangerous than it probably was. After all, Shaq could do the same thing naturally.

"Clock's ticking," I said, falling into the closest seat. We were in the first of the glass-partitioned rooms, David hunched behind the terminal, staring at the display and occasionally scribbling something onto the same slab that held the Grimoire. Having watched him work a few times, it was probably another equation or a value for a variable. When he said he was close, I think we all thought he would solve the puzzle in a day or two.

That was ten days ago.

"Good news," Keep said, "is that Gia's made progress on identifying who built the blueburn's hull. According to her search algorithm, the tolerances suggest it's a modified version of an SR-90 Star Racer."

"Star Racer?"

Keep smiled. "Oh, you haven't seen the star races yet. You'd actually make a good racer pilot. It's pretty much what it sounds like, except there's a set course and obstacles along the way. Not that unlike what we went through getting here. Racers are faster and more agile than most ships."

"And we needed an algorithm to make that guess?"

He chuckled. "Racers are also about a quarter of the size of the blueburn. I probably should have said custom built instead of modified. They used the same basic principles and Gia thinks only an experienced racer builder could have made the ship." He shrugged. "But what do I know? Any ship that gets me where I need to be is a good ship. Bad news for our lollipop queen, though. The Royals traced her traffic redirection trick back to her servers. They don't think she's responsible yet, but they're trying to get in touch with her to ask some questions. And they want physical access to her systems to investigate. Obviously, she can't do either of those things from here, which only makes her look more guilty."

"And she did that for us," I said. "She's giving up a lot."

"For you," he corrected. "Because she cares about you. All of us do."

"You included?"

"You've always been something special to me, kid."

"And you always answer similar questions with a generalized statement that could have multiple meanings, depending on the context in which you made it."

"Bingo."

"So you think Gia will get us a lead without David's help?" I asked, not pressing him for a direct answer I knew he would never give.

"Sure seems that way. You may need to make a choice, Bennie."

"What choice?"

"You have a few options. We could pack up early to go after her lead while David keeps working on *Head Case* and hope for the best. Or Matt could take the others and head off in that direction while we stay behind. Or we could all continue waiting."

"Matt's in charge when we're not on the ship," I said. "That would be his call."

Keep laughed. "Since when is Mattie in charge of anything? The crew follows him when you do, but if you ever countered him they'd all fall in line behind you and leave him sitting wherever with his thumb up his butt. It's not his fault. Don't tell him I said this, but he's got a lot of great qualities, especially with a rifle in his hands. But he ain't you, kid. Like I said, you're something special."

I leaned back in the chair, putting my hand over my mouth to cough and doing my best to ignore the burning in my lungs and the blurriness in my vision. "I'd choose the first option. I don't want us to split up. And if we have a chance to catch up to Prince Hiro, we need to take it, even if it costs me my life."

He smiled, his voice more serious. "I knew you'd say that. You've grown up a ton since we were stuck in Sedaya's dungeon together, Ben. Honestly, no matter what happens, it's a privilege to know you."

The statement caught me off-guard, enough so that tears welled into my eyes in response to his kindness. Subconsciously, a part of me had come to see him as the father I never had growing up, and his acceptance and friendship meant more to me than I knew how to express.

David burst into the room anyway, before I could reciprocate. "Hey Ben," he said offhandedly, focusing on Keep. "Mr. Keep, you need to see this."

CHAPTER 34

Keep and I followed David back to his workstation. He had set up his laptop on one corner of the table. A wire that Alter had made connected it to the network interface for the station's mainframe, allowing him to run his simulations and calculations. I expected to see his software up on the display, showing the sigil he was working on that he hoped would be the equivalent of *purify*. Essentially, a passive sigil that would return my cells to their natural, unmutated state. I knew it built on the lines used for *calm*, which is how he came up with *calmed-to-death*. But of course, it wasn't that simple. Not that any sigil was simple.

There was no sigil on the screen. No running simulation of the possible effect of the action. Instead, a slightly heavyset woman with dark olive skin and dark hair stood frozen on the screen. The same lab we were standing in was in the background.

"Priya," Keep whispered beside me, his huge bag of emotions giving off a charge that brought goosebumps to my skin. "Where—"

"I needed a break from the equations," David said. "So I started digging around in the station mainframe. I know you said everything was erased, but on Earth, data that's wiped is sometimes still recoverable. I thought maybe if I could get back some of what was lost, it would give me a clue to what I was missing. Especially the *restore* sigil your wife gave you."

"The data was supposed to be encrypted and then wiped," Keep said, looking at him. "How did you recover this?"

"That's the thing. I didn't. I found it hidden with the operating system files. Oh, yeah, I did root the OS. I can't believe you're still using Linux all these years later."

"David, you could have crashed the entire mainframe," I said.

He smiled and shrugged. "It wouldn't be the first time."

"You do realize the mainframe controls life support, right? Our air supply? Keeping the airlocks sealed so outer space doesn't come in?"

The smile vanished, face paling. "Uh. I wasn't thinking about that. I should probably back out—"

"No," Keep snapped. "You didn't break anything."

"Yet," I said.

"I won't touch it anymore," David said. "I promise."

"She left a video for me," Keep said. I had never seen the expression he wore before. He looked like he had just been kissed for the first time. "Play it."

"I already did. She says—"

"Play it," Keep repeated more forcefully.

"Sure," David replied, tapping the enter key on his laptop.

"This is a message for my husband, Orban Card. If you aren't Orban, you might be watching this hoping for some clue or information about this place or about my work. You won't get that here. What you will find instead is something much too lacking in the Hegemony right now. Love. More specifically, the love of a wife for her husband, even though that husband is on the opposing side in a war that never should have happened. A war whose foundation is built upon technology that never should have existed, and has no place in this universe or any other. I'm responsible for creating some of this technology, and now I'm also responsible for helping to destroy it. You won't find any of the answers you seek here."

Her expression and voice softened, her eyes latching onto the camera as though she were looking her husband, whom she called Orban instead of Avelus, in the eyes. "Orban, I don't know how many years may have passed before you returned to this place. I don't know what trials you've endured as a result of the experiments we undertook together. I know you never wanted us to be parted and you always hoped we would find our way back together one day. No matter what has become of me, today is that day when we are reunited, in spirit if not in physical manifestation."

She paused, eyes welling with tears. "Whatever has happened to you, I always knew you would return one day. I always knew you would see this. I want you to know that I'm sorry for the burden I placed upon you. For the lives we were forced to live. My entire life has been a series of mistakes, taking something beautiful and making it into something grotesque. I've spent all of our last days apart fearing I've done the same to the only thing that has truly ever made me happy and whole. You. By your return, I know you haven't forgotten me. I know you still care for me. And I beg your forgiveness for the decisions we made.

"Just standing here, thinking about you seeing me again, as you last knew me, brings me a joy I can't describe. As you've heard me say so many times, all of the energy in all of the universes is connected, which means even in death we are connected. If you feel the same joy that I do, wherever my energy is, I will feel it. I will know you. And when your journey at last comes to an end, I will be here waiting. I love you eternally, my darling husband."

The video stopped on a frame of her smiling brightly at the camera, moist eyes filled with emotion. Glancing at Keep, I could tell he was struggling to keep his own emotions in check.

David sighed. "That is so touching. I almost cried the first time I watched it, and look at me." He wiped his eyes with his shirt. "Waterworks now. Damn."

"Could you shut up?" Keep growled. "I'm having a moment."

"A beautiful moment," David agreed. "It kind of makes everything I went through to be here worthwhile."

"David!" I snapped.

"Sorry. I talk when I'm emotionally uncomfortable." He clamped his lips together and wiped his eyes again. Keep just stared at the last frame of the recording, tears running down his cheeks. I'd never seen him cry before. Not even a hint. He stayed that way for nearly a minute.

"Can you copy that to *Head Case's* datastore?" he asked.

"Sure," David replied.

"Are you okay?" I asked Keep.

He nodded. "Better than ever, kid."

"I guess your real name is Orban? Orban Card? Not Avelus Keep?"

"When you're a thousand years old, you need to keep reinventing yourself. Otherwise people get suspicious. I've had plenty of names before Keep. But my given name is Orban Card."

"It's too bad she didn't leave us anything we can use," David said. "Like her equations for *restore*. That would have been helpful." Keep glared at him. "Right. I don't mean it like that. You know, I'm just saying."

"Some things are more important than sigils," I said.

"Some things are more important than life. You're lucky you got to have that."

"Exactamundo," Keep replied. "I am lucky. Luckier than I even knew."

"That's all I found," David said. "I'll get out of the operating system now before I kill all of us."

"Wait," Keep said, eyebrows crinkling in thought.

"Why?" David replied.

"Maybe she did leave us something more that we can use."

"I heard the message twice, Mr. Keep. It's very emotional. No math whatsoever."

"All of the energy in all of the universes is connected, which means even in death we are connected," he answered. "You told me the base sigil is used to allow the catalyst to draw in energy. Every sigil contains that simple geometry."

"Sometimes it's more hidden, but yeah. So?"

"So take what I just said and turn it into a sigiltech equation."

David raised an eyebrow. "But she said death. We want the opposite."

"Do we? How far has that gotten you?"

David shook his head. "How could your wife leave a message for you a thousand years ago that's relevant to our specific situation today? That's impossible."

"She didn't. She left me a clue on how to reverse the sigil she put in my head. A way to end the *restore* so I could die naturally. You're already close with *calmed-to-death*. Let's call the target sigil *decay*. If you can reverse that, then you're back at *restore*. Badabing badaboom."

"It doesn't exactly work like that."

"But it's something, isn't it?"

"Yeah, it's something. But how would your wife know

that you would know that's a clue? Or that you would be able to make a new sigil?"

"Why else would I come back here? To reminisce about her untimely demise?" He smiled. "She thought I would come back here to die. She was trying to offer me a softer way out. I'm sure of it."

David shrugged. "If you say so. I mean, I can try it. It's not like I've had so much success with the path I've been on." He looked at me. "But if it doesn't work, I might not be able to backtrack in time to save your life."

I looked from him to Keep, meeting his gaze. I could see the resolve in his eyes, certain that was the message she was trying to send. It was hard for me to wrap my mind around, but I'd never loved anyone the way she seemed to love him. So what did I know?

"Do it," I said with equal conviction, recovering much of the hope I had lost over the last week in a single moment.

"Doing it," David replied with a smile, switching back into his simulator.

I clapped my hand on his shoulder. "You're going to do this, David. I know it."

"Thanks for the vote of support, Ben. I *am* going to do this."

The main door to the lab slid open and Matt walked in. His expression was a sharp contrast to mine, as down as I had ever seen on him. He spotted me and hurried over, nearly colliding with the glass door in his impatience for it to open.

"Ben," he said.

"Matt, what's up?"

"We have a problem."

"No, we have a possible solution," I countered. "David and Keep think they've figured out how to get to a sigil that'll help me."

"That's great, man. But it doesn't solve our problem. It actually makes it worse."

"What do you mean?"

"Zar, Druck, and I finished cleaning everything else, so we figured we'd check in on Storage. Keep, you said there should be catalyst, or materials for catalyst in there, right?"

"Yeppers," Keep answered. "More than enough to make one sigil."

Matt was already shaking his head. "The storage room is empty. Cleaned out."

"What?"

"My thought exactly. Is it possible the scientists took it with them when they left the station?"

"Nope. They left cups of coffee on their desks, they didn't stick around to load heavy metal into their escape craft."

"Then where did the catalyst go?" I asked.

Keep stared at me, dumbfounded. "I have no idea, kid. At all. Did you check the assembler?"

"Quasar's checking it now," Matt said.

As if on cue, the lab door opened again. Quasar and Druck hurried in, Shaq on Zar's shoulder. She shook her head emphatically, indicating the assembler was also empty.

"Shit," Keep seethed in a rare display of frustration. "How the hell can this be possible?"

My stomach sank, and I slumped to a sitting position on top of the table, lowering my head into my hand. A major potential breakthrough, and then this? It was so damn unfair.

"Are you totally sure those were Royal Guard drones out there?" Matt asked. "Because it sure seems like someone else was here."

"That's impossible."

"And yet, all the catalyst is gone."

Keep shook his head. "Then it doesn't matter if we come up with the sigil. Without catalyst, we're done."

"Maybe we can find some," Quasar said.

"And how do you propose doing that?"

"I don't know. We should have checked Storage as soon as we got here."

"There was no reason to think it would be empty," Keep replied defensively. "Who could have known this place existed, let alone found it, got inside, and took all the catalyst without disturbing anything or leaving a trace?"

"One name comes to my mind," Matt said.

"Begins with suck and ends with ass?" Druck asked.

"Yeah. He seems to know quite a bit. Maybe as much if not more than you do, Keep. And we did take the catalyst materials he collected on Earth out of play."

"I can't even begin to tell you how bad it would be if you're right," Keep said. "Not only can he make a shipload of sigiltech devices, but the fact that he didn't stick around to use the assembler means he likely has one of his own."

"There's no material for Ben," Matt snapped. "That's as bad as it gets."

We fell into a tense, brooding silence. I closed my eyes, coughed a few times, and otherwise felt like I was ready to die right now so I wouldn't have to go through another round of disappointment. Finally, I let loose a resigned exhale and lifted my head. The fates had already decided I was meant to die. I couldn't fight it anymore. "It's over, crew. I'm sorry you wasted your energy unpacking. It's time to pack it back up and move on."

CHAPTER 35

The others stayed behind in the lab to vent their frustrations, argue whether or not we should leave, and otherwise bicker back and forth in a way they had rarely done before. They all knew what it meant for us to give up here, though the reasons for their upset varied. I was sure Gia would have a couple of cents to add for herself once she heard the news. Keep had said the crew would do whatever I asked them to, but they didn't even notice when I left.

Shaq stayed with me as I made the walk from the lab to the hangar, pausing a couple of times to cough and steady myself. After Matt, I would miss him the most. Though we could barely communicate, he was always there for me, offering a nuzzle to my neck or just perching on my shoulder, ready to defend me from any threat we faced no matter how dangerous. We didn't need a lot of words to be close.

"Ben, is everything okay?" Matt asked over the comms, having finally realized I'd left.

"As good as it gets," I replied. "I just don't have the energy to listen to you all argue. It's not going to change anything anyway."

"We're going to figure something out. If Gia can track down another shipment from Sedaya, we might find some catalyst on board and—"

"Matt," I interrupted. "I know you want to save me, and I appreciate the hell out of it. But I can tell I don't have any time left. I'm done."

"I don't accept that."

"And you won't, even after I'm gone. I wouldn't if the situation was flipped. But that doesn't change anything."

"Keep said we should be able to modify the assembler to break down his sleeve and reassemble it with new sigils. Because of the sickness, he'd need to use the sigil on you to have an effect, but it could work as a short term fix."

I should have felt hopeful about that idea, but my heart just wasn't in it. "I don't want a hack or a patch to stay alive. I just want to accept it at this point. I want to be able to make peace with the fact that I'm going to die instead of fighting it forever. I know that's not what you want to hear from me, but I need your support."

"I want to support you, Ben. I do. But we're still brainstorming. I'll let you know."

I sighed. "Okay. I'm going to shut my comms off so I can rest. We can talk later." I turned off the comm and sighed again.

"Are you okay?" Shaq buzzed.

"I don't know what I am right now, bud. Too many conflicting emotions."

I couldn't understand his response. That he didn't offer platitudes meant a lot to me. "I'm sorry I won't have a chance to learn your language."

"Me too," he buzzed back. Out of everyone, he seemed to be the only one who accepted my decision with grace. Who wasn't in denial about the fate that waited for me sooner than I wanted to admit.

"You're going to keep an eye on Matt for me though, right?"

"Mmm--hmmm." He said more, buzzing out one of the longest diatribes I had heard from him. He knew I wouldn't understand, but it seemed like something he really wanted to say, and when he finished he pressed himself tighter against my neck, emitting a high-pitched buzz that I took as sobbing. The mournful sound brought tears to my eyes too, and I rested my hand over his warm, soft body, appreciating the moment.

Reaching the hangar, I came to a stop in front of *Head Case*, looking up at the ship. The ears were in rough shape, but the rest of the spaceship looked just like it had the first time I saw it. It had only been a couple of months, but right now it felt like my entire lifetime.

"We had a pretty good run, didn't we?" I said, placing my palm against the ship's skin, twisting my mouth to mimic its open grin. I laughed at the stupidity of it before ascending the ramp into the hangar. My heart ached as I made my way to the elevator. Not that any of this had been easy, but I was already missing it.

I stopped in the lounge to sit while I waited for a bout of dizziness to subside. From there, I headed to my room, plopping down at the edge of my bed. Shaq jumped off my shoulder and sat beside me, his quizzical look bringing a smile to my face.

"I know it's not intentional, but you look so damn cute like that," I said.

"Shut up," he buzzed, embarrassed.

We both laughed.

I glanced at my nightstand, gaze lingering before I pulled open the drawer to reveal Bill and George's gift. Just in case. In case of failure? In case of death? I never really knew what that meant. I had probably thought about it a lot more than the two men had ever intended or considered

I might. They were both surprised I hadn't already opened it. What had I been saving it for, anyway? Maybe the gift itself meant more to me than the contents. So much that I didn't want to ruin the idea of the present with the outcome of whatever waited inside.

Picking it up, I looked at Shaq. "What do you think, bud? Should I open it?"

"Mmm-hmmm," he buzzed emphatically.

"Okay," I agreed. I removed the tag and pulled the ribbon to untie it.

"Seriously?" Shaq buzzed in response to my fastidiousness.

"Yeah, you're right," I agreed, smiling as I tore off the wrapping paper like it was Christmas morning, revealing a child's shoe box underneath. I was pretty sure George hadn't given me a pair of Kyrie's shoes. I grabbed the lid and lifted it off, staring down at the contents.

Shaq let out a shrill buzz and began bounding around my bed excitedly, as if he had a case of the zoomies. Fresh tears sprang to my eyes, only this time they weren't out of sad hopelessness.

A small chunk of rock the size of a golf ball rested on top of a bunch of newspaper and cotton balls stuffed into the box. A golden color with flecks of silver and black, I recognized it right away. We had thrown all of it out of the back of the Humvee at Alonzo Dellaqua's processing facility.

Or so I had thought.

My hands shook as I reached for a note folded beside it. Shaq returned to my shoulder to read as I unfolded the paper.

Ben,

We don't know if this will be useful to you at some point in the future. All we know is that it seemed valuable even though Avelus didn't want you to have it, so we had to make it a little less obvious that we kept a small piece (George shoved it in his pocket when you emptied out the Hummer. LOL). If nothing else, you can use it as a paperweight (do they even have paper in the Spiral?) or just a little tchotchke to remember us by. Anyways, best of luck on your adventures. We hope to see you again sometime. You'll always be welcome at either of our farms.

Best wishes,

The Frasiers and the Ackermanns.

I glanced at Shaq, face moist. "They have no idea what they just did."

He buzzed back something that sounded like, "you should have opened it sooner, dummy." But maybe that was just my translation given the situation.

I turned my comms back on. "Keep, Matt."

"Ben," Matt replied, concerned. "What's wrong?"

"Nothing. I'm fine. Better than fine." I started laughing. "You're never going to believe this."

CHAPTER 36

Thanks to Bill and George, we didn't pack up. Instead, we doubled-down. All of our focus turned to providing Keep and David anything and everything they needed so they could keep working on the sigils. Somebody was always on gopher duty, ready to provide them with coffee, snacks, meals, or whatever else they might request.

Meanwhile, Gia announced she had compiled a list of four companies she believed might have constructed the blueburn. Intriguingly, one of them was under Sedaya's flag and two were in Nobukku's territory. The last had a manufacturing facility on America, the third settled world in the Hegemony which sat within the Empress' immediate sphere of influence and direct rule.

I didn't really see most of the developments that followed my reveal of the catalyst material Bill and George had gifted me. Cancer was like a snowball, and now that it had built momentum it sent me downhill at an ever increasing pace. I spent most of my time *calmed* to sleep. Keep slowed the runaway train as best he could while he and David raced the clock.

"Ben," Matt said, shaking me out of my unnatural slumber. "Ben. Wake up."

I looked up at him. He had a huge grin on his face. In fact, I don't think I'd ever seen him happier. "What's going on?" I asked, getting excited for what I expected he might say.

"He did it," Matt answered with a laugh. "David actually did it."

"What?" I said, practically jumping out of bed. "Are you serious?"

"That's what he said. As long as the simulation's good, he found a solution."

I knew all of his test simulations had been accurate to date. Using the symbols we knew against his program, they had all output the desired effects. The whole idea of testing a sigil seemed so crazy, but then again, that was the difference between magic and technology. One could be described by equations and proofs. The other wasn't real.

"Why are we standing here then?" I asked. "Let's go."

I tried to hurry away from the bed, forgetting my shoes in the process. The room started spinning, and Matt caught me before I fell flat on my face.

"Whoa, not so fast," he said, easily holding me up. Two weeks since we had arrived on Omega Station, and I had lost all of the muscle it took me two months to gain and then some. "Keep's running your catalyst material through the assembler. He said that'll take a little while. Alter's working on an interface so David can upload the sigil to the etcher from his laptop."

A chill ran through me with his mention of the etcher. Standard sigils were etched into catalyst material by the assembler during their construction, outputting a full device. Gilding was different. Instead of producing a functional piece, the assembler would provide a liquified catalyst composed primarily of the chunk of ore combined with some other minerals we had fortunately been able to scrounge up from other places, palladium from one of *Head Case's* turret controllers, for example. That molten gold would be loaded into the etcher, which turned out to be a component of the dentist's chair in the lab. The sigil—or sigils, in the case of a full Gilded—would be loaded into the machine and a robotic arm would get to work making precise cuts in the subject's flesh to create the sigils, injecting the catalyst behind it

Most importantly for a passive sigil, the catalyst had to go deep to reach enough blood supply to power it continuously. And any kind of anesthetic or even *calming* could mess with the outcome. In other words, I was going to feel every single slice, plus the hot metal pouring into the wound. As I had seen on Alonzo Dellaqua, those cuts could be overlapped to use the same lines for multiple sigils in what Keep had called a construct. That would reduce the overall pain, but was small comfort.

That it might save my life was pretty motivating, at least. "No pain, no gain, right?"

"Right," Matt agreed.

I put on my shoes and let him support me as we made our way from my small room in the station's living area to the lab. David jumped up from his workspace when he saw me enter, running over to me as Matt and I approached him.

"I told you I would do it, and I did it," he said excitedly. "Nailed that son of a bitch!"

"I knew you would," I replied, matching his enthusiasm as I clamped my hand on his shoulder and gave him a small shake to show my appreciation. "I only doubted you for a few seconds."

He laughed and waved me toward his setup. "Let me show you."

Mechanic Alter crouched between his desk and a

cabinet next to the dentist chair, rigging a wire between his laptop and the box. She didn't look up at me when I entered the room. I shuddered at the chair as we passed it before turning my attention to his screen. The sigil's shape didn't mean a whole lot to me, but it was more intricate than any of the others I had seen.

"Pretty cool, huh?" David said. "Do you recognize it?"

"Should I?"

"Looks kind of like an ocean wave," Matt said.

"Close. It's a dragon curve. From chaos theory. Only I invented this specific type myself. Well, actually the equations for the sigil effect dictated the shape but, you know, I came up with it so it was me."

"This is *restore*?" I asked.

"Pretty much," David replied. "I don't know if it's the same *restore* Keep has but it does the same thing."

"And it'll cure my cancer."

"It should, yeah. I mean, ideally we'd build an extension to my software to run it against models of your cells and all that, but we don't have three years. And also, your blood is atypical and doesn't match anything I'm running the simulation against so there's that too. It's the best chance you have, but it's still fifty-fifty that it'll kill you."

"I'm willing to take that risk," I said.

"I figured you would be." He leaned over the table to look at Alter. "How much longer do you think you need?"

"Almost done," she replied without looking at him. An array of tools were spread out at her feet. She dropped one and picked up another, crimping the wires. "Few more minutes."

"That'll give Avelus time to finish assembling the catalyst," David said. He motioned to the dentist chair. "Feel free to sit. Did you decide where you want it?"

"How big will it be on my skin?"

"About six inches by two inches. Orientation doesn't matter."

"I was thinking my back would be the best spot then."

"Sounds good to me. You'll need to take off your shirt."

I nodded, pulling it off and falling into the dentist chair as another wave of dizziness hit me.

"Man, you lost a lot more weight than I realized," Matt said on seeing me shirtless.

"I can gain it back if this works," I replied.

"Done," Alter announced, standing up. "See if you can connect."

"Etcher-921?" David asked.

"That's it."

"Yeah, I've got a link. I'm uploading now."

The main lab door parted again. Keep entered the area, a large vial of liquid gold in hand. He smiled when he saw me, picking up his pace to get to our part of the facility.

"Here we go, kid," he said. "Enough Gilded catalyst for one person. Badabing badaboom."

"If you had known Bill and George took the chunk, would you have made them throw it away?" I asked.

He shrugged. "I plead the fifth. I'm just glad they kept it a secret from me. That's all I'll say." He went around the back of the chair and opened a panel on the side of the etcher to push the vial in place. "Catalyst juice locked and loaded."

"The upload's nearly finished. Ben, this is extremely important. Once I start the etcher, you can't move under any circumstances. If the lines are wrong or incomplete, there's no telling what might happen. Best case, you die quickly. Got it?"

"Got it," I replied, sitting back in the chair. Clamps on the arms, legs and headrest would keep me mostly pinned once they were locked.

My heart pounded with anticipation, a grin crossing my

face. After everything we had gone through to get to this point, I still couldn't believe it was about to happen.

"Upload complete." David announced. Standing over his laptop, his hand lowered toward the enter key as if it were moving in slow motion. "And here. We. G—"

I didn't hear the last part. Klaxons hidden in the walls began screaming, instantly drowning him out. The overhead lights changed from white to red, flashing furiously.

What the hell was going on?

CHAPTER 37

"Ben, Matt!" Gia cried through the comms, her voice nearly lost in the noise from the security alert. "I'm not sure who's doing it, but the outer hangar bay doors are opening."

I put my hand over my eyes. Between the klaxons and flashing lights, I thought I might have a seizure.

"It sounds like we're going to have company," Matt replied over the din. "Zar, Druck, meet me in the corridor leading to the hangar. Bring your guns. And Shaq."

"Copy that," Quasar replied. "We're on our way."

"It has to be Sedaya," Keep said. "Or Sucaath. Whoever it is, they're using sigiltech to pry the doors open."

"Just great," I groaned. "Could their timing get any better?"

"Alter, Keep, come on," Matt said. "Ben, David, wait here."

"I'm not waiting here if we're about to be attacked," I said.

"What are you going to do? Cough on them?"

I hated to admit it, but he had a point. "David, how long will it take to etch the sigil?"

"An hour at least," David answered.

Too long for me to be able to help. Too long to risk even starting. "I'm not completely useless," I said, reaching into my pocket. Pulling out my phone, I tapped my way into *Head Case's* remote operations. I could still help defend the station with the ship.

"We'll be back before you know it, kid," Keep said, joining Matt and Alter as they rushed out the door.

I focused my attention on my phone's screen, using my thumbs to adjust my view through *Head Case's* cameras. I watched the hangar bay doors spread apart against their will, the same way Keep had done it to get us here. Looking past the slabs of metal, I spotted the interloping ship hanging above the entrance to the station. My blood ran cold.

"Shit," I cursed through the comms, heart pounding. "It's *Dominator*."

"What?" Matt hissed back. "You've got to be kidding me. How the hell did they find us here?"

The large sigiltech ship obviously hadn't been destroyed by Archie's candy bomb. It loomed over the station's hangar, the lines of its sigils glowing softly. Whenever an asteroid appeared ready to collide with *Dominator* it changed course suddenly, *reflected* away from the ship.

This was bad. Very, very bad.

A smaller landing craft swept in front of *Dominator*. The size of a school bus, angled and menacing in appearance but visibly unarmed, it vectored toward the hangar. I tapped on the screen, activating the fire control system. I wasn't about to let the ship inside without a fight.

"Matt, we're in the corridor," Quasar reported.

"We're almost there," he replied.

"I've got the landing craft in my sights," I said as the turrets swiveled toward the incoming target. "Firing."

I hit the trigger button.

Nothing happened.

What the hell?

I knew Alter had scavenged some of the parts of one of the turret controllers to help make the catalyst. I didn't expect that gun to work. But the rest of them should have fired. I hit the trigger button again. Same result.

"Something's wrong," I said as the landing ship reached the hangar doors. "The guns aren't working."

"Check the diagnostics," Alter suggested.

"There's no time. They're about to touch down." I resisted the urge to hurl my phone against the glass wall of the room, settling for punching the arm of the chair instead. "Damn it, damn it, damn it!"

"We need to cut them off," Matt said. "Let's go."

I couldn't see Team Hondo, but I imagined them running to the blast doors leading into the hangar, waiting for the bay doors to close and the atmosphere to pour back into the space. It wouldn't take long. The outer doors were already sliding shut again, the landing craft safely inside. Its skids hit the deck, and it too remained static, waiting for air.

"Gia, can you prevent the system from refilling the hangar?" I asked.

"Of course," she replied.

"Hold that thought," Keep barked. "They just forced open the hangar bay doors. You don't think they can open the other doors and vent this whole place while they're nice and cozy in their ship?"

"What are we supposed to do?" I asked.

"Not that," he answered.

"If they can do that, why haven't they already?" Matt asked.

"Why do you think, Sherlock? They want at least one of us alive. And I'll make you a million dollar bet I know who."

I turned my head, eyes landing on David.

"What?" he asked, unable to hear the conversation over our embedded comms. "Why are you looking at me like that?"

"I think your mother sent word to Sucaath that we had you, and he passed it on to Sedaya," I explained. "And he sent his goons to pick you up."

David's face paled. "You're kidding."

"I wish I was."

I could tell by his expression he was thinking hard about what I had just said. Working through the problem like he had the sigils. "It doesn't make sense. Can it be a coincidence they showed up right after I solved your sigil?

I kept staring at him, shaking my head. Sedaya probably wouldn't mind eternal youth like Keep, but I doubted *restore* was his primary goal. "No, it would have taken him time to get here. Not *restore*." Fear sent a shiver across my body. "*Calmed-to-death.* You proved you can create new offensive sigils. He wants you to make more for him." A second wave of fear shot through me. "He waited for you to advance your work. Which means—"

"We have a spy in our midst," David finished.

"Gia," I said, struggling to accept what I knew had to be true "What did you do?"

"What?" she replied. "Ben, it wasn't me."

"Bullshit," I shouted back. "You're the only one with a network link. The only one with the means and opportunity to communicate with Sedaya from here."

"No. I swear—"

"You played me so perfectly with your sob story about how Sedaya killed your parents and you went through so much trouble to get your revenge. Is your algorithm even real or was this whole thing a setup?"

"How could that be? I led you to the space dock. I gave you the evidence—"

"How did *Dominator* get away from the explosion? Why didn't the Empress accept the evidence we provided? You knew she wouldn't."

"No," she insisted. "I…"

"None of this matters right now," Matt growled. "The air's pumping back into the hangar."

"Gia, where are you?" I seethed.

"The command center," she replied. "Ben, I didn't do this. I'm innocent."

"That's what they all say," I growled back. "We'll deal with you later."

"Team Hondo, we're going in," Matt said.

I looked down at my phone, switching my view so I could see the landing ship and the inner hangar door at the same time. The ship's ramp had already lowered as the door slid open and Matt and the others moved in, rifles up and ready for whoever came into view. Keep had put on the sigiltech glove, and both it and his sleeve were already glowing.

A pair of feet appeared on the ramp, connected to lithe, bare legs that flowed into a knee-length pencil skirt, which connected to a dark, short-sleeved jacket with a nehru collar. The woman's face was narrow and pointed, her eyes sharp, her hair short. She didn't seem bothered by the guns aimed in her direction, or Shaq bunched on Quasar's shoulder, ready to strike. She reached the bottom of the ramp and came to a stop.

"Who the hell are you?" Matt asked.

"My name is Admiral Lyke," she replied. "I'm here on behalf of Duke Sedaya. He's interested in making a trade."

"He couldn't be bothered to come himself?"

"He has other important duties," Lyke replied. "And I'm quite certain we can come to an agreement without his personal attendance. I have full autonomy regarding the negotiations."

"And what is it you want to trade?"

"Simple enough. You give us David, and we spare your lives."

Matt laughed. "Did you practice that beforehand? A cliche line gets a cliche response. Go to hell."

"There's no need to be brash, Matthew," Lyke said. "You wrang what you needed out of him. Now it's our turn."

"Except we're not using him. We're his friends. Something you and Sedaya probably don't understand the meaning of."

"Oh, we understand the meaning all too well," she replied. "We both know that friendship creates weakness. Otherwise, I wouldn't be here."

"Yeah, you managed to plant a spy among us. Congratulations. Why don't you march back up that ramp into your ship and go home?"

She was kind of pretty when she smiled, in a Stepford Wives way. "I'll be leaving with David one way or another. I strongly recommend that you accept my offer. If you make me go through you, I promise that you *will* suffer before you die."

"That doesn't seem like much of a negotiation to me," Keep said. "You're supposed to make an offer. We make a counteroffer. So on and so forth. Then we come to an agreement. Badabing badaboom."

"Fine, Avelus. You caught me. It's not a negotiation. It's an ultimatum. By the way, you'll suffer the most. Duke Sedaya is very unhappy with you."

"Good."

"You're going to get through all of us?" Druck barked. He shifted his head around, trying to look past her. "You and what army?"

"I don't need an army," she answered. "I have something better."

"Gilded, am I right?" Keep said.

"You aren't wrong," Lyke agreed, raising her hand. All of Team Hondo's guns were yanked from their hands before they could react.

Keep raised the glove and thrust it toward her, but she flicked her other hand as if she were swatting a gnat, seeming to knock aside whatever effect he was going for.

"I'm not my second-in-command, Avelus," she said. "I've been doing this for a long time. Not as long as you, of course. But long enough." She flicked her finger, and Keep launched into the bulkhead, hitting hard enough that he didn't get back up.

"No!" I shouted. "I have to go help them." I tried to stand up. My legs buckled, and I fell back into the chair.

The others were able to do what I couldn't. Even without weapons, even though they probably didn't stand much of a chance against Lyke, they still charged, trying to bum rush her before she could turn her sigils on them. Druck slid a knife from a sheath on his thigh and whipped it forward, and Shaq launched from Quasar's shoulder behind it.

Lyke raised her hand toward the blade and it quickly melted, superheated steel splashing onto the deck, leaving a smoking puddle at Matt's feet. He would have stepped right into it, but somehow Keep managed to push him aside, sending him tumbling.

Shaq got within inches of Lyke's face before he was pulled upward, lifted toward the overhead hangar doors and pinned there, buzzing and squirming in a futile effort to break free. Lyke caught Druck and Quasar in the same grip, yanking them to the deck and holding them there.

A flash of energy caught her in the shoulder, and she cried out but didn't lose her concentration, keeping her hold on the others while ripping the blaster from Matt's hands before pinning him too.

"Lyke!" Keep shouted, back on his feet and limping

toward her, his leg probably broken. His glove and sleeve both glowed brightly, ready to give everything he had to keep the woman from getting to David.

"Hey Ben," David said, watching the fight unfold over my shoulder. "Where's Alter?"

CHAPTER 38

I was so busy watching the action, I hadn't even realized Alter wasn't part of it until David pointed it out. Quickly scanning the hangar, I didn't see any sign of her.

"Maybe she ducked into *Head Case*," I said. "If she fixes the ion cannons, Admiral Lyke is toast."

Keep continued limping toward Lyke, who let him approach with a smug expression on her no-longer-pretty face. The others were all down, or up in Shaq's case, held in place in the same manner I imagined Commander Kray had done on the cargo ship. They had given their all, but they were no match for a Gilded, especially this one. Despite Keep's desire, I knew he would lose too. Just like he had lost to Kray.

"Alter, did you get it yet?" I asked, firm in my belief she had snuck into *Head Case* to fix the guns. "We're running out of time."

"Correction," Alter said. But not over the comms. My head whipped up from my phone, finding her just outside the room. What was she doing here? "You are out of time."

"What are you doing here?" I asked. "You should be in the hangar, helping the others."

"Now why would I want to do that?" she replied. She entered the room, eyes fixed on David. "You're coming with me."

"What?" David answered. "Coming with you where?"

"Alter!" I snapped. "What's the matter with you?"

"Nothing," she replied. "Never been better. I'm especially enjoying this part." She thrust a finger toward David. "You. Grab your laptop and let's go. Now." I tried to stand up again. Her hand lashed out, shoving me back into the chair. "Seriously Ben? You're so sick you can barely stand. And you're going to stop me? You don't have any catalyst on you."

I stared at her, frightened and confused. Of all my crew, only Matt had more of my trust than she did. And now she was betraying me?

"Why?" I asked as she rounded on David, ready to force him into compliance. She glanced my way.

"Because I am not who you think I am," she replied. The answer sent shockwaves of cold through my body, and I started coughing again. She grabbed David and threw him against the table next to his laptop. "Don't make me hurt you, David. Because I will. The laptop is enough to satisfy Duke Sedaya."

"I can't believe you've been lying to us this entire time," I said. "How can that be? Twenty years on *Head Case* with Keep, and it was all bullshit?"

David grabbed his laptop, quickly pulling the makeshift wires from its ports. Alter crouched beside him and opened the side of the etcher, reaching in for the gold catalyst. "I might as well help myself to this, too. You can never have too much." She stood up and grabbed David's arm. "Are you done?" Pulling him roughly by the arm, she dragged him past me without answering my question.

"Alter!" I shouted between coughs. "Wait."

She turned back toward me, shaking her head. "It must

be the brain tumor," she said, her body changing form faster than I had ever seen before, growing and morphing into a specimen of a man, with short black hair and light gray eyes. "Alter's gone, Ben," he continued, smiling widely. "She made for a tasty snack, but now there's only me. I am Blorb."

"Your name is Blorb?" David said, as if he wasn't sure he had heard it right. Probably because it sounded ridiculous.

"Funny," Gia said as the doors to the lab slid open. "All I see is dead meat."

She had a rifle in her hands, and she opened fire, sending a burst of bolts into Blorb's face. They punched right through while I cringed and tried to shout. "Gia, the gut. Aim for the gut." I couldn't get my voice loud enough for her to hear.

Blorb tossed David aside like an old shoe. He changed into its natural form and rushed Gia. She was too slow to adjust her aim. Unlike Alter, Blorb's tentacles had barbs on the end. They whipped out toward Gia, lacerating her face and ripping into her body. She dropped beneath the onslaught, her demise over in seconds.

The Aleal regained its male form, turning back to David. "Let's go," he said again.

"Wh…what about Ben?" David asked.

I wanted to wring his neck. Was he asking this thing to kill me?

"He's already dead," Blorb replied. "And he'll spend however long he has left alone, with nothing to occupy his mind beyond knowing that everyone he cares about in this galaxy is suffering more than he is. And everyone he cares about back on Earth will join them soon enough." An impossibly wide smile split Blorb's face. "You never should have crossed the ruler of the Hegemony, Benjamin."

"He's not the Emperor yet," I replied, as if there was anything else I could do to stop him.

"No?" Blorb replied, morphing into a regal looking woman in a white gown. I recognized her immediately. The Empress Li'an.

Glancing down at my phone, I saw my crew floating behind Admiral Lyke, held in place by the sigils etched into her body. Keep among them. They vanished up the ramp into her ship.

"Poor Ben. All of your effort to stop us from ruling the Hegemony. And little did you know, you're already too late. Enjoy what's left of your life. I know I will." He grabbed David's arm again, dragging him out of the lab.

Leaving me there alone.

"Nooooo!" I shouted as loud as I could, forcing myself out of the chair. My legs refused to support me, and I fell forward onto my hands and knees. I didn't give up. I couldn't. I was on the verge of losing everything, and I wasn't ready to let it end like this.

We were so damn close.

I didn't move quickly, dragging along the deck, heart pounding so hard I could barely breathe. Every cough brought up blood, and I started seeing double, then triple, then too many copies of the room in front of me—along with Gia's ravaged body—to count.

I stopped fighting then, dropping onto my stomach and sobbing openly and loudly, not that anyone was around to hear it. Who was I kidding? We had never been close. Sedaya had been one step ahead of us from the beginning. All the way back to Gia's parents, murdered by a second Aleal. Alter was gone. Keep was gone. *Matt* was gone, along with Shaq and the others.

More importantly to the Hegemony and Earth, he had David, and with him access to new and terrifying sigils that, along with *Dominator,* would make him truly unstoppable.

It was over. We'd lost. The best I could hope for now was that I would die straight away, so that I wouldn't have time to drown in the truth of the pain to come for the people I loved the most. I closed my eyes.

If there was any mercy left in the universe I would never have to open them again.

Thank you so much for reading Blue Burn! I'm sorry. I know I left Ben in a bad state, but this isn't the end of the series! For more information on the next book, please visit mrforbes.com/starshipforsale6.

OTHER BOOKS BY M.R FORBES

Want more M.R. Forbes? Of course you do!
View my complete catalog here
mrforbes.com/books
Or on Amazon:
mrforbes.com/amazon

Forgotten (The Forgotten)
mrforbes.com/theforgotten
Complete series box set:
mrforbes.com/theforgottentrilogy

Some things are better off FORGOTTEN.

Sheriff Hayden Duke was born on the Pilgrim, and he expects to die on the Pilgrim, like his father, and his father before him.

That's the way things are on a generation starship centuries from home. He's never questioned it. Never thought about it. And why bother? Access points to the ship's controls are sealed, the systems that guide her automated and out of reach. It isn't perfect, but he has all he needs to be content.

Until a malfunction forces his wife to the edge of the habitable zone to inspect the damage.

Until she contacts him, breathless and terrified, to tell him she found a body, and it doesn't belong to anyone on board.

Until he arrives at the scene and discovers both his wife and the body are gone.

The only clue? A bloody handprint beneath a hatch that hasn't opened in hundreds of years.

Until now.

Earth Unknown (Forgotten Earth)
mrforbes.com/earthunknown

Centurion Space Force pilot Nathan Stacker didn't expect to return home to find his wife dead. He didn't expect the murderer to look just like him, and he definitely didn't expect to be the one to take the blame.

But his wife had control of a powerful secret. A secret that stretches across the light years between two worlds and could lead to the end of both.

Now that secret is in Nathan's hands, and he's about to make the most desperate evasive maneuver of his life -- stealing a starship and setting a course for Earth.

He thinks he'll be safe there.

He's wrong. Very wrong.

Earth is nothing like what he expected. Not even close. What he doesn't know is not only likely to kill him, it's eager to kill him, and even if it doesn't?

The Sheriff will.

Deliverance (Forgotten Colony)
mrforbes.com/deliverance
Complete series box set:

The war is over. Earth is lost. Running is the only option.

It may already be too late.

Caleb is a former Marine Raider and commander of the Vultures, a search and rescue team that's spent the last two years pulling high-value targets out of alien-ravaged cities and shipping them off-world.

When his new orders call for him to join forty-thousand survivors aboard the last starship out, he thinks his days of fighting are over. The Deliverance represents a fresh start and a chance to leave the war behind for good.

Except the war won't be as easy to escape as he thought.

And the colony will need a man like Caleb more than he ever imagined...

Starship Eternal (War Eternal)
mrforbes.com/starshipeternal
Complete series box set:
mrforbes.com/wareternalcomplete

A lost starship...

A dire warning from futures past...

A desperate search for salvation…

Captain Mitchell "Ares" Williams is a Space Marine and the hero of the Battle for Liberty, whose Shot Heard 'Round the Universe saved the planet from a nearly unstoppable war machine. He's handsome, charismatic, and the perfect poster boy to help the military drive enlistment. Pulled from the war and thrown into the spotlight, he's as efficient at charming the media and bedding beautiful celebrities as he was at shooting down enemy starfighters.

After an assassination attempt leaves Mitchell critically wounded, he begins to suffer from strange hallucinations that carry a chilling and oddly familiar warning:

They are coming. Find the Goliath or humankind will be destroyed.

Convinced that the visions are a side-effect of his injuries, he tries to ignore them, only to learn that he may not be as crazy as he thinks. The enemy is real and closer than he imagined, and they'll do whatever it takes to prevent him from rediscovering the centuries lost starship.

Narrowly escaping capture, out of time and out of air, Mitchell lands at the mercy of the Riggers - a ragtag crew of former commandos who patrol the lawless outer reaches of the galaxy. Guided by a captain with a reputation for cold-blooded murder, they're dangerous, immoral, and possibly insane.

They may also be humanity's last hope for survival in a war that has raged beyond eternity.

Man of War (Rebellion)
mrforbes.com/manofwar
Complete series box set:
mrforbes.com/rebellion-web

In the year 2280, an alien fleet attacked the Earth.

Their weapons were unstoppable, their defenses unbreakable.

Our technology was inferior, our militaries overwhelmed.

Only one starship escaped before civilization fell.

Earth was lost.

It was never forgotten.

Fifty-two years have passed.

A message from home has been received.

The time to fight for what is ours has come.

Welcome to the rebellion.

Hell's Rejects (Chaos of the Covenant)

mrforbes.com/hellsrejects

The most powerful starships ever constructed are gone. Thousands are dead. A fleet is in ruins. The attackers are unknown. The orders are clear: *Recover the ships. Bury the bastards who stole them.*

Lieutenant Abigail Cage never expected to find herself in Hell. As a Highly Specialized Operational Combatant, she was one of the most respected Marines in the military. Now she's doing hard labor on the most miserable planet in the universe.

Not for long.

The Earth Republic is looking for the most dangerous individuals it can control. The best of the worst, and Abbey happens to be one of them. The deal is simple: *Bring back the starships, earn your freedom. Try to run, you die.* It's a suicide mission, but she has nothing to lose.

The only problem? There's a new threat in the galaxy. One with a power unlike anything anyone has ever seen. One that's been waiting for this moment for a very, very, long time. And they want Abbey, too.

Be careful what you wish for.

They say Hell hath no fury like a woman scorned. They have no idea.

ABOUT THE AUTHOR

M.R. Forbes is the mind behind a growing number of Amazon best-selling science fiction series. He currently resides with his family and friends on the west cost of the United States, including a cat who thinks she's a dog and a dog who thinks she's a cat.

He maintains a true appreciation for his readers and is always happy to hear from them.

To learn more about M.R. Forbes or just say hello:

Visit my website:
mrforbes.com

Send me an e-mail:
michael@mrforbes.com

Check out my Facebook page:
facebook.com/mrforbes.author

Join my Facebook fan group:
facebook.com/groups/mrforbes

Follow me on Instagram:
instagram.com/mrforbes_author

Find me on Goodreads:
goodreads.com/mrforbes

Follow me on Bookbub:
bookbub.com/authors/m-r-forbes

Printed in Great Britain
by Amazon

20501702R00164